THE GHOST AND THE WOLF

THE BROKEN SERIES

1

SHELLY X. LEONN

OWL HOLLOW PRESS

Owl Hollow Press, LLC, Springville, UT 84663

The Ghost and the Wolf

ISBN 978-1-945654-37-4 (paperback)
ISBN 978-1-945654-38-1 (e-book)

ISBN 978-1-945654-98-5 (paperback)

Library of Congress Cataloging-in-Publication Data
The Ghost and the Wolf / S.X. Leonn. — First edition.

Summary:
A student reporter and a paranormal investigator follow the clues of a twisted scavenger hunt from a secret organization of teen urban explorers until they realize—too late—that the group's plans are much more deadly than they'd realized.

OHP

I dedicate this story to my family,
who sees the beauty in my broken.

BROKEN APP: LEADERBOARD, ROSTER

The following information is for members only. If you're reading this and you're not one of us, we'll have to kill you.

LEADERBOARD

1. Riot, led by Griffin
2. Ozone, led by Haze
3. Void, led by Titan
4. Nova, led by Avriel
5. Pitfall, led by Mumble
6. Crux, led by Essence
7. Myth, led by Rhapsody
8. Kharma, led by Symmetry
9. Entropy, led by Anax
10. Pack, led by Wolf Cub

PACK TEAM ROSTER

Wolf Cub: Elijah Atkinson

Garnet: Helena Proctor

Drips: Mason Morston

Nail: Nate Robinson

Skin: Seth Robinson

Zig: Xavier Pichardo (transitioning out)

Zag: Yuma Rivera (transitioning out)

1

UP FOR IT

Penelope drummed her fingers on her desk. Arriving first made her feel lonely. While stomps and chatter spilled through the open door, the room itself was silent. A few seconds passed, and still, no one entered.

Might as well make use of the time, she thought.

With care and precision, she removed the journalism class folder from her book bag and set it on the desk. Next, she pulled out a mechanical pencil and a pen. The pen's color was the same lively green as her hair. She placed the final item, a planner, on the left corner of her desk and flipped it to the correct date. Today was empty of all notes except one word in the corner written in her tight, neat script. *Birthday.*

She checked her cell phone. No texts. It was just as well. She double-checked that the phone was on silent, then secured it in its inner pocket of her book bag.

"Waiting to hear from someone?"

Penelope turned toward the voice. Elijah, a junior, plopped into the desk next to her.

She swallowed, her tongue suddenly thick in her mouth. In the high school social structure, Elijah outranked her in every way. He and those of similar popularity usually ignored her. His sudden interest made Penelope squirm. Ignoring her mounting social anxiety, she decided to keep her reply simple. "No. Why?"

He pushed his long, stringy hair away from thick, black-rimmed glasses, and grinned. "I saw you checking your phone. You're not sneaky." He plopped his book bag on the floor.

"Well, the teacher didn't see. That's what matters," she replied, smoothing her hair into place.

Elijah, never the kind to stay on one topic for long, kept his tone low as more student reporters wandered into the classroom. "Hey, we're getting the results today." As he spoke, he tied his rebellious strands into a low ponytail.

Penelope felt the color drain from her face. "Today? Are you sure?"

"Oh, trust me. I'm sure." He leaned even closer. "I saw Taylor with a big stack of something. Looked like certificates."

Her stomach knotted up, and her breath escaped her nose in tiny, short huffs. It was too much to process. But it wasn't cool to freak out about something like journalism awards.

Say something, her brain shouted at her. "Uh, wow. That was fast."

"Yeah, for real." His attention had already shifted, half on her and half elsewhere. "But don't worry. Even if you don't win anything, it's not like she's gonna give you a hard time about it. She's always had a soft spot for you, being the first freshman in, well, *ever* to make the *Bulletin*."

"Yeah, but that was last year," Penelope said, although she could feel her insides warming at the compliment. "Trust me, it's been no mercy this year."

He flashed her a grin. "Then you're just like the rest of us."

You think so? Penelope wanted to ask. At first, the other reporters had seemed so much more mature, skilled, and connected. She didn't think she'd ever reach their level in writing or reporting. Despite her doubts, she had stepped beyond her comfort zone—way beyond—and, after hours of deliberating, entered a profile on the marching band's drum major in the annual regional student journalism competition. And today she'd find out the result of that risk.

"I'm sure you're going to get something big," she said.

"Huh?" Elijah looked up from his phone.

It's like we weren't talking a second ago. "I said I bet you'll do well. Your spread was amazing." She pulled her own phone out again to avoid eye contact. She'd been meaning to let Elijah how much she liked his submission but had never quite found the right moment—or worked up the nerve. Now, staring at her phone screen, she vowed to eat an extra piece of birthday cake to congratulate herself.

"Oh, hey, thanks. Yeah, that was crazy to shoot." Elijah was the photo editor for the newspaper, and according to their teacher, he was "going places." Everyone knew he would do something with his talent, maybe even become a real photojournalist some day. For the contest, he had submitted a photo spread of flash flooding in the St. Louis area.

It had been weeks since she'd seen it, but Penelope could still recall some of the details of the spread. The submerged cars, surrounded by frothing, brackish water. The mold-caked ceilings glistening with beads of moisture. The piles of debris spread across a barren, water-logged field of dead grass. Somehow, Elijah had photographed the disaster in a way that captured its destructive force but also its somber beauty.

An annoying *tap-tap-tap* came from Penelope's left, and she looked over to see Jonathan, the news editor, absently bouncing his pencil on his desk. Penelope realized she wasn't the only student feeling the pressure. Other classmates fiddled with the edges of their notebooks and chattered about something else, *anything* else.

Sometimes, she forgot Journalism Production was just another class on the schedule. For the next ninety-minute block class period, she and her classmates were journalists.

The bell rang, silencing any lingering whispers. Taylor, the editor-in-chief, rose from her desk and fingered through a folder of newspaper clippings and certificates.

"Hey, guys." She brushed a curled, black strand of hair from her caramel cheeks. "So listen, the results are in. And I think many of you are going to be really happy." Penelope wanted some sign from Taylor that she had gotten an award, but the editor didn't look at anyone in particular. "So, how should we do this? Highest to lowest, or lowest to highest? Anybody have opinions?"

"Highest to lowest," Jonathan called out.

"That's one vote. Anybody else?"

Xavier, a beefy senior with a mop of curly hair, shot his hand up. "No, lowest to highest. You gotta build up the suspense."

"Spoken like a true sports editor," another reporter said with derision.

"I know," said Lacie, another senior. She flipped her gauzy scarf over her shoulder with a flick of her wrist. "Let's throw them all into the air. Let fate decide which awards are revealed first."

There were a few groans. As the features editor, Lacie was supposed to be the creative one, but she often took that aspect of the position to unexpected—and, in Penelope's opinion, unnecessary—extremes. Penelope, a features contributor, often had to answer to her. Her mood swings were irritating and the opposite of helpful.

Taylor shrugged. "Well, I guess we can't come to a consensus here. Penelope, what do you think we should do?"

All eyes and bodies turned to Penelope. She felt herself shrinking in her seat like a wet sponge left on hot pavement. Taylor never singled her out. Why now?

"Umm, well..." Trying to think, she swallowed her initial shock and anxieties. Some wanted highest awards announced first. Some wanted lowest. Lacie, of course, wanted anarchy.

"How about we fan them all out, face down?" A faint smile touched her lips. "Everybody lines up by, hmm—"

"Birthday?" Elijah suggested, flashing Penelope a hint of a coy smile.

How would he know that? Wait, he can't know, Penelope thought in alarm. "Uh, sure, birthday. And then we each grab one, announcing whatever it says to the whole class."

Taylor nodded. "Perfect. I love it. Let me count these first." She held the folder close to her chest as she counted the papers inside. "There are seven. So everybody can pair up and take one. Mr. Jaeger, you gotta play too, all right?"

The teacher, feet propped on top of his desk, nodded. He was always listening, even while he just sat in the front of the room reading the newspaper.

"Front of the line is January. Back is December. And no talking. No mouthing words, either. That's cheating. You gotta sign it with your hands, just like summer camp."

Penelope smiled at Taylor's additions. The editor-in-chief must have sensed the mounting tension in the room and was trying to lighten the mood.

"Ugh, I'm gonna lose," Elijah whined.

"Just don't talk, Elijah, for like, two minutes. Now, go."

Penelope slid out of her seat to move closer to the front of the room. Andrew, another photographer, had also started moving to the front. He flashed a two with his fingers, and she held up three fingers. He moved in front of her. Paul came up next and showed them three.

Another March birthday, Penelope thought. She answered him with her own three, and he responded by flashing five fingers three times—March 15th. She held up seven. His eyes widened as he stepped behind her.

After a bit more shuffling and snickers, the students formed a straight line running from the front to the rear of the classroom. Even Mr. Jaeger was in the line at the back.

Taylor narrowed her eyes. "Mr. Jaeger, did you really play, or did you just go straight back there?"

"My birthday is December twenty-first." His voice always sounded more like a groan than regular speech. "Need my driver's license?"

"I'll let you go with a warning this time, Mr. Jaeger." Taylor winked. "Is everybody ready? Pair up."

Penelope tried to avoid partnering with Paul, but the four people ahead of her left her with no choice. He wasn't deterred by her lack of eye contact.

"Hey, you didn't tell us it was your birthday," he exclaimed.

Penelope stared at the paint marks on her flats. She could sense Andrew in front of her turning around to look at them.

"Yeah, it's not a big deal." Penelope wished she could melt into the floor. *Leave it alone, Paul.*

"Doesn't everybody make a big deal over birthdays?"

"Not me."

"Oh."

The couple ahead of them moved away with their certificate. Penelope looked up to see Taylor fanning the certificates facedown in front of them. Paul snatched up the closest one, and the two found a spot in the back of the room. Paul didn't try to peek at the award, but Penelope could tell how tightly he clutched it from his white knuckles. At least it had made him shut up about her birthday.

After what seemed like hours, all the certificates had been handed out.

"Come on, let's do this already." Taylor snapped her fingers at the group. "Xavier and Yuma, since you're the front of the line, you get us started. Ugh, you two are so cute it's gross. Even your birthdays are similar?"

"January," they both replied in unison. They were neighbors, had grown up together, and had been a couple since middle school. To Penelope, they seemed lost in their own world, keeping to themselves and shutting out nearly everyone else. The one exception was Elijah, whom they would often pull aside for quiet, intense conversations. Probably gossip.

Xavier and Yuma each held a corner of the certificate as they read the printed words in perfect unison. "Jonathan Thomas, news writing, Best in Show."

The entire classroom erupted into applause. A Best in Show award was the highest honor an individual story could receive in a division. Jonathan, his face alight with pride, accepted the certificate from Yuma and Xavier.

"Jonathan, I have your plaque right here, too." Taylor lifted it from the desk behind her and displayed it for the class. "Let's keep going. Any February birthdays?"

The advertising editor and Andrew both raised their hands. The editor turned it around and read, "Xavier Pichardo, sports writing, first place."

Yuma squealed in delight and threw her arms around her boyfriend as Xavier broke into a dance. "Yes, yes, yes!" he shouted.

Taylor couldn't restrain her smile. "Enough. Moving on." She had to repeat the request a few times before Yuma grabbed Xavier by the shoulders and shoved him back into his seat. "Who's March?"

"We are," Paul said before Penelope could worry about what to say.

"Happy birthday month," Taylor exclaimed. "What do you have for us?"

Paul held up the certificate like it was a children's book so the entire class could see. He read, "Penelope Pine, features writing, second place."

A combination of nerves from the attention and shock at the award had an unusual effect on Penelope's body. Her mouth went dry, and her heart sped to an allegro tempo like it was the lone drum trying to beat life back into a symphony. She had the presence of mind, barely, to hold the certificate in her fingers when Paul handed it to her. She managed to force her lips into a smile and nod in acknowledgment to the applause.

Penelope clapped, smiled politely, or said congrats as necessary for the remainder of the awards. As expected, Elijah had placed in news photography—third. And Taylor, of course, won first place in investigative reporting. Moreover, the entire staff was excited to hear they had received third in overall newspaper production, which recognized the quality of the entire newspaper.

As the excitement began to wind down, everyone made their way back to their desks, and Taylor addressed the group again. "So, like I said, it was a great year for us. I'm happy, but I'm sad, too. We are losing two of our editors, along with one of the best editor-in-chiefs this newspaper has seen." She brushed her shoulders off, and a few people snickered. The other seniors, Lacie and Xavier, cheered. "I know we still have three months of school, but it's time to start thinking about who is going to fill these editor slots. Who wants them? More importantly, who's ready?"

She was quiet for a moment, letting that thought settle inside the underclassmen. "It's a lot of work, but it's worth it. But for now, we have a paper to put out. Deadline for rough drafts is this Friday. Let's get to work."

She started to walk away from the front of the room, but she turned back as if she had just remembered something. "Oh, and Penelope? I need to see you. Come back when you get a second."

Elijah slapped a hand on her desk. "Ooh! What did you do, Penelope?"

"Elijah, shut up." Taylor crossed her arms in front of her chest. "The only one around here who's gonna be in trouble is you if you don't give me that spread on the freshmen." With that, she hustled to the back of the classroom where a storage closet with an old teacher's desk acted as the journalism student office.

Penelope glanced at the wall clock mounted over Mr. Jaeger's head. 10:19. She would wait until 10:23 before she moved—no reason to make the editor think she was nervous or too eager. She pulled her planner to the center of her desk and flipped to the notes section where she had written the questions for her interview the next afternoon. Keeping one eye on the clock and the other on her paper, she rose from her desk as soon as the minute hand reached her designated time.

When Penelope opened the door to enter the office, Taylor greeted her. "Hey, Penelope, have a seat." She gestured to one of the two blue cafeteria chairs in front of her desk. At least twenty pictures in colorful frames decorated the work surface. Half of the pictures featured the newspaper staff. Penelope was only in the shots of the entire staff posing in lines. She recognized some of the other shots from journalism group get-togethers that she had declined.

Penelope took a seat in the chair closest to the door. "You needed to see me?"

"Yeah, for sure. Thanks for coming back. I know you're super busy on your next profile." Taylor gestured to the whiteboard drilled into the dark purple wall, which listed the upcoming assignments. In the Features column, "clown girl" was written next to Penelope's name. "I think it's going to be a great story."

"Thanks," Penelope said, perhaps too curtly.

Taylor leaned back, her orange desk chair emitting a loud squeak that both girls ignored. "You're good at finding interesting subjects, Penelope. Seriously. Like Lilliana, a random girl who wants to be a clown someday? And does clown acts for sick kids at the children's hospital? That's so cool. How did you find her?"

Penelope frowned. She realized there were answers she was supposed to say, like a mutual friend. Except Penelope didn't have many friends. Instead of spending an uncomfortable amount of time thinking up the right reply, she went with the truth. "I just listen to people a lot, I guess. I heard someone talking about this girl from school visiting her kid brother when he had appendicitis."

"So you chased that lead and found Lilliana?"

"Yeah." Penelope averted her gaze, her cheeks flushing.

She could hear the smile in Taylor's words. "See, that's what makes you different. That's why you won second place. Because you listen. I'm not gonna waste your time, Penelope. I called you back here to congratulate you and to encourage you to go for features editor. I think you could be amazing."

Penelope's eyes widened, and she looked up. "Really? Me? But I'm—"

Taylor waved a dismissive hand. "You're an introvert. So what? That's why you understand people. Introverts can be great leaders too. We will be distributing the applications next month, so you have plenty of time to think. Just promise me you'll consider."

Penelope nodded. She opened her mouth to say thank you, but the door opened and Lacie stuck her head inside.

"Hi, Taylor, sorry to interrupt. Just want to talk to my reporter for a second. Hey, Pen," she said, her voice rising and falling in a sarcastically sweet singsong. The tone reminded Penelope of stale, crusty syrup. "Great win there. Honestly. Second place, wow. Hey, listen, I have a story idea for you. You up for something a little different?"

Taylor arched one of her sculpted eyebrows. "Different, huh? If it's so *different*, why aren't you taking it?"

Penelope thought she had a good point.

Lacie sighed through her nostrils and rolled her eyes. "Ugh, I'm so busy with graduation."

Taylor's eyebrow arched up even farther. "That's three months away."

Lacie walked toward Taylor's desk and sat on its one empty corner. "Taylor, relax. Can't I give our promising young reporter the story tip of the school year here?" She brushed Penelope's shoulder. "Come on, Pen, let's go talk in the hallway for a second." Without waiting for Penelope's answer, Lacie strode out of the office.

Penelope stood to follow Lacie, but first she turned to Taylor. "Thank you. I'll think about it."

Taylor smiled and nodded, and Penelope left.

Ghosting through the classroom, she exited into the hallway. A few students rummaged through their lockers and one strolled to the restroom, but the corridor was almost empty.

Penelope walked to where Lacie stood along the wall of painted cinder blocks, a sterile white and lackluster yellow, and tried her best to make eye contact with the features editor. This was harder than usual because Lacie wore bright-red contacts to match the red polka dots on her navy scarf.

Lacie put a hand on Penelope's shoulder, and Penelope had to focus on not shaking it off. "So let's talk, Pen. You won second. That's a big deal for a sophomore. But don't you wonder why you didn't get first like Taylor? Or Best in Show like Jonathan?"

"Well," Penelope said, forehead furrowing, "they are incredible reporters. And I still have a lot to learn."

Lacie squinted her eyes and tucked her fist under her chin as she pretended to analyze Penelope's words. "Yeah, yeah, maybe. I'm sure that's all it is. They're just older than you. Don't worry about it." After another moment of scrutiny, Lacie smiled sweetly. "You know, I can squeeze in the story myself." Lacie began to turn to the classroom door.

Penelope shook her head in confusion. "What do you mean?"

She turned back, lower lip out in a pout. "By what, Pen?"

"That you're sure 'that's all it is.'" Even as she asked it, Penelope knew she shouldn't have. That she wouldn't like the answer.

"Oh, well, that it's just a matter of them being older than you. It's not like you're just not a good enough writer, right? I mean, I'm sure you'll catch up some day."

Lacie's tone communicated far more than her words—she clearly thought Penelope would never catch up, that Penelope was incapable of catching up. The idea burned Penelope like a lit match buried into her neck. "What does this have to do with your story lead?"

"Well, it's an intense and interesting story. Your stories are..." Lacie paused and tilted her head, then snapped her fingers. "I know the word I'm searching for. Typical. Your stories are typical. Like the drum major story." She shrugged. "That was just boring and typical. And juvenile. Any kid taking a high school journalism class could have produced something like that. And my story—it just needs something more. Like I said, no big deal."

Penelope felt the tears welling up. She took a deep breath and forced them back. "What's the story?"

Lacie turned back once more, all innocence. "Oh, so you think you're up for it? Cool. I'll text you tonight with everything you need. It's not like you'll be doing anything anyway, right? Great, it's settled. Thanks, Pen."

Lacie's red boots reverberated down the hall as she traipsed back into the classroom.

BROKEN APP: MESSAGES

Monday, 5:15 p.m.

Drips: *Wow, you were right. This girl has been through some stuff.*

Wolf Cub: *I knew she was one of us.*

Drips: *You can always tell, Wolf.*

Wolf Cub: *We find our own. It's what we do.*

Garnet: *Did that basic twit with the crush on you talk to her today?*

Wolf Cub: *Of course. People looking to impress others are easy to manipulate.*

Drips: *Don't you feel a little bad for playing her like that?*

Wolf Cub: *Not really.*

Drips: *That's cold, boss. Really cold.*

Garnet: *So do I text her tonight?*

Wolf Cub: *Yes. Wait for word from me. Then start the initiation.*

Garnet: *You sure? You might scare her off.*

Wolf Cub: *She won't scare easily. I can tell.*

Garnet: *But she hasn't met me yet.*

Wolf Cub: *True.*

Drips: *I've known Garnet for three years, and she still scares me.*

Wolf Cub: *Just promise me not to hold back with her tomorrow. If she agrees to go, do everything you can to shake her up. And be ready. I'll send directions to the first location soon.*

Garnet: *Was there a change?*

Wolf Cub: *Yes. Alpha himself rewrote the test over the weekend. It's starting somewhere a little outside of our norm, but I like it.*

Garnet: *We'll be ready.*

Wolf Cub: *I'm counting on you, Garnet, to keep the rest of them in line.*

Drips: *What's that supposed to mean?!*

Wolf Cub: *Shut up, Drips. Just follow Garnet's lead tomorrow.*

Garnet: *That's if she even agrees to go.*

Wolf Cub: *She will. I know it.*

2

I DON'T TRUST REPORTERS

Cold chocolate marshmallow birthday cake—spongy, moist, and her favorite flavors. Two pieces sat on the birthday plate she had pulled from the cupboard as a way to celebrate her party of one. Still, there was something missing. No, not presents and people. She preferred time alone.

But somehow, even though she enjoyed the solitude, Penelope couldn't taste that birthday magic she remembered from birthdays past. Eating cake in her room by herself was like going to an amusement park with the stomach flu. You should be thrilled, but something just makes you want to throw up about the whole thing.

After taking the bus home, Penelope had dumped her book bag on the kitchen counter and opened the refrigerator. Inside, her chocolate and marshmallow cake had been waiting, accompanied by a note written on bright green stationery in darker green pen: *Happy Birthday, Penny! We love you!!!! Be home soon. Love, Dad and Dad.*

After tucking the note in her pocket, she served herself two enormous pieces and carried the plate and a big glass of milk up the stairs. Her nightstand served as her food tray, just as it did most nights when her parents worked late. She ate the birthday meal lounging on top of her bed's fuzzy purple comforter.

From the outside, her house resembled many others on the block—shutters on the windows, neutral siding, clean landscaping, a doormat declaring "Welcome" to all who sought entry. Nothing stood out except perhaps the bright-red door. Inside, the house revealed the true personalities of its owners.

Her two dads, Mike and Henry, had acquired many treasures during their lives and careers. Each item had its own symbolism or story. Mike, a theater event coordinator, had one living room wall filled with celebrity autographs scripted on napkins. The kitchen walls were covered with framed playbills. Henry, as an anthropology researcher and professor, had a display case in the dining room with fishing rods and lures from around the world. The bathroom featured devices used as toothbrushes or toothpicks by different global cultures. Penelope cringed every time she imagined certain ones scraping along her gums.

After six years of living with her dads, Penelope was beginning to acquire her own mementos. Sections of her room were devoted to each of her passions—one corner had a desk, desk lamp, computer, notebooks, and a bookshelf; another housed an easel, paints, brushes, and smock. Journalism and writing were her career goals, but painting was her hobby.

Some of her front-page newspaper stories hung from her door. The murals and portraits she had deemed worthy of display hung above her bed.

Her own room. Her own stuff. All thanks to her dads. She had been adopted when she was ten, but there were moments when it still didn't feel real. Her past self lingered under the surface—a cold, deep abyss churning beneath a thin layer of smooth, white ice. It had taken her years to learn how to be a good daughter in a good family. After her adoption, she had to acquire skills most people learned in childhood, like how to make a bed and cook a balanced dinner.

Emotional gaps took even longer to fill. There were still moments when she opened the kitchen pantry and stared at all the boxes, bags, and containers of food in awe. And when she made what she considered stupid mistakes, like throwing her clean laundry in a corner instead of folding it, she wondered when her dads would realize she wasn't "right" for them and return her to foster care. Those thoughts had haunted her daily during the first few years with her new family, but now they just rose to the surface during her weakest moments. She had come a long way, but she still needed her parents' support and reassurance.

And even though her parents loved her and would go to the moon and back for her, they had to work long hours sometimes. It seemed as if they worked late on the nights she needed them the most. Or maybe it just felt that way because it was her birthday. Maybe Lacie's little meeting in the hallway had affected her more than she cared to admit.

Penelope caught a glance of her reflection in the full-length mirror across from her, and she smirked at herself and her lonely cake pile. Her bobbed green hair framed her chin. Rebellious bangs slipped out from behind her ear and blocked her view of her left eye. Her right eye, large and dark, looked back at her from pointed facial features—high cheekbones and a sharp chin. Ripped jeans and T-shirts of various bands and plays—gifts from Mike—made up the usual wardrobe for her slight body. Today, a purple beanie she had knitted was pulled over her green hair, and her favorite orange studs poked out beneath it. She had kicked her flats, the ones covered with paint drops, into her closet before she had jumped on the bed.

"Well," she said to her reflection, "guess it's just you and me. And who else is going to eat all this if we don't?"

With grim determination, she dived into the cake. Holding her fork in one hand and her phone in the other, she pounded away the dessert while scrolling through social media posts, flipping through Top Ten lists, and skimming personality surveys. Most evenings she would use her phone to read news and features stories from national newspapers. That evening, she was done thinking about journalism. All she wanted to do was shove bites into her mouth and play with her phone. It was brainless and pointless, but her phone provided her with what she needed at the moment—easy, instant entertainment.

She didn't want to think about her birthday, or her previous birthdays, or her second-place award, or Lacie.

Especially not about Lacie.

Her phone chirped and a text notification popped down from the top of the screen. Penelope groaned when she saw who it was from.

Lacie: *Hey, Pen! You're going to be getting a text from an Unknown Caller in a minute. Don't block it, k? It's the story of the school year contacting you!!!*

Penelope's stomach contracted around the chocolate cake. She hadn't really thought Lacie would follow through. After making her cry in the hallway, the witch was giving Penelope a story lead. And Lacie hadn't receive an award. None of it made sense.

Was Lacie trying to punish her? Was she that petty?

Penelope tried to think of something to text back. Something cruel and clever? Confront her about what happened in the hallway? But Lacie would deny she had meant anything negative by it, and she would make Penelope look like a touchy underclassman. Lacie's fake cheerfulness had backed Penelope into a corner.

Penelope: *K.*

Penelope ate three more bites of cake, trying to enjoy the overwhelming sweet richness. She didn't want to admit she was nervous. Just a story lead, right? A trap, most likely, but still. Just another story.

It didn't take long for her phone to ding.

Unknown: *Are you that reporter?*

Penelope scrunched her lips together. That reporter? What had Lacie told this person about her? She decided to proceed with caution.

Penelope: *What does that mean?*

Pause.

Unknown: *It means I don't trust reporters.*

Penelope swallowed a big gulp of milk. *What a jerk.*

Penelope: *Why?*

Pause.

Unknown: *Because they just ask questions, never answer them.*

Penelope scoffed. What was this person's problem?

Penelope: *I'm a student reporter for my school paper, but I don't know what you mean by "that" reporter.*

The replies were coming faster now.

Unknown: *Do you want a story?*

She shoved a huge bite in her mouth before she replied.

Penelope: *I always want a story.*

Unknown: *That's another reason I don't trust reporters. Everything is just a story to them.*

With a huff, she reflected upon the mysterious texter's accusation. Her first reaction was to defend herself, but she realized she had nothing to say that wouldn't affirm this person's belief.

Penelope: *You're right. I'm a reporter, and I like stories. That's what I do. So do you have a story for me? Or is this just a trick from Lacie?*

Unknown: *Who's Lacie?*

Penelope placed both hands on the phone, cake and fork forgotten.

Penelope: *Quit playing. Whatever. It doesn't matter. What's your story? Answer me, or I'm blocking you.*

Unknown: *This isn't the type of story I can just tell. I have to show it to you.*

Penelope: *I have pictures from unknown callers blocked. How are you going to show me this story?*

Unknown: *You're sure?*

Penelope stared at those words for at least a minute. Something told her she shouldn't "be sure" to this, whatever it was. However, she couldn't help but think of Lacie's words. *Boring and typical. And juvenile.* Yes, Lacie was rude, but she had a point. Penelope needed a story that would get her noticed, something different and exciting. And already, this texter had livened up her dull night.

She replied before she could ponder any further.

Penelope: *Yes, I'm sure.*

Unknown: *Great. Here it comes. See you at the pickup site tomorrow. DON'T be late.*

Unknown: *Happy Birthday Penelope*

Penelope's eyes widened in surprise, but before she could process the last text, her phone's screen flashed and went red. Then it omitted a long, shrill cry. She dropped it onto her comforter.

"What?" It sounded like the noise phones made during an Amber Alert, but higher pitched and angry. Penelope tried pressing a few buttons, but nothing would respond to her touch. Even the "off" button wouldn't react. As the noise continued to stab her eardrums, Penelope tapped the touch screen with her index finger five more times before giving up. With a final groan of frustration, she fumbled with her phone case, trying to slide it off to get to the battery.

Just as she managed to unsnap the case, the noise stopped.

She stared at the screen, the sudden silence making her feel jumpy. It was still red, but words began to appear. One word at a time, repeating over and over.

WE

ARE

THE

BROKEN

WE

ARE

THE

BROKEN

"We are the Broken?" Penelope whispered. Along the bottom of the screen, she could see a downloading status bar. There was no percentage, just a black rectangle outline slowly filling with black.

Penelope could do nothing but watch the heavy black words on the red background cycling through their cryptic message. Worry gripped her as she waited. Was this a virus? She had heard of hackers who could get into phones and then use them to access a family's entire wireless network. How would she explain this to her parents?

When the download bar filled, the red screen disappeared. Her phone's home screen appeared unchanged. She touched a social media app. Everything came up like normal. She closed the app and swiped her finger to the right. And then she saw it, next to a game she had downloaded the previous day. A new app with a small red square and the words "The Broken" written in a blocky black font.

She tapped it. Nothing happened.

Then, the phone screen went dark. Small white letters materialized like floating faces in a deep pond. Each sentence appeared for a few seconds before dissolving to reveal the next sentence.

Broken App: *Penelope, welcome.*

We are honored to have you as our guest.

Tomorrow evening, wait at the gates of the Bellefontaine Cemetery at 8:30 p.m.

Bring nothing but this phone.

Tell no one.

Heed our instructions or face the consequences.

WE ARE THE BROKEN

The app closed, returning Penelope's phone to the home screen. When she swiped to the right again, the only app was the game. She checked her list of recent downloads—nothing.

Searching for "broken" or "the broken" in the app store didn't turn up anything.

Before she could overthink it, she grabbed her phone and called Lacie. The senior picked up on the second ring.

"Well, hey, Pen. What a nice surprise to get a phone call from you. I mean, whoa! Who calls anymore, right? You really are traditional."

"Just listen for a second, Lacie." Penelope tried to keep her voice calm, but her volume increased as she spoke. "What did you just put on my phone?"

"Me? Sweetie, listen. Don't be so loud. I have sensitive ears. Honestly, you're getting mad for no reason."

"No reason? My phone was screaming like a stupid tornado siren, and now there's some app on it that disappeared. And it's telling me to meet strangers at a cemetery. Are you kidding me? I want a story, but I don't want a worm virus. I definitely don't want to get stabbed by some crazy person."

"Honey, you need to calm down. Don't you worry about everybody thinking you're a freak anyway? Calling people and accusing them of stuff isn't going to help."

Penelope pulled in a breath and exhaled it at a measured rate. "Please, just answer me. Did you just give my phone and my house's computers a virus?"

For a moment, there was silence on the other end. When Lacie spoke, her voice's pitch was lower, and some of the condescending sing-song tone had evaporated. "Ask Elijah."

"Elijah?"

"Yeah, ask him. He knows more about this than I do. But for real this time, Pen. Just because something is a little scary doesn't mean you shouldn't do it. And if you're not going to meet up with these guys at the cemetery, tell me tomorrow. I'll go."

"No," Penelope said, realizing she had already decided what she would do. "No. I'm going. And I'll ask him."

"Great. Awesome. Don't call me again. Text. Perfect. I'm glad we could have this talk. Bye, honey."

The call ended. Penelope scowled a little. She checked her phone's screen to the right again, but the app was still missing. With a few quick swipes and taps, she searched her Internet browser for Bellefontaine Cemetery. An elegant website featured beautiful photography and historical stories about the cemetery's more interesting and noteworthy residents. They included William Clark of the Lewis and Clark Expedition, beer legend Adolphus Busch, and author William S. Burroughs.

This place seemed pretty interesting for a cemetery—at least, during the daytime. Wandering around cemeteries at night wasn't Penelope's idea of a good time. She shuddered when she imagined all those monuments and obelisks looming above her in the moonlight.

When she checked the historical site's address, her frown deepened. The cemetery was located on the north side of St. Louis, far away from her home, her school, and any other place she frequented. Mike would want to know why she was leaving the house so late on a school night. She needed to think up an excuse, and fast.

Her favorite thinking place, however, wasn't inside the house. After grabbing the plate of unfinished cake and pulling on some flipflops, she threw open her bedroom window and climbed onto the garage roof. Its slight slant made the perfect seat for writing or listening to music while gazing at the sky.

The evening chill helped to clear her head, and she absently chewed another bite of cake as she pondered. She didn't have a lot of believable excuses, and she only had her anti-social self to blame. A journalism staff get-together? No, her dads knew she never went to those.

Before she could form another idea, Mike's car pulled down their street. The roof rumbled beneath her as the garage door opened and the car disappeared inside. Before it had a chance to close, Penelope was through the window and out of her room.

Peering over the banister, she saw Mike enter through the garage door into the mudroom. "Hey, Dad."

"Hey, Penny." He smiled with warmth. "Did you see the cake I made for you?"

"Yeah, I did. Thanks. I ate two huge pieces."

"That's great. Hey, we will do dinner this weekend. Henry will be home from his lecture series by then, so we can make it a real family outing. And you're sure you're cool with waiting to get your presents until he gets back?"

Penelope nodded. "Yeah, of course. That's totally fine."

He shrugged his leather messenger bag off his shoulder. "Monday birthdays suck, huh, Lucky Penny?"

"Not really."

"Oh? Did you have a good day today?"

"Yeah," she replied, surprising her dad as much as herself. "Yeah, I did." An idea popped into her head. She never attended the staff social get-togethers, but she *would* attend a more formal recognition event. "Hey, some of the other newspaper students want to do something after school for all the award winners. Can I go? I might be out late."

"Wait. Slow down. You won something?"

She rolled her eyes, faking apathy. "Yeah, it's no big deal. Second in features writing. Seriously, can I go?" She repeated the question quickly, hoping to monopolize on his joy for her birthday and big win.

"It's a school night, Penny." He said it because he had to. "Just be careful. And home by midnight. And no, that's not your curfew. I guess we will have to set you a curfew. But this is a one-time extension, got it?"

Penelope smiled. "Got it."

3

FIND THE GRAVE

As twilight faded over the cemetery, Lex performed his equipment check. The zipper on the ripped backpack resisted his pull, but a swift tug released it from the fabric that had caught it. Lex checked the five items within. First, the flashlight. On, off, on, off. It worked. To the normal observer, it resembled any other flashlight. But Lex had strict requirements, and this beauty met all of them, including a lifetime warranty.

He slid the flashlight into its protective case and pulled out the next item, a digital EMF and temperature meter. EMF, or electromagnetic fields, could be emitted by TV antennas, electrical sockets, and even thunderstorms. Those weren't the types of EMF readings he wanted, though. The device resembled a 1990s cell phone due to its clunky buttons and blocky shape. Because it combined two functions into one, he could keep one of his hands free.

Before putting it back, he ran his check. On, off, on, off. The temperature meter showed 43 degrees when on. No problems.

The last electronic device was an EVP recorder wristband. From a distance, it resembled an expensive fitness tracker. The recorder had enough memory to be left on all night. He would dump the audio files into his laptop at home for analysis.

He dreaded that part of the work. Listening to hours of his own shuffling footsteps and breathing could be dull. It was like hunting for the proverbial needle in the haystack. However, he had found a few needles. And what fascinating and mesmerizing needles they were. They made it all worth it.

After securing the recorder to his wrist, he pulled out a long, skinny item wrapped in a dish towel. Setting the towel in his lap, he uncovered an object that resembled a giant wishbone. Lex didn't use it often, but the dowsing rod had helped him out of a few rough spots. With care, he returned the rod to the backpack.

The last item was the most precious. It was a creased, leather-bound journal. Letters had been pounded into the cover and filled with gold leaf to spell out "Julian James Sterling." Inside, half of the pages were filled with his father's looping handwriting, while the other half were covered in Lex's chicken scratch. After returning the journal, he zipped the backpack and stood up from the wooden bench.

Lights from a golf cart bounced in his direction. He turned his head away from the glare, allowing his hoodie to shield his face.

His outfits rarely varied beyond his black hoodies, jeans, black skater shoes, and ripped backpack. And, of course, he was an African-American male teenager wandering around by himself at night. That made some morons nervous.

People. Ugh.

The golf cart stopped, and the driver turned off the headlights and the engine. Before his eyes could adjust, a voice called out. "Hey there, Lex."

He sighed and smiled. "Hey, Gladys."

An elderly woman with wispy white hair and thick eyeglasses stepped out. Around her neck, she wore a badge that read "Bellefontaine Cemetery Volunteer." She sat on the bench and patted the spot next to her. "Have a seat, young man. The night is young."

"Yes, ma'am." He shrugged the backpack off and joined her.

In the quiet between them, he relaxed his shoulders and his breathing. Gladys, with her apple cheeks and eye-creasing smile, had always been a source of comfort for him. Glancing at her out of the corner of his eye, Lex reflected upon the first time they met. It was a night much like this one, with dusk giving way to complete darkness and temperatures falling with the surety of a rock dropped in a pond.

He had been skulking around some of his favorite headstones, knowing full well it was two hours after closing but unable to resist the lure of recording one more EMF spike. Gladys spotted him before he spotted her. No one ever managed to sneak up on Lex, but somehow, she had managed it. He didn't know what she saw in him, but instead of kicking him out, she invited him to join her on her golf cart for her evening rounds of grounds clean-up and guard duty. He found himself bonding immediately with the grandmother figure. They had been friends ever since.

It wasn't just Gladys that allowed him to release the tension in his muscles. The setting itself put him at ease, as well. He had been in scary cemeteries. Bellefontaine wasn't one of them. This one radiated peace and belonging. The headstones, mausoleums, and tombs seemed as naturally placed in the environment as the tall, ancient trees.

Overhead lamps lit the cemetery's main paths, so the graves themselves were blanketed in soft shadows. The evening calls of the birds, the chirping of a nearby frog, and the hum of nocturnal insects created their own soft music.

"I found your skateboard by the entrance. I moved it inside the gate before locking it for the night."

"Thanks, Gladys."

After a few more minutes of sharing quiet space, Gladys asked, "How's school?"

"Not great, ma'am."

She smiled at him and patted his knee. "I know." She gestured to the surrounding graves. "Who are you visiting this evening?"

"Probably Kate Brewington Bennett again."

"You do love a tragic female, don't you? I hope the same isn't true for your love life."

He scoffed. "Love life? I don't need a love life. My ladies on the other side take all my time."

"A lady like Kate, though? I don't know if she's someone I would court more than once. Vanity is a wretched sin, and it killed her. She claimed to be the most beautiful woman in St. Louis. And what was her beauty secret? Arsenic. Not a smart choice. Dead in 1855 at the age of thirty-seven."

Lex smiled in appreciation. "Do you have all their stories memorized?"

Gladys chuckled. "Oh no. There are 87,000 stories laid to rest in this cemetery. I just remember the noteworthy or historical ones for the tours. And a few extras for my own amusement."

Using the arm of the bench for support, Gladys stood and glared down at Lex. She took on the voice and posture of an angry guard. "Ahem. Young man, you are to vacate the premises this instant. I'm not responsible for the consequences if you get caught again."

He sighed. "I know. Don't worry. I won't get you in trouble, Gladys. Just me. I'm used to it."

She examined him over the rim of her glasses, scowling a little. She almost said something but stopped herself. "Good luck on your date."

"Thanks." He hurried over to give her a hand into her golf cart. She started to reach for the keys, but Lex said, "Hey, Gladys?"

"Yes, Lex?"

"Why do you volunteer here?"

She reached out and patted his cheek. "The same reason you chase them. I can't let go of somebody." The little engine flared to life, and Gladys nodded in goodbye.

Lex watched her taillights disappear around a bend. Gladys's words swam like little fish inside his gut. She had seen right through him. He tried to force the discomfort away, but his grief didn't work like that. It came and went, and he just had to live with it. This wave washed over him, full of memories and pain, and he breathed through it. When it ebbed, he slung his backpack over his shoulder and approached his chosen subject for the evening.

After the puttering of Gladys's cart faded to nothing, Lex couldn't hear any other vehicles. Any lingering guests had vacated the cemetery at closing time. The volunteers and staffers who remained, he knew, would be few, and Gladys had his back. With a little caution and awareness, he should be left undisturbed.

Undisturbed by people, anyway. The weather was already getting on his nerves. His hoodie had felt too warm on him earlier in the day, but with the sun setting, the temperature plummeted. Late winter and early spring in St. Louis could bring snow, rain, hail, sunshine, ice. Any of it was possible in March, sometimes in the span of one week. Tonight, the forecast predicted freezing rain after midnight.

Because Mrs. Bennett's monument sat beside a chapel that drew tour groups and funerals, Lex approached with care. He watched the little building for a few minutes, lingering in the shadows behind an old elm. No movement or light betrayed any delinquent visitors. With quick, long strides, he slinked around the right side of the chapel and hurried to the grave.

She rested atop her ornate four-poster canopy bed of white marble, the top of which rose high above Lex's head. It wasn't her, of course, but her likeness carved into the gravestone. Her husband had wanted to preserve her beauty forever, so he had purchased the massive, bleak tribute to her. Time had worn away the details. All that remained of Mrs. Bennett's legendary beauty was an old, white statue lying on a creepy stone bed. A similarly worn figure of an angel watched over her.

Many cemetery visitors stopped by the huge marble artwork to see the macabre lady. Lex had seen it plenty of times before, so the novelty had worn off. He sat in the grass, leaning his back against the grave on the side that faced away from the chapel and road. Then he set to work. After he flipped on the digital EMF and temperature meter, he rested it in a crevice of the stone folds of her dress. The dowsing rod and flashlight waited in his lap in case he needed them. After gathering his thoughts, Lex pressed the EVP recorder's "on" button.

"This is Alexander 'Lex' Sterling. The date is Tuesday, March eighth. Time is 20:15 Central Military Time or 8:15 p.m. Central Daylight Time. Location is Bellefontaine Cemetery at the monument of Kate Brewington Bennett. This is my third visit to Mrs. Bennett, and both previous visits have been completely unsuccessful. No temperature changes. No unidentifiable sounds on the audio. Not even a weird EMF reading. I'm not too optimistic about meeting the missus tonight."

He adjusted his position to warm himself. "Honestly, I never get anything when I come to Bellefontaine. Probably because this is sacred ground. But I'm bored. My home life sucks, school sucks, and it's Tuesday, so it's not like I can schedule a real investigation. And this place is on an easy bus route from my house, so what else am I going to do? I'll start the observation now. After adding notes to the journal, I'll make my first attempt at contact."

Using his father's system of abbreviations and shorthand, Lex spent less than a minute writing a status report in the leather journal. Then he tried to settle himself in the appropriate frame of mind.

His father had narrated most of his hunts by hand, only using an EVP recorder for communication with "them." Consequently, Lex had spent countless hours poring through every one of his father's words in his journals, trying to piece together his methods and habits.

One such method was the meditative mind. To reach out to his desired subjects, Lex needed to open his awareness to possibility. He had to turn off the churning, whirling, chugging thoughts inside his head as well as steady his emotions.

Lex had plenty of practice at this, and he didn't view it as a chore. It was part of the escape. He could leave reality behind as he relaxed his muscles, steadied his breathing, and slowed his heart rate. Even the chill outside lost some of its bite as he fixated on reaching outside of himself.

With this heightened focus, he sought out Kate. He tried to imagine her as she would want to be imagined—youthful, charming, and stunningly beautiful.

"Kate Brewington Bennett. Mrs. Bennett. Kate. Tell me your story."

He glanced at his EMF and temperature meter but observed no change.

"Tell me your story," he repeated. He waited, letting the silence of the cemetery settle around him. He imagined grasping her lily-white hand, helping her to emerge from a shadowy gloom. "Show me your face."

After a few more minutes of inactivity, he spoke again, but this time in a drier tone. "No readings noticed. Contact will be attempted again in sixty minutes. Any voices heard in between now and nine twenty-one are not my own unless identified."

He leaned against the stone but maintained his meditative mind. It was not a sleepy feeling, but he wouldn't describe it as relaxed, either. He felt alert and reflective. He hovered in between the world in front of him and the gateway to the other roads that opened within him and extended outward.

His eyes remained open so he could glance at his meter and recorder, but only half his mind processed what he was seeing. The other half was searching for Kate.

The flow of time lost its power. During past hunts, Lex had allowed entire nights to pass while in meditative mind. He had only realized he was going to be late for school when the sun touched his face.

Tonight felt no different. Even though the wrist recorder showed the time, he didn't pay attention to it until he was due for another communication attempt. As a result, he didn't know how long he had been sitting by Kate's grave when he heard footsteps.

Footsteps.

For a second, his heart soared. But then he saw a flashlight's beam. His subjects didn't carry flashlights.

"Dammit," he seethed between clenched teeth.

Irritated, he made sure his belongings were tucked close to him so he couldn't be spotted from the road. Keeping the hood pulled low over his face, he peered around the corner.

It was a girl, at least he thought it was a girl, and she was coming right for him. In one hand, she carried the flashlight. The other hand glowed with the murky light of a cell phone. He watched her strides for a moment. She appeared to be in a hurry, but her rigid posture as well as her frequent stops to check landmarks and road signs suggested she was both nervous and lost.

Lex began eliminating possibilities. She wasn't a regular volunteer or employee, and she didn't resemble the trespassers or thrill seekers that sometimes crossed his path—they usually preferred black over green hair. Idiots liked cemeteries and old, abandoned houses. Lex didn't like idiots, but this girl, judging by her frantic searching, wasn't the usual idiot.

Lex watched her approach until she was about the length of a school bus from him. Then, her wandering eyes found Kate's bed, and she began to hurry toward it—and him. Lex ducked behind the grave.

I'll wait her out, he decided. *Hopefully, she'll glance at the grave and walk away. She might not even come around this side.* He turned his meter over to hide the screen's light, curled his legs close to his body, and held his breath.

The footsteps came so close that Lex could hear individual leaves and sticks popping under her shoes. Then, he could hear her huffing and puffing. She was right there on the other side, her flashlight shining on the grave itself.

"Kate Brewington Bennett, found you." The footsteps circled closer. "Now, where is the—oh, oh shit!" That quickly she had spotted him.

With a groan, Lex stood up. He kept the hood over his face so the only feature she could see was a deep frown.

The girl swallowed and stepped away from him. "Do you, do you work here?"

"No. Do you?"

"No. No, I don't."

He could see her better now. Choppy green hair, thin face, short stature, skinny jeans, and a zippered windbreaker. She was young, either his age or a year younger.

"So." He raised an eyebrow as he scanned her over. "What are you doing here?"

She rubbed her forehead. "Well, I'm trying to solve a puzzle so I can find this, this group, I guess, but—hey, what are *you* doing here?"

He folded his arms across his chest. "Talking to Kate. What else?"

"Oh. Well, I guess I won't interrupt your conversation. I just need to see the month of her death, fifth letter." She stepped forward with hesitation, straining to see the details of the monument.

Lex held up a hand to stop her. "It's M. She died in November. What are you spelling?"

"It's supposed to tell me where to meet with these people, and I have to be there by nine oh eight. I already have the letters H, U, and M, so now I need to find the grave of—"

"Don't bother. It's Humboldt. It's the cemetery entrance that dumps into Broadway Avenue, but it's locked. I bet your friends are waiting there." He glanced her over. "Pretty crappy friends, sending you on a scavenger hunt at night by yourself."

She shook her head. "They're not my friends. It's for a story. I'm a student journalist."

Mumbling and grumbling to himself, Lex packed his backpack and walked closer to her. "My EVP recording is all shot to shit anyway. Come on. I'll take you over there. It's a long way, and you're short on time."

She looked genuinely surprised. "Wow. That's nice. What's your name again?"

"Don't worry about it." Without checking to make sure she was following, Lex began moving toward one of the roads. "Just keep up. And please, please don't get all freaked out or something. They're just graves. But," he turned back to her, his eyes boring into hers, "if you see anything *unnatural*, let me know right away."

He flashed his teeth at her, more of a grimace than a smile, and started jogging.

BROKEN APP: MEMBER PROFILE

Name: Garnet

"Legal" Name—SECRET: Helena Proctor

Membership: Three years

Allegiance: The Pack, led by Wolf Cub, ranked tenth of ten teams

What makes you one of the "broken"?

You guys shouldn't get to hear anything about me. That's my personal business. My Pack knows. That's what matters. Not every loser who somehow manages to scrape through initiation should get to hear what makes me messed up. Yeah! I said it! Scrape through.

I'm sick of all these teams filled with people who don't get who we are and what we're trying to do. Some of you losers are in this because you think urban exploration is super edgy. Are you trying to get more subscribers, you damn posers?! NOBODY CARES ABOUT YOUR VLOG. Ugh, you all make me sick.

Alpha Wolf and Wolf Cub didn't make this organization so you could start a new hipster hobby. Yeah, we explore abandoned buildings. But most of you don't get the WHY part. And I'm not going to explain it to you. If you don't know, GET OUT and make room for people who actually need this organization.

Wolf Cub said I need to go back and add something about why I'm actually here. Let's see. My parents are jerks. I've been kicked out of my house three separate times. My face is more pierced than a porcupine handler. Both of my older brothers are in and out of rehab. I hate school, I hate adults, and I hate 99% of people I meet. How's that for an answer?

Why is the Pack at the bottom of all ten teams?

Nobody cares about those rankings. But since you asked, let me just make this as clear as I can. The other teams have a problem with us because we're led by Alpha's little brother. They're jealous. I don't blame them. Wolf Cub is awesome. Basically, they hate us cuz they ain't us.

They search out every opportunity to drag us down. Like the time we got an "anonymous" tip for a location overgrown with poison ivy. Or that time a bunch of our recent location visits got "accidentally" deleted from the app. Keep trying to tear us down, losers. The Pack just comes back biting.

What was your favorite location you ever visited?

We got into an abandoned school, but the inside was pretty boring. We had heard there was an empty pool inside. That turned out to be complete crap. Outside, though, there was a busted up, overgrown track. We raced on it, all seven of us. Moon was up. Night breeze. Sneakers pounding away. All of us fighting for that first-place finish like it was the outcast teen Olympics or something.

Guess who won? Me. Guess who tripped on a crack and got bloody shins and elbows? Drips. What a klutz. Hah!

4

THE REAL TEST BEGINS

Penelope inhaled through her nose and exhaled through her mouth. Holding her dollar-store flashlight in one hand, she struggled to maintain a steady pace while watching the ground in front of her. She considered herself in decent shape thanks to fairly regular jogs around a mile loop in her neighborhood—Mike was a runner and had got her started—but she found herself huffing and puffing more than she cared to admit. And flats weren't exactly ideal running shoes.

She didn't have enough energy left to be frightened. The terror of searching alone, every sound sending cold tingles of panic down her spine, had exhausted her. The dropping temperatures, the darkness, the twisting paths, and the hundreds upon thousands of graves. None of it was safe. Now, she had something to focus on—keeping up with the long-legged, hooded figure.

As she adjusted her stride to maintain the stranger's pace, Penelope focused on the task at hand—finishing the scavenger hunt. She was nervous but also eager to finish. At the end of this insane chase, she would find the subjects of her big story, who remained a complete mystery to her despite efforts to unearth information. Lacie had instructed her to ask Elijah if he knew anything about the Broken, and she had done so earlier that day in class. Elijah responded with a puzzled expression, and then stated he had never heard of it before pulling out his phone and forgetting about her. Penelope wasn't buying it.

But this could be the incredible story that would make her feel worthy of the title features *editor.* It wasn't that she had any competition. No other journalism student in her class cared about features stories as much as she did. Her biggest obstacle was herself. She thought she lacked the communication skills, experience, and writing prowess to deserve the title.

Lacie's rude comments in the hallway had poked a hole in her thin self-esteem, spurring her to chase after a story lead at night in a cemetery. She knew it was illogical, but Penelope wanted to be good enough for the editor role. She wanted to believe Taylor, who clearly had faith in her abilities. Before any of that could happen, she had to believe in herself.

If I can pull this off, she thought, *I'll feel like I really did something big. I'll be worthy of leading others.*

Any misgivings she had about following Lacie's sketchy lead had vanished with Taylor's announcement that day that names for prospective editors were due Friday. The original April date had been moved because Mr. Jaeger was going on leave for surgery. Penelope had only the remainder of the week to decide whether she wanted to be the features editor next school year.

She didn't know if she could convince herself that she would ever be good enough. But one solution to her swirling doubts became fixed in her mind: Get the story.

Then, somehow, everything would fall into place. Just get the damn story.

No one had told her it would require so much running, though.

Her guide turned around, jogging backwards. He pointed the light of his large flashlight on the ground in front of her. "Eight minutes until 9:08."

He accelerated his pace.

Penelope groaned. She couldn't maintain a faster pace. Did she really need him to lead her? Surely she could figure out how to make it to the gate by following the signs. Just as she prepared to call out to him, he sprinted off the path and disappeared.

She froze in her tracks, breathing hard. "Hey? Hey, guy! Where did you—"

"Shh!" he hissed. "Over here."

She spotted his light around the corner of a squat, square grave. Penelope skidded into a sitting position next to him and pulled her legs to her chin. "What happ—"

"Shh." He gestured with his chin in the direction they had been running. Headlights from a slow-moving vehicle approached. A golf cart puttered by them. After the blinding headlights had passed, Penelope could make out the dark blue uniform of a guard driving the vehicle.

It turned a corner, and her guide held up his hand, signaling her to remain in her spot. This close to him, Penelope could see he was only a bit older than her. She caught a glimpse of his eyes, which looked as sharp as shattered stones.

"Come on. We'll cut through the grass. Shortcut."

She realized how much she had been wheezing while they waited. Avoiding his glances, she stood up and fell in step alongside him.

The stranger led her through a maze of headstones, family crypts, and towering monuments. In some places, churned earth signaled the locations of fresh bodies just beginning to rot. She hadn't noticed any of these unsettling details while she was running, and she'd really rather not notice them now.

When imagined arms of decaying flesh began reaching for her ankles, Penelope blurted, "I don't do stuff like this a lot." As soon as the words left her mouth, the graveyard reverted to its normal, eerie self. *Whew.*

"I noticed," he deadpanned.

In a rush, Penelope told him of the odd events that had led her to this point. "Well, it's a group, and it's supposed to be a great story. They sent me this app, and I was told to meet them here at eight thirty. I parked the car at a gas station and walked up to the front gates. Of course, it was already locked. My phone started going crazy. It was the app they sent me. It told me to go in the cemetery. Luckily, I found a break in the fence. The app gave me these instructions for a scavenger hunt with timed tasks. That's when I found Kate. And you."

When she finished, she closed her lips as tightly as if they had been sutured. Despite the chill, her face flushed with heat. *Why did I just tell him all of that?* She cleared her throat. *I must be more nervous than I thought.*

The stranger briefly turned his head in her direction, and his dark eyes scanned her expression with a discerning eye. "Well." His voice bespoke caution but also reassurance. "It's not like I was finding anything good out here, anyway." He flashed her a lopsided smirk. "Besides, I'd be a complete asshole if I didn't help you."

Despite herself, Penelope grinned, some of her embarrassment forgotten. "Well, thanks for not being a complete asshole."

"Hey, you know," he teased. "It's the little things." He paused by the slender trunk of a tree and held up a hand. "Wait here for a second."

Cold, icy fingers of fear began inching up her throat again. Spreading out from the tree were grassy knolls and shadowed tombstones—no path in sight. "By myself?" Her voice cracked.

He gave her a puzzled look. "You were by yourself before, and you were fine. We're close to the gate now. I want to check things out first. I have a bad feeling."

"What? Are your ghost hunter senses tingling?" Penelope asked before she could stop herself.

He didn't return her mirth. "Something like that." After a few steps of a jog, he vanished into the blackness.

Standing alone, she remembered the young man's words to her before they departed Kate's monument. *Anything unnatural.* What exactly did he mean? Would something move, approach her, or touch her? A gust of wind rattled the empty tree branches over her head. Tiny frozen darts of precipitation began to sting her skin.

Shivering from both the cold and her nervousness, Penelope leaned against the tree. It didn't provide the same cover as a grave, but she wasn't about to snuggle up next to one of those things.

Her phone buzzed. She pulled it out with her free hand, trying to keep the sleeve covering most of her fingers.

Mike: *Penny, I hope you're having fun! Love you.*

The phone made a louder, angrier buzzing noise as if she had just slapped a beehive. The Broken app opened itself, bleeding red over the text from her dad. Three words filled her screen.

FIVE MINUTE WARNING.

She looked up just the stranger reappeared in front of her, and she stumbled backward in surprise. "Jeez!" she exclaimed, catching herself on the tree. "Quit popping up!"

"Listen. We don't have much time. There is a car with four people wearing ski masks."

Her stomach clenched. "That's sketchy."

"Exactly. Here's my plan. I'm going to hand you one of my business cards—"

"You have business cards?"

"Just listen. I'm going to do it where they can see me. They'll probably take it from you because they will want to know who's been hanging around. Memorize it before we get close. But here." He crouched in front of her and unclipped a rubber bracelet from his wrist. He went to clip it around her ankle but looked up at her before touching her. "May I?"

"Sure?"

He rolled up her pant leg, latched the bracelet around her ankle, and pressed a button on it. He unrolled her pants to cover the device. "That's an audio recorder. When these freaks drop you back off tonight, throw this in the bushes by the cemetery's front entrance. I'll pick it up before school to listen to everything that happened and give you the important details." He stood up. "And one more thing."

Her eyes had widened while he spoke. She felt irrational relief at finding this unexpected ally. "What?"

"You gotta text me when you get home. If I don't hear from you by morning, I'm calling the damn cops."

Before she could agree, he reached into his back pocket and pulled out a business card. It had a gray, swirling mist background. In purple letters, Penelope read, *#paranormalex: comprehensive investigation services* as well as his phone number, email, and various social media identifiers.

Despite everything, Penelope got a little thrill at receiving a guy's contact information. *Hormones*, she thought. *Go figure.*

"Lex? Is that your name?"

He nodded. "Let's go."

They hurried forward. As they moved, Penelope glanced at the business card, trying to soak in as much as the information as possible. She had the phone number down by the time she caught sight of the tops of a wrought-iron fence. As they descended a small hill, she could make out an idling, beat-up car parked on the other side of it, lights off. The people inside must have spotted their flashlights. Three of them came out and stood with their arms folded. Penelope discreetly slipped the card back into Lex's hand.

"Lex?" she whispered.

"Yeah?" he replied.

"If this gets too weird, I'm out. I'll go home. But I make that call, not you."

"If you say so."

The three masked people stood still as the pair approached the fence line. They all wore black. The overhead street lights created long shadows, like slim, dark guards, behind each figure. Penelope found she was glad a fence separated her from them.

When Penelope and Lex were close enough to smell the car's stinky exhaust, one of them spoke.

"We told you to come alone, reporter girl." It was a younger man's voice pitched low.

"She did," Lex said. "We bumped into each other."

"In a cemetery? You expect us to believe that shit?"

"It's true," Penelope said. "He was working."

"Working? You a grave digger or something?"

"You a bank robber or something?" Lex gestured to their masks. "Nobody wears those anymore. You know that, right? You look like an eighties movie villain."

A girl spoke, her tone laced with anger. "Shut up, freak. No way am I trusting any of this now. We told her to come alone, and she didn't. She can't follow simple directions, and I won't risk us being exposed. I'm gonna call all of this off."

Lex, eyes narrowing, pulled a business card out of his pocket. "Here," he said, passing the card to Penelope. "Even though they don't believe me, you at least can see what I do."

Penelope reached for the card, but the first one approached the fence. "What is that?" he demanded. "Give me that right now."

Lex shrugged with feigned nonchalance. "Just a business card."

The three strangers burst out laughing. It was an odd sight, laughter transforming three dark figures into teens playing dress-up. Except not being able to see their mouths while they rocked back and forth was a little disturbing.

The girl caught her breath and extended her arm through the gate. "Give it up, reporter girl, or no story." She chuckled with derision as Penelope gave her the card. The streetlights lit up her green eyes as she read it. "Paranormal Lex? Oh my God! Oh my God. Too funny."

The third figure wiped tears of laugher from his eyes, then shrugged. "Well, at least the dude checks out. Are you good with this now?"

This speaker was also male, but his speech was slower and more level than the first boy. Also, he directed the question to the girl. She must be in charge.

"Yeah, I guess so," the girl muttered in reply, although she didn't sound happy about it.

The first boy nodded in agreement. "Paranormal Lex, or whatever your real name is, you're staying here. She's coming with us. That is, if she still thinks she can handle it."

Penelope nodded with more confidence than she felt. "I can handle it as long as I'm still getting a story."

The girl grunted in agreement. "Let's get this over with. Make yourself useful, knight in clearance rack hoodie. Help her over the gate."

Lex narrowed his eyes but escorted Penelope to the fence line.

As the three of them shrieked with more laughter, Lex knelt down and grasped one of Penelope's feet. He hoisted her over and whispered, "Whatever happens, don't let them find the recorder. Text me later."

After landing lightly on the other side, Penelope turned around. Lex had already disappeared. As she searched the cemetery for any sign of him, the laughter died off behind her.

"Did that dude run off that fast?" the first voice asked. Penelope turned to see them studying the cemetery as she had been.

"Guess so," the third voice said. "Can't lie. I'm a little impressed."

"Whatever, bro. Let's just go."

The fourth person, the driver, unrolled the window and stuck his head out the car. Unlike the others, he only wore an eye mask, and his wide Afro formed a semicircle around his face. "Come on, you buttholes. We're on a schedule, and I am not going to be late for curfew again."

"Shut up, Drips. Jeez, you always gotta ruin the atmosphere."

The girl, who positioned her legs in a wide power stance, glared at each of them, last of all Penelope. "You will complete a test. If you pass it, we will tell you our story."

"Well," Penelope asked, "how do I even know I want this story? And I doubt that his real name is Drips. I can't use aliases if I'm going to get this printed."

"We are an underground network of teenagers with members at every high school in the St. Louis area. Basically, we're every parent's worst nightmare. Two kids who go to your school are willing to give their names. Does that answer your question, reporter girl?"

"Ooh! Give her the code name!" Drips called out from the car.

"Drips, shut up!" the girl said. "Right. Introductions. I'm Garnet. These are Skin and Nail, and they're twins. And you, you're not Penelope anymore. While you're with us, you're Lois."

"Why—Oh. Because I'm a reporter. Funny."

"There's one more of us, but you won't meet him until you're initiated. Put this on." Garnet held out a long strip of black fabric. It took Penelope a second to realize what Garnet wanted her to do.

Penelope stopped. The car, a Toyota Corolla, was in worse shape than her Tempo, which she hadn't thought was possible. Flaking paint, stained seats, and a cloth ceiling sagging down were the more obvious cosmetic problems. Penelope hated to think about mechanical issues. All four of them were still wearing masks. The blindfold was the last straw.

"No. No way." She shook her head back and forth and stepped away. "I'm out."

"I guess she doesn't want the story that badly," Nail jeered. "Told you she couldn't take it."

Drips groaned. "Jesus, Garnet. Don't be like that. Just give it to her, Nail."

Nail reached in his pocket before handing Penelope a black canister about as long as her palm. Penelope recognized it immediately as mace. "At any point, you can tell us to take you back here. We get you wouldn't wanna take our word for it. So if at any point somebody tries something, you can spray us all like wasps. Cool?"

"Spraying that stuff in a car with me in it would hurt me, too," Penelope said with an arched eyebrow.

Nail sucked his teeth in irritation. "What do you expect us to do, give you a knife? That would just be dumb of us. We don't know you either, remember?"

She rolled her eyes. "Fine. I'm still in," she murmured. After Garnet took her flashlight, Penelope snatched the blindfold from her as well as the mace from Nail.

"Put it on," Skin said, almost sounding bored. He seemed to be the least stressed of the three.

Penelope placed the fabric over her eyes and tied it around the back of her head. Nail wrapped his hand around her arm and guided her into the front passenger seat. The pressure of the seatbelt across her hips was followed by the buckle clicking into place. The car smelled like any teenager's car—old French fries and stale latte.

Penelope muttered, "I guess I should have asked you about your driving record before I agreed to this."

"Guess you should have," Drips said with a laugh as he started the engine. She heard the other three pile into the backseat and slam their doors shut. The car began moving, but it didn't feel to Penelope as if Drips were doing anything too outrageous or drastic.

"Where are we going?" Penelope asked.

"The cemetery was the first test. Technically, you passed it," Garnet said, grumbling with annoyance. "But getting help was against the rules."

"When did you say that?"

"When you were told to bring no one," she snapped. "That hoodie freak knows too much. It's too late now, though."

"Can I take my mask off?" Drips whined. "It's itchy."

"No," Garnet said. "It stays on the entire night. Those were the orders."

Without pausing for a breath, Drips rolled into his next question. "Whose turn is it to choose the music? It's mine, right?"

"Drips, you always say it's your turn," Skin said. His even cadence came from directly behind her.

"Well, this is my car, so it should always be my turn. Okay, wait. Technically, my aunt owns it. But, whatever. I've had it so long, it's basically mine now."

"So, *technically*, wouldn't that mean your aunt gets to pick the music?" Skin asked.

"Ugh. Skin, always with the logic. Nobody cares about logic. Haven't you realized that? How about this for logic? I'm driving. I'm the boss man. I pick the music."

"How about this?" Garnet cut in. "I get to pick it because I'm second-in-command. I'm the one who had to remind you idiots this was even happening tonight, too. It's my turn."

"Always gotta pull rank, don't you, Garnet?" Nail said with a snort as something solid—presumably Garnet's shoulder—brushed Penelope's arm. Within seconds, the car's speakers boomed with a bass drum. It was a steady beat, a calm before a storm.

"Do you like heavy metal, Lois?" Garnet asked.

"Actually, I—"

"Oh, wait. I don't care," she said just before the guitars screamed like undead cats, then shifted to white man groaning over the bashing of trash can lids. Penelope wanted to cover her ears, but she didn't want to look that lame.

As the music played, the group remained mostly silent. The one exception was Drips, who complained about Garnet's taste every time a song ended.

Penelope kept track of the time by counting the songs. By the end of the seventh song, the car came to a stop. Drips turned off the engine. Car doors opened, and someone unbuckled her and placed her cheap flashlight in her hands before leading her a few paces away from the car.

"Now the real test begins, Lois," Nail said. "Take off your blindfold."

BROKEN APP: MEMBER PROFILE

Name: Drips

"Legal" Name—SECRET: Mason Morston

Membership: Three years

Allegiance: The Pack, led by Wolf Cub, ranked tenth of ten teams

What makes you one of the "broken"?

Well, my Pack family is always mean to me. That's really rough on my self-esteem. I mean, I'm a sensitive guy. Also, I'm in an abusive relationship. My girlfriend is mean to me every day. Look, I know I seem all super cool and together on the outside, but I'm soft and squishy on the inside like a breakfast pastry. Chocolate flavored, in case you were curious, ladies!

Oh yeah. Every time we go to a location, I have to pick out my Afro. Do you know how long it takes to get loose sheet rock out of my epic hair?

When I ask one of my Pack members to help me, they say my hair is my problem. My problem? Uhhh, I thought we were family, guys. I thought you supported me. I shouldn't always be the one to do this. If anything, you should be honored I'm allowing you to touch the holy relic that is this masterpiece on my head.

I just got in trouble like Garnet. I'm supposed to open up a little bit. I'm with Garnet on this one. It's nobody's business except my Pack. But since Wolf Cub is asking me to do this, I'll do it. Let me just sum it up: School is a struggle for me.

Did you know that school computer systems code you? It's true. I have two codes by my name—one for my 504 plan (a fancy adult label for the "How to Handle This Crazy ADHD Nutcase") and another for my Gifted and Talented Program test results. My discipline record is lengthy, to say the least. I have trouble regulating my emotions, apparently. I'm a musician, too. When you mush all that together, you get me. Super talented. Super smart. And super screwed up in the head.

At least, that's what most people see. Most people don't get me at all. My Pack does. That's all that matters.

Why is the Pack at the bottom of all ten teams?

What do you mean, "why"? Don't you mean "why not"? Oh, I know what you mean. You mean "how." HOW are we so awesome that we're at the bottom? I can't say I blame you for being jealous. We're an organization for broken kids. We're the biggest losers in an organization built for losers. Do we get a special prize for that? No? Well, screw you guys. By the way, we're coming for you, Riot team. Don't get comfy up there in the number one slot.

What was your favorite location you ever visited?

The city sewers. No, not working sewers. They're historic. I love them because they're under the ground. There's this entire cathedral of beauty under everybody's feet at Forest Park, and nobody even knows about it.

5

JUST A BASEMENT?

"Lilliana, I'm so sorry. I am," Penelope pleaded for the fifth time into the receiver. Mr. Jaeger glared at her. For a moment, her tired brain focused on the three coffee stains that marked his teal polo. With a shake of her head, she shifted to face the back of the classroom. There, Lacie tried to hide her amused expression under one of her layers of jet-black hair. Penelope could still see the corners of her smirk.

"I brought clown feet to school," Lilliana cried—loud enough that Penelope held the phone away from her ear. The whole class could hear their conversation. "Everything. My entire outfit and all my props. I lugged that bag around all day. A senior in chemistry asked me if I had killed somebody. It was so embarrassing."

Penelope shifted the receiver to avoid the stares of her classmates and teacher. That slight body movement sent a shockwave of pain up her right side, but she did her best to hide her wince. "I know, Lilliana. I'm so sorry. Listen. I'll come to you. Tell me where. I'll come to your next visit at the hospital. Just tell me what I can do to make this up to you."

"You said Tuesday after school by the buses. I waited there with my bag for twenty minutes. You never gave me your cell phone number, so I couldn't call. I even went to the journalism office but didn't see anybody."

The one day nobody stayed after school to work on the paper, Penelope thought in frustration. She struggled to maintain her focus and not melt down. It was difficult on fewer than two hours of sleep. The events of last night were still so fresh, all she had to do was close her eyes to begin replaying random scenes as if it were a movie stuck on a loop. Even though she had almost fallen asleep in all of her classes, the scenes had kept her from resting.

That was a good thing, she supposed, but she wondered if she would ever sleep peacefully again.

"I really, really screwed up," Penelope said calmly. "I know it's not a good enough excuse, but I had some stuff going on yesterday. I just forgot. It was no one's fault but my own. Please, please can we reschedule for any time this week? I want to do what I can to make this story work. Tell me your favorite coffee drink, and I'll bring it to our second interview. Please, just let me try again."

Lilliana was silent for a second, and Penelope realized the entire class was silent as well. Everyone was listening in. Mr. Jaeger, still next to her, took a long, noisy sip from his mug.

Why did Lilliana have to call on the teacher's classroom phone? Penelope mourned.

Dead air hung between them for a few moments. Lilliana sighed. "I gotta think about it. I'm not saying yes, but I'll be at the children's hospital Friday at four thirty. *If* I let you try again, you come to me this time."

"Thank you for considering, Lilliana. I'll call later in the week. By the way, here's my personal number." The girls exchanged contact information, and Lilliana hung up.

Penelope carefully placed the receiver back on Mr. Jaeger's phone.

"Interview room. After class," Mr. Jaeger rumbled at her.

"Yes sir," she muttered. She glanced up before making her way to her seat and wished she hadn't. Twelve pairs of eyes tried to find somewhere else to look. Keeping her gaze on her flats, which were now splattered in mud as well as the dried paint, she shuffled to her desk and wrote down the second interview in her planner. Every movement brought fresh stabs of pain, but she had been dealing with that all day. She was almost used to it.

She had never missed an interview. Ever. Now she was a complete failure.

But last night… Maybe she wasn't such a failure after all.

A faint smile touched her face.

For the remainder of class, she sat at the computers and struggled to compose something resembling a first draft. The deadline to section editors—in her case, Lacie—was Friday, but Penelope only had one interview's worth of material. Lacie would butcher her crappy writing with joy.

The bell rang as she hit the period key on the final sentence.

As everyone filed out, Mr. Jaeger squeezed in between the students' desks and waddled into the interview room. He didn't bother checking on her. He knew she would follow.

Penelope saved the story file to her account and packed her belongings. When she entered the tiny room, Taylor and Mr. Jaeger were already seated. Taylor, dressed in a black T-shirt and yellow bracelets, leaned toward her as she entered, and smiled. Mr. Jaeger leaned back in the extra chair and had his arms folded across his expansive stomach.

"What is your next class, Penelope?" he asked as Penelope claimed a seat across from them.

"Advanced Painting with Ms. Collins." She studied her flats as the scratching of Mr. Jaeger's pen wrote out late passes for her and Taylor.

Taylor cleared her throat. "Penelope, we are so sorry that happened to you in there."

Penelope looked up in shock. She had expected to be reprimanded. "No, I completely deserved it."

"Oh, well, to be clear, Lilliana is justified to be upset. It's just, you know, all journalists get that call sometimes. We all make mistakes and miss appointments, but you had the entire class listening in."

"I never make those mistakes. And I won't ever again," Penelope declared.

"Lighten up a little, kid." Mr. Jaeger waved his hand toward her. "You got talent. A real knack for this. Mostly because you never drop the ball. Other teachers don't trust kids to interview them. Too many mistakes." He pointed the ball point pen in her direction. "Except for you. They trust you. That means something."

Taylor nodded. "Don't get discouraged. And don't let this change your decision about going for features editor on Friday."

Penelope nodded dumbly. "Of course. Thank you both so much."

Mr. Jaeger gave her a final nod of dismissal. Penelope hurried out of the editor suite and classroom. The hallway hubbub during class changes was already starting to die down as students filled the classrooms surrounding her.

Even though Penelope could have used a restroom break and a visit to her locker, she had been waiting for her art class all day. After the public fiasco with Lilliana, her need to paint was almost overwhelming. Painting required nothing from her other than inspiration and honesty. She was definitely inspired, and she needed to be honest with someone or something.

Before turning into the art department hallway, she paused to remove a bottle of pain pills from her backpack. She popped two of the brown discs into her mouth and swallowed them down with a few gulps of water from the drinking fountain.

As Penelope entered the art room, she saw that all the other students were sitting in little clusters, chatting and texting. Penelope dropped her backpack on one of the splattered student tables and rushed to the painter's easels, dodging other students along the way. Breathing shallowly helped reduce the pain in her side.

By the time class had started, Penelope's brush had already placed some dark, sweeping strokes of purple paint across her blank canvas. Somewhere in the background, Penelope heard Ms. Collins calling out attendance. She held herself out of complete concentration until her name was called, and then she succumbed to the previous evening's memories.

Wind. My God, such a cold wind. That was her first thought as someone guided her out of the car, the blindfold still in place. The temperature had dropped even more since the cemetery, and each gust carried with it stinging darts of ice. Penelope had brought only a thin zip-up jacket with no hat or gloves, and she hugged her arms around herself as her guide led her up an incline.

Her flashlight was pressed into her palm. "You ready?" That was Nail's voice, a smirk in his tone.

"I guess so," she muttered.

The blindfold fell to the ground. In front of her, a hill rose from the earth in front of a moody, churning sky. Long grass shifted and leaned in the gusting wind, the dry branches of elm trees clacking around her. Barely visible against the stormy sky, the silhouette of a farm house rested on the peak of the hill. The car's headlights revealed a narrow gravel drive leading up the hill.

Her back pocket vibrated. Penelope jumped, then scoffed at her own foolishness. It was just her phone. After sliding her flashlight into her other back pocket, she pulled the phone out. The starting rumble of a car engine made her turn around before she could glance at it.

The rest of the group had already piled into the car, a hundred feet behind her. Their black-masked faces leered at her through the dirty windows.

"What the—" she cried. "Hey!"

The tires squealed and rocks sprayed as Drips peeled out. From partway up the drive, Penelope watched as they turned onto a country highway. In less than a minute, she couldn't even see their tail lights. One set of headlights flew by on the highway in the opposite direction.

Then all light disappeared.

She was alone.

But she smirked. Penelope had remembered the audio recorder after the car stopped. While pretending to straighten the cuff of her jeans, she had taken it off her ankle and slipped it under the front passenger car mat.

She hoped the little device could pick up sound through the fabric and plastic. She hoped Lex would have an entire evening's worth of their conversation to analyze. She hoped she'd get out of this mess.

Shaking herself from her thoughts, she checked her phone. The Broken app had reappeared, but it was doing something new. In the upper right-hand corner, a timer ticked down from thirty minutes. Phrases in a jagged font appeared in the middle of the screen. Every time she tapped a phrase, it dissolved and another replaced it.

Broken app: *If that which is bent never breaks, what happens to those who are already broken? Are we the failures? Society's forgotten? Something inside us broke. Were you asked to bend and bend until one day you broke? Do you hate yourself for it, or have you learned to find Beauty in the Broken?*

The screen changed again, showing blocky instructions above a box that showed the view of her phone's camera—currently, the blurry outlines of her fingers.

Broken app: *Find a tapestry in the family room.*

The family room? But I'm outside, Penelope thought in puzzlement. It dawned on her. *Oh, wait. Of course. The test is inside the house. The creepy, abandoned house.* It waited for her at the top of the hill, a dark outline that seemed to grow as it loomed over her.

She tried to close the app to text Lex, but the phone refused to obey her commands. Shivering in the driveway, she considered her options—wait for the timer to run out or go inside to follow the clues.

A part of her was terrified to approach the house. Everything about the situation reminded her of every scary movie she had ever seen. She could almost hear the killer's chainsaw revving up.

But another part of her was excited. She was surprised she felt this way. Her heart pounded, her legs trembled, and her hands shook... but she was curious. What adventure awaited her? What did this app have planned for her?

She decided to capitalize on her own recklessness before it went away. After putting her phone in her back pocket and retrieving her flashlight, she pulled her jacket around her scrawny frame as best she could manage with one hand and began to trek up the hill. Her flats struggled to find a solid grip on the loose rocks. The wind whipped the droplets of cold precipitation into her squinting eyes, and her nose dripped. Yet, she forced her feet to move, one step at a time, up the slippery incline.

The house greeted her at the top—what was left of it, anyway. Peeling, drooping shutters decorated the windows, all of the glass either cracked or broken out completely. Vines climbed up the drainpipes and between the decayed wooden siding. The front door creaked open with each intense blow of wind, revealing nothing but perfect blackness. A deflated basketball rested in an oily puddle beside a crooked porch banister.

I already decided to do this, she reminded herself. *No use backing out now.*

The pep talk worked. With a rush of energy, she sprinted across the overgrown front yard, over the porch, and into the house, banging the creaking door against the frame as she entered.

She skidded to a halt in the front room. Everywhere her wavering flashlight beam fell, it revealed something ruined. A sofa, turned upside down with springs and stuffing ripped out from its underside. A particleboard entertainment center, sagging with water damage. An analog TV with a spider web of cracks. An overturned bookshelf torn from the wall left holes in the flowered wallpaper and drywall. The carpet was ripped and stained, and yellowing, crinkly novels were strewn everywhere. A ceiling fan with a light fixture swayed from the ceiling by its wires.

What happened here? Penelope wondered. *Who would leave all their things like this?*

Directly across from her, a doorway gaped, leading into a corridor that her weak flashlight beam barely illuminated. She'd investigate that later. This space seemed like the family room, so her first task had to be completed in here. But what she had been directed to find made little sense.

A tapestry? Penelope pondered. *Nothing in this room resembles a tapestry.* Judging by the belongings and the condition of the house, she doubted this family could afford fine art.

She once again focused her flashlight on the floor. This time, she tried to notice details instead of letting her attention be absorbed by the larger, more conspicuous objects. A battery-powered alarm clock. An empty soda bottle. A child's white dress shoe. A refrigerator magnet. All the random, little things that make up a family, a life, just left here to die.

A memory surfaced from its burial place in her mind, nearly pushing Penelope over. A detective with a big calloused hand gripping her much smaller one. The crunching of warped, fire-damaged linoleum under her feet. Her young eyes stinging from the smoke that still hung in the air. All of her belongings, strewn across the floor of her childhood home, soiled with ash and soot.

That was the last time she would ever see that house.

But there was no fire damage here, she reminded herself. Her eyes stung slightly from the cold, not from smoke.

"And that was a long time ago," she murmured aloud.

She cordoned off the memory and scanned her flashlight across the room again—and she saw it. A dish towel draped across the back of a sunken arm chair. A cross-stitched outline of a cottage graced the front, and the words "God Bless This Home: The Brinkman Family" encircled the house. Someone had spent many hours hand stitching the towel.

Maybe it wasn't a tapestry, but she knew it was important to the family who had once resided in the house. She retrieved her phone and lined up the towel in the viewfinder and pressed the camera button. The screen changed to the word *Pending*, then flashed the word *Accepted*.

The camera reopened, but there was a different instruction across its top.

Broken app: *Find stained glass in the kitchen.*

Penelope smiled. Beauty was here, even if it wasn't immediately apparent. To see this beauty, she would have to forget the shivering cold, forget her fear, and forget her own memories. She had to be present in this place and see that broken things have their own poignant beauty.

She tiptoed around the obstacles and entered the corridor, treading carefully as her flashlight beam slowly illuminated what lay ahead. Four closed doors, two on each side, hid their rooms. As she passed one, she noticed deep gouges slashed into the wood and continuing on the wall. Her flashlight followed the gash, and the cuts and wild streaks spread and multiplied all around her. She reached forward to finger one of the marks left on the wall. It was so deep, it slashed through the wallpaper straight through to the drywall.

In the utter silence, she listened. For what? She wasn't sure, but she felt the need to make sure she was truly alone in the house.

The rain came into focus, heavier now and beating steadily on the roof. Her own breath came in audible gasps. The loose door banged in the wind, making her start. A quiet dripping drifted down the hall from whatever was at the end of the corridor. She shone her light forward, trying to see through the thick darkness. The linoleum floor of the space beyond reflected points of her beam.

With a deep breath, she passed through the corridor and exited into a small kitchen, which had probably been a lovely, airy room a long time ago. Large broken windows offered a wide view of the backyard to anyone who sat at the small table with aluminum chairs arranged next to them. Faded homemade curtains of a cheery white with a pattern of yellow lemons dangled from their skewed rods. The red cabinets and green refrigerator once provided pops of color, but now only added to the murkiness. Mangled cabinet doors sprawled across the warping linoleum, the refrigerator lay on its side in the middle of the floor, and rust-colored stains splattered the little curtains.

Stains.

She approached the curtains over a small window and the sink. An occasional drip from the faucet fed into a dark brown goop that filled the sink to the brim. The original substance had solidified into something with the consistency of pudding. Even the broken windows and wind couldn't mask the rotting smell from this close, and Penelope held back a gag.

The glass in the window above the sink was cracked but intact. The brown substance splattered across the windows, blocking the view of outside. When she pointed her flashlight at the window, the cracks in the glass lit up like strands of pure light. The contrast of the bright strands against the brown smudges looked almost beautiful.

She held her phone up with her other hand and snapped the picture.

Broken app: *Pending. Accepted. Find a mosaic in the bathroom.*

Emboldened by her success so far, she walked back into the corridor and opened the one closest to her. It was the bathroom. Someone, probably a vandal, had smashed the porcelain toilet and had ripped the shower curtain from its rod. Under the debris, intricate tile work constituted the forgotten flooring.

An easy one. She aimed the camera and pressed the button.

Broken app: *Pending. Accepted. Find calligraphy in the basement.*

Suddenly, all of her courage seeped out of her.

The basement.

She squeezed her eyes shut but her mind played the memory anyway. A bed, a small bed in the corner of a basement room. Her bed. Her room, or more really, her corner of the room. The bed's blankets that smelled like mildew. The single pink pony poster she'd secured to the wall with super glue—tape didn't stick to the concrete—before her aunt caught her. That bed had been where she spent most of her waking and sleeping hours. Her "guardians" had locked her down there to keep her away from the constant parade of strangers who came in and out of the house.

As a child, she never understood why she couldn't meet all of those new people. Now, she knew her aunt and her boyfriend had made her a captive so they could conduct their "business."

She hated them. She hated them so, so much.

And just like that, the curiosity about this Broken organization vanished. What did any of that matter? Did she think she'd actually be able to level up her writing with this story? It was all pointless.

Biting into her cold bottom lip to stop her tears, Penelope tried to fight against the depression that always came with thoughts of her childhood. But the basement… Maybe she had done enough by discovering three of the pictures. Surely, she could wait for the car to return to pick her up.

She glanced at the time remaining on her phone. About fifteen minutes. Futilely, knowing it wouldn't work, she tried to close the Broken app. It refused to budge.

Somehow, she knew Lex was worrying about her. He would be wondering why she hadn't texted him yet. And thinking of Lex, a stranger who helped her for no reason, gave her strength.

Maybe the fastest way to get it to close is to finish all the damn tasks, she thought. She was, after all, a perfectionist. She hated leaving tasks unfinished.

That meant going in the basement.

She curled her hands into fists. "It's just a basement," she shouted into the empty house. "Just another space in a house. Not tied to my past in any way, right? Right? I can do this."

Her declaration rang false in her own ears, but she latched onto her bravado. She burst out the bathroom and opened the door across from it. Completely bare, likely used as a bedroom. The next door revealed the same. When she opened the final door, a black nothing greeted her. Her flashlight could barely penetrate the darkness, revealing only the first few steps. She could not see what waited for her at the bottom. She gulped down her fear and took her first step downward.

For an elongated second, the stair groaned. Penelope froze, but it was too late. The stair cracked, then shattered.

She fell into the darkness.

6

PAIN IS SUBJECTIVE

She landed on her side in a pile of decaying wood pieces that stirred up a cloud of dust and dirt that coated her. She couldn't seem to register anything else, her senses failing her as her brain tried to work around the pain. The lack of air.

Her mouth opened, but she couldn't breathe. Her lungs refused to draw in oxygen. The wind knocked out of you—that's the old idiom everybody used to describe the feeling. But this wasn't just wind. Not to her. It felt as if someone had knocked her life essence out of her, and she was struggling to suck it back. When she finally gasped in a choking breath of dust, the pain in her right side spiked, and she cried out.

But her brain needed air, so breathe she did. Gasp. Pain. Gasp. Pain. Forcing her body to repeat the cycle, she gradually began to hold more air. A piece of wood jutted into her back, and when she shifted, she heard her pants rip.

As she sat there, carefully hunched and cradling her right side, the shock wore off enough to realize she had dropped the flashlight. And her phone. Neither shone with any light visible to her.

She was sitting in the basement in complete black.

Her anxiety ticked up, the absolute darkness magnifying the pain, the lack of air. Her hard-won deep breaths reverted to gasps.

Desperately, she began rummaging through the broken wood pieces that had been the tops of several basement stairs. She wasn't sure how many had come down when she fell. Every time she twisted her torso, another paralyzing spasm ground on her right side. Still, she dug through the rubble. Dust flew into the air, causing Penelope to cough.

"Ohh," she moaned as tears began to flow freely. Coughing hurt worse than a dagger stabbing her flesh.

She must have bruised or cracked a rib. She had cracked a rib before she was adopted, so this pain was familiar. Somehow, it brought her some comfort to know what was happening, at least to her body. Her rib would heal and nothing else felt seriously injured. She would be fine.

Feeling calmer, she began to move each piece away from her with deliberation, making a small stack.

"Lois, are you there?"

Garnet's voice. Muffled but recognizable. It sounded much less gruff and much more frantic. Penelope cocked her head, trying to hear where it was coming from.

"Lois, answer us!"

It was close, but she still couldn't—

Penelope smiled despite everything. She reached underneath her rear and pulled the phone out. Two thin cracks ran across Garnet's masked face on the screen.

"Dammit," she muttered, rubbing at the cracks. "Hey, Garnet." Her voice broke on "hey."

"Holy shit, Lois! Are you okay?"

"I think so. I fell through the stairs. Might have cracked a rib. I haven't tried to stand yet, but—hold on."

"Just wait there! Don't move! We're coming to get you."

Penelope ignored her. She refused to wait in that dark basement, her memories lurking in every shadow, until they returned. Keeping her torso as still as possible, she put her left hand against the wall and slowly stood up, using mostly her left leg. Her right side screamed at her, a sharper pain than she remembered from her childhood injury. She couldn't breathe. Couldn't see. She bit into her lip so hard she tasted blood. She leaned against the wall, breathing shallowly, until the pain stabilized.

"Dude, she's so hardcore," she heard Drips exclaim. "Lois, you're a badass."

"Drips, shut up," three voices yelled.

Garnet's voice. "Lois, seriously, just wait there. We'll get you."

Penelope wiped tears from her face with her free hand, feeling grit smear across her cheeks. "No."

Garnet's green eyes widened. "Listen, Lois. You don't have to prove anything to us, to me. Just stay there. We're coming."

"I said no. I want to finish it."

"I told you she was hardcore," Drips shouted. He pushed Garnet aside so Penelope could see nose and lips. "You're awesome, Lois," he shouted into the screen.

Garnet shoved him back. "No, you idiot."

"It's my choice. I'm fine. I can finish. Put the task back on the screen."

Garnet covered half of her face with her free hand and sighed.

"Let her do it, Garnet," Drips said.

"She's determined. Just let her," Nail's voice chimed in.

"Let me contact Wolf first," Garnet said.

"No." Skin's voice. "That will take too long, and you know it. Just let her do it. And you know that's what Wolf would want too."

"Fine," Garnet shouted. "You're crazy, Lois, but we all are. See you in thirteen minutes, I guess."

"See you in thirteen minutes," Penelope said.

Giving a final frustrated groan, Garnet disappeared, and the screen once again showed the countdown and the camera. Her phone emitted a slight, dull light, enough that she could see her hands and sleeves. It wasn't enough to continue the search, but she cringed away from the idea of bending down to search for her flashlight in the rubble.

The flashlight on her phone, however, could be accessed by swiping up, regardless of what app she had open. She tried it.

"Yes!" she exclaimed when the command options appeared. For once, the phone had obeyed a touch that wasn't part of the app. She pressed the flashlight icon, and a piercing beam of white light illuminated the dusty air in front of her.

Slowly, careful not to twist her right, she moved the light around the room. Behind and above her, the door to the basement stood ajar. The lower half of the stairs remained intact, the rest a jumbled mess on the floor around her. The space itself had a low ceiling, so low she would have to duck in some spots.

A water heater and furnace stood in the far right corner. Two file boxes sat along the right wall, their lids askew, paper spilling onto the floor. Directly across from her, a door led, she presumed, outside.

To her left, she saw it. Scrawled across the left wall were the words "You Can't Have It!" The red declaration consumed the entire space.

Penelope had seen good graffiti before. It was easy to dismiss graffiti artists as vandals, but Penelope was one of those few people who saw something more than just mess.

This, however, was not graffiti art. These words were scrawled in haste, the strokes of uneven thickness and consistency. Someone had sprayed this protest without caring about how it looked.

The word *calligraphy* referred to artistic handwriting, usually on paper. She had no doubt they wanted her to take a picture of the words to complete the task. But that didn't seem right to her. This wasn't beauty to her. She wasn't sure what the writer had meant by "You Can't Have It," but she felt certain someone experiencing a personal tragedy had sprayed those words.

She knew a few things about personal tragedy, and it wasn't beautiful.

Maybe she could find something else to use. Placing each step with deliberate care, she lurched toward the file boxes. The thought of a misstep terrified her. If she fell, she doubted she would be physically capable of getting up again.

Once she was through the broken wood of the steps, she faced another problem. At this end of the basement, the pipes, wires, and duct work of the house hung low. She bent over into a slight crouch, but her ribs protested that choice. A curse almost left her lips, but the pain stole her voice from her, reducing the word to a startled squeak.

Instead of curling at the midsection, she tried a shuffling squat that allowed her torso to stay straight. It wasn't comfortable, but it would work for moving to the other end of the basement.

Once she reached the file boxes, she tossed the lids to the side. Both of them contained a collection of crumpled paper balls wadded with the care of someone forming a snowball. She reached for one ball but stopped.

Is this right? she asked herself. *Is snooping through someone's trash any less invasive than taking a picture of their emotional graffiti?*

But she wanted to know. Maybe the papers contained the answer to why this house was abandoned, why all the rooms were such a mess, why those words had been left on the wall.

A journalist's curiosity, maybe.

Carefully, she pulled apart one of the paper balls. It was a property appraisal dated 2012. Property appraisals, Penelope knew, provided homeowners with the value of their home, and are usually completed during a home's sale. Most people didn't get their property appraised for no reason. She laid the paper next to her and opened another.

It was labeled "Foreclosure Mediation." While she had never seen those two words together, she knew the meaning of the words individually. Scanning over the document only verified her theory. It was a revised payment plan for the house's mortgage. The bank had offered lower monthly payments when the homeowner couldn't pay the original amounts.

She flipped the paper over to read where the document had been signed by the bank as well as a Gerald Brinkman. The signature was tidy, professional. She remembered the hand-stitched towel in the living room.

That must have been the dad's name—Gerald, she thought.

She felt her heart lurch as she pieced the clues together. She had a good idea what had happened to this family. The next couple of papers were budgets, mortgage statements, and revised foreclosure mediation documents. The sixth paper ball verified her theory. "Judgment of Foreclosure" titled the wrinkled sheet. The bank had taken this family's house after they couldn't make the payments on it any longer.

That explained why every room was trashed but nothing of real value was left. It also explained the words on the wall. The bank had seized the property, but she wondered how long it had taken the family to actually leave. Maybe they waited until they were actually evicted.

She turned this document over and examined Gerald's signature. There was nothing tidy or professional about his signature this time. It was almost scratched into the paper, and it was so large that it covered up some other text. It looked as if a child had written it. Obviously, it was Gerald's private way of giving the entire foreclosure process the middle finger.

His rebellion was beautiful.

Penelope held up the phone and snapped the picture.

Broken app: *Pending. Rejected.*

Once again, she saw the same instructions.

Broken app: *Find calligraphy in the basement.*

It was waiting for her to take a picture of the graffiti, which she refused to do. She took a picture of the signature again.

Broken app: *Pending. Rejected. Would you like to receive the next task? YES NO*

Penelope touched the "Yes."

Broken app: *Find the landscape panorama.*

Unlike the other tasks, this instruction didn't provide her with a room. But Penelope knew where she was supposed to go. She had seen all the rooms in the house, including the two small bedrooms next to the basement door. A panorama view could only be seen from a roof.

The only problem would be getting up there.

Moving in her crouching shuffle, she reached the basement door she presumed led outside. Here the ceiling was higher, so she slowly straightened her legs, keeping her midsection as still as possible. Once she was standing, she leaned against the basement's cement wall for a moment, catching her breath.

"Pain is subjective," she said aloud. "Mind over matter. Mind over matter."

As she spoke, she realized something. Garnet, Nail, Skin, and Drips could hear everything she was saying. They could probably see her actions through the camera phone too. That was the only way they could have known she had fallen through the stairs. They were watching her.

Might as well make the best of it, she decided.

She brought the phone up to her face. "Guys, are you ready to go on the roof?" No reply, of course. She unbolted the basement door's lock, opened both it as well as the screen door, which squeaked horribly, and stumbled into a small concrete room.

Or maybe room wasn't the best description. Ahead of her and to her right, a gray retaining wall reached above her head. To her left, concrete stairs led up to the backyard. An aluminum trash can lay on its side at the bottom of the stairs. The freezing rain fell in a steady stream now, but the retaining wall and the roof's overhang provided some shelter from the drops' bite. The stairs, she noted, were covered in a thin sheet of ice.

Penelope knew she couldn't keep her balance on the stairs while also trying not to move the upper half of her body, but that was easy to get around. She approached the stairs and gingerly righted the trash can. Then she turned around and eased herself down on the third one. She began to go up the stairs one at a time, first pushing up with her arms, then moving her feet. It was just like how her toddler cousin moved down steps. Who knew it would work for a teenage girl with a cracked rib on icy stairs?

When she reached the top, she rested. Now that she was out of the basement and all its darkness and memories, exhaustion threatened to overtake her. More than anything else, she wanted to curl over, rest her face in her hands, and close her eyes. But she had a job to finish, and they were watching.

No longer near the retaining wall, Penelope was left exposed to the icy precipitation. The drops almost hurt when they hit the bare skin of her hands and face, and she could feel her clothes becoming saturated. The ice of the step soaked through her jeans, its biting cold touching her skin.

She managed to stand using only her knees and her balance. Her feet stood on a narrow, broken sidewalk. The edge of the roof, which sloped gently upward in the center, was about nine feet off the ground. Illuminating the yard with her phone flashlight revealed overgrown grass. There was little to see and even less left behind.

But there was one useful item. Turning back toward the basement stairs, she saw it—the intact aluminum trash can. She grimaced as her plan formed, but she didn't see any other option. And she would have to hurry—only seven minutes remained.

The first task was bringing the trash can up the stairs. She went down the steps the same way she came up except facing forward. Her pants and jacket were soaked by the time she reached the bottom. The coldness on her ribcage actually soothed the ache there—a little. Remaining seated, she reached for the trash can's handle with her left hand and pulled it close to her. It scraped along the concrete with a metallic scream.

Placing her left hand around a side handle and her right hand on the concrete basement wall for balance, she used her reverse toddler technique to shuffle up one stair at a time, trash can bouncing up behind her. On the last stair, she carefully stood and pulled the trash can over the ledge. Her teeth chattered, and she had lost feeling in her hands. Proper outerwear and tennis shoes—something to remember for next time. If there was a next time of whatever this was.

But there was no time to reflect. She pulled the trash can to a level part of the sidewalk and flipped it over so that she could stand on its base. Now she just had to climb up. No big deal, right? The phone went into her left pocket, blocking the crew's view of anything about to happen.

She put a steadying hand on the siding of the house as she hoisted a knee onto the trash can.

No breath. Again. And lights, sparks, flashing in her vision. She couldn't see.

But rather than rest—which she knew would be far worse—she leaned up on the knee and brought her other foot onto the trash can, then stood up and gripped the drain on the edge of the house for balance. It was slippery, so slippery she struggled to maintain a grip with her numb fingers. But she knew her choices were cling on or tumble off the trash can.

She breathed through the pain in her side until it faded slightly. The trash can, resting on cracked concrete, wobbled and swayed every time she shifted her body weight.

She knew what she had to do next. Dreaded it but knew it.

Tears streaming, she bent her knees and jumped.

Her upper half dangled on the edge of the roof, elbows bent and midsection leaning on the gutter. Without her injury, it would have been uncomfortable. Now, it was agony. Never in her life had she felt pain this intense. This pain snatched her words and snatched her thoughts, replacing everything she knew and felt with itself. Pain like this was greedy.

But she straightened her arms and heaved her legs over the top. Since she was already on her side and belly, she stayed in a crawling position and scrambled up the slanted roof. In the center, the roof reached its peak. A small chimney provided her with the needed support to sit, catch her breath, and turn toward the view.

Despite the pain, she beamed.

The St. Louis skyline. In the distance, she could see the shapes and lights of the city's downtown center. The Arch, of course, dominated all the other nondescript high rises. The landmark, a sweeping curve of silver, had always defined the city. It seemed to glow in its own ball of warm light. Seeing this skyline, which had been her home for six years, filled her with a sense of calm.

She pulled the phone from her pocket. Even through the cracked screen, the city looked perfect to her. The picture almost took itself.

Broken app: *Pending. Accepted. All tasks complete. Wait for further instruction.*

She sighed and realized the tears had stopped. The pain was still there, but at least she had finished . . .

Penelope completed the painting just as Ms. Collins told the class to start cleaning up for the day. Never had she been able to fill an entire canvas in one class period. Before the teacher could notice, she popped a few more pain pills. As she put the finishing touches on the painting, she realized there were a few students standing behind her.

One said, "Wow, Penelope, it's—"

"It's beautiful," she finished.

On the canvas, in bold purple strokes, was the abandoned house, the St. Louis skyline in the background.

BROKEN APP: MESSAGES

Wednesday, 1:18 a.m.

Garnet: *We're back. Sorry it took a little bit to contact you. Drips and I were delayed.*

Wolf Cub: *I was lying awake worrying about everyone. Now I hear the only reason is because you two decided to get "de-laid"?*

Drips: *Hah! Punny.*

Garnet: *Please don't start with me, Wolf. It's been a rough night.*

Wolf Cub: *What happened? Did Lois pass?*

Garnet: *Oh, yeah. She definitely passed. With a fast time. And she gets it. She understands the deeper meaning of the whole thing. That wasn't the problem. Or problems.*

Wolf Cub: *What were the problems?*

Garnet: *First, she didn't come alone.*

Wolf Cub: *Are you kidding me? I thought you told her to tell no one.*

Garnet: *I did! That was the weird part. She said she just randomly bumped into this dude in the cemetery. He's a complete freak, too. He was there one minute and disappeared the next. I'm serious.*

Wolf Cub: *Do you believe her story?*

Garnet: *Nope, not at all. I don't like this guy. But we did take his business card from her.*

Wolf Cub: *He had business cards?*

Garnet: *Like I said, he's a freak. I left it with Drips so he can do some checking on him.*

Drips: *Guys, can we wrap this up? I'm tired. We have school tomorrow.*

Wolf Cub: *Just hold on, Drips. Did you research this guy from the cemetery?*

Drips: *A little bit. I'll dive into it more tomorrow. I found his paranormal investigation site. It's pretty legit. I'll message when I get more.*

Wolf Cub: *That was the first problem. We can figure out what to do with him later. What about the second?*

Garnet: *The stairs to the basement broke, but she begged to finish the test anyway. She passed out. It was a pain in the ass getting her down from there.*

Wolf Cub: *Wow. Well, that decides it.*

Garnet: *What?*

Wolf Cub: *She's in. As long as nothing goes ridiculously wrong at the mall, she's part of the Pack now.*

Garnet: *Can we just wait and see what Drips finds on this freak Ghostboy first? I smell something funny.*

Wolf Cub: *Of course.*

Garnet: *Wolf, I don't mean to be a hater, but are you sure about that location?*

Wolf Cub: *If we don't start taking some risks, we'll always be the tenth of ten teams.*

Garnet: *You're the boss. See you Friday.*

7

THE GHOST HUNTER

The text came at 12:37 a.m.

Unknown: *Hey, it's Penelope. I'm safe.*

Lex paused the game, slid the headphones off his head, and laid the controller on the floor. He had regretted letting Penelope go the moment he hoisted her over the fence, his guilt keeping him from sleeping until he got the text. Now that he had received it, he wasn't sure how to reply.

He went with the truth. He tended to go with the truth, even when it got him into trouble.

Lex: *I'm glad. I was worried.*

Unknown: *Why?*

Lex: *I feel responsible. I shouldn't have let you go.*

Unknown: *Well, it was never your choice. It was mine.*

He felt he had somehow wronged her. He didn't want to make her upset.

Lex: *True. I'm sorry.*

Unknown: *Don't apologize. Thank you for everything. I left the recorder where you said. Can we talk tomorrow after school? I'm exhausted.*

Swallowing his nerves and fighting back the rising heat in his chest, he carefully constructed his reply.

Lex: *OK. Sleep well.*

Unknown: *You too.*

After adding her number to his contacts, he let the phone fall out of his hand. He groaned. With a final huff, he turned off the console. There was no way he could play now. He just needed to think—close his eyes and let his thoughts swirl. Maybe something solid would materialize out of that chaotic spinning.

He slid out of his gaming chair and jumped into bed. There was little else in his bedroom except for his juiced-up desktop computer in the corner. If he made his room too appealing, he would be tempted to stay in it. He couldn't do that, not when there was so much work to be done.

His father Julian, one of the original paranormal investigators before every cable station had a "ghost" show in its programming, was a legend in the paranormal community. Before he succumbed to sickness, Julian taught Lex everything he knew about the scientific approach to paranormal investigation. Yet, despite all his skill and fame, Julian never managed to capture irrefutable evidence of the existence of the paranormal.

After his father's death, Lex vowed to honor his memory by continuing his work. The paranormal world existed, just like the "real" world around him existed. He just had to prove it. Anyone who ever doubted his father—his mother among them—would have to eat their damn words.

As a rule, his investigating backpack stayed propped by his bedside. In the morning, it would be his school book bag, and he would add a few notebooks and folders to the items already inside.

In October, some moron had called in a bomb threat and school security had searched everyone's belongings at the school entrance. Lex could still see the security guard's face when he pulled out his digital EMF and temperature meter. Nothing in his investigation kit was against school safety policy exactly, but it was hard to convince the uneducated. It resulted in a parent meeting.

He remembered his mom trying to explain his "condition" to his principal. "His dad passed away a few years ago before we moved to St. Louis," she had said. "This is how he stays close to him. It's been a natural outlet for his depressive behavior."

With his elbows on his legs and his hands covering his eyes, Lex had wished he could disappear. Slipping into the realm of the unknown he had vowed to spend his life unraveling sounded appealing at that moment. "I'm right here, Mom. Don't talk about me like I'm not. Right. Here."

His mother whipped her head around, giving him that look he knew all too well.

Principal Peeler had intervened before the conflict escalated, though her words did little to diffuse his mom's concerns. "Lex is a brilliant student. A four-point-oh GPA since his freshman year. And while his disciplinary record is impeccably clean, we've received eleven separate complaints about him. His solitary habits have alarmed other students. He never talks to his classmates or raises his hand. We are constantly forced to remind him to keep his hood down. His teachers tell me his written insights are astounding, but they are worried about him due to his lack of interaction with—well, anyone.

"Lex, why not join a club?" He could hear the forced smile in her voice. "You're a junior, and with your grades, you could get into any school you want with scholarships. Schools want well-rounded students, which means you need some extracurriculars. I'm sure the theater department would love someone with your technology skills—"

"Not interested," he said, his face still buried.

"Alexander," his mom exclaimed. "Pick your face up."

Lex lifted his face and forced his lips into a slight grin. With staged formality, he recited, "I regret to inform you I'm not interested, ma'am."

That whole episode had resulted in his grounding for a month. No investigations for a solid month, during October no less, had almost killed him. At school, he had been forced to attend weekly sessions with the dopey school counselor. The overscheduled fool's counseling sessions had consisted of him talking to himself for thirty minutes about random topics he probably had pulled from teen self-help books, like self-esteem and body hygiene.

Other than his weekly counseling, life had fallen back into its regular routine by November, which included investigations, gaming, homework, and chores. It was the best he could do to make his mom proud, though he knew he fell far short of the perfect picture she wanted to stage after his dad's death. His mom was a Washington University professor, author, and researcher—a book jacket cover personified. His sister Nadine was majoring in pre-med at the University of Missouri-Columbia. He and Nadine had always been close, close to the point of dependency on Lex's part. But she was two hours away in Columbia, and texting wasn't the same as having her at home. In the end, Lex was the underdeveloped son in the portrait of his mom's success.

"All those brains, Lex, and all you want to do is run around graveyards," his mother always said.

Then he'd run off to a graveyard.

Other than those periodic run-ins with his mom, things had been normal.

But now?

When he closed his eyes, he saw the eyes of another—big, startled, eager eyes. He tried to invent a reason to text her again, but he couldn't come up with anything.

She had said she needed sleep.

Sleep, he resolved. *Probably a good idea.*

Computer Science served as a daily joke class. The teacher had made the mistake of providing them with the class curriculum at the beginning of the semester. It was one of those "project-based learning" classes, which meant Lex's entire grade came from the completion of a few basic programs with elementary school coding.

He had completed all the assignments by the first week of February, and now he used class time to listen to his investigation audio files collected with the EVP recorder. Any time the teacher circulated to his computer, he changed the computer screen to one of the projects in its earlier stages of development. No reason for the teacher to know he was done, and with how many hours of recordings he took, he needed the time to listen.

Today's recording was not typical. Before school, he had sneaked out to Bellefontaine to retrieve the EVP recorder, making it home before his mom woke up to drive him. The file, he quickly discovered, was about twenty minutes of heavy metal, thirty minutes of the four buffoons who had picked up Penelope chattering away, and another twenty minutes of her telling them everything that had happened.

Most of the conversation without Penelope present was a lot of shouting, teasing, and hollering at someone named Drips to shut up. But not all of it. About five minutes of dialogue proved useful, and he replayed it three times just to be sure he had heard correctly. Each time he heard the section again, anger coiled tighter in his stomach. He had to tell Penelope.

Keeping one eye on the teacher, he pulled his phone out of his backpack. The front pocket of his hoodie doubled as a perfect cell phone concealer. He sent a quick message.

Lex: *Do not do anything they say. They're playing you. We have to talk.*

Penelope: *One more class before I'm done. Do you want to meet?*

Lex: *Yes. Where?*

Penelope: *Laumeier Sculpture Park? I just realized I don't even know where you go to school.*

No, Lex hadn't told her his school. He couldn't drop that on her, not yet anyway. There was also no way he could tell the cute girl he didn't have a car. His mom wouldn't allow it because she didn't trust him not to drive to remote cemeteries in other states. By the time you were a junior, no one was supposed to ride public transportation, but he did. Ask him a bus route, and he probably had it memorized.

He needed a plan.

Lex: *Mom, you're off today, right?*

His mother replied within minutes.

The Mother: *I'm preparing for my conference, honey. Why are you texting in class?*

Lex: *We have a project at Laumeier Sculpture Park. Could you pick me up from school so I won't miss it?*

The Mother: *All the way out there? Why?*

Lex: *Please, Mom? The other kids need me.*

He felt a little guilty for the manipulation. He knew she would agree because she would be so happy to hear about him working on a school project with other "peers his age."

Sure enough, his mother agreed to drive him as long as he found a ride home.

Riding in a car alone with Penelope had its own terrifying appeal.

Lex: *I can meet you, but I need a ride back.*

Penelope: *No problem. Meet me at the spring bathhouse at 4.*

For the rest of class, he listened to the last twenty minutes of the file. His jaw tightened when Penelope described her fall, her broken rib, and blacking out on the roof. But he admired her, too, for her courage and her creativity. When the other members asked why she refused to photograph the graffiti, they were impressed with her reasoning. It sounded like no one else who had gone through the trial had realized the home was abandoned due to foreclosure.

Little was said during the drive from his high school to the sculpture park. His mom was playing an audiobook released by one of her colleagues, so Lex updated his social media pages and replied to comments posted by fans from across the country. Some of his recordings and photographs had gained him some notoriety. Also, the fact he was the late Julian Sterling's son retained the attention of people who had followed his dad's work.

The sculpture park's lot was empty. They had beaten her.

His mother paused the audiobook. "Home by ten, Lex. I mean it."

"Yes ma'am," he said with an eye roll as he shut the car door.

The park included rolling hills and winding, looping, wooded trails. Statues, metalwork, whirligigs, and other works of art were scattered throughout the park. Their placement seemed to complement the scenery, as if nature had formed the sculptures in its womb and spat them out of the earth.

It took him awhile to find Penelope's requested meeting location. It wasn't a large sculpture that dominated the landscape, like the massive, bloodshot eyeball or the red behemoth that resembled a giant's toy blocks arranged in a sloppy pile. The bathhouse, if it could be called that, was hidden along a narrow, wooded path. Beneath an overhanging rock, walls of natural stone formed a room of three sides, about seven feet deep and six feet high. The fourth side opened to a view to the trail. Two stone benches welcomed travelers along the back wall. There was a hole in its center, which Lex avoided as he entered and sat down.

The air was warmer and melting ice and last night's rain had turned the dirt trails to a muddy goop. But the bathhouse's interior was noticeably cooler. He doubted many visitors found this secluded spot, and if they did find it, they probably wouldn't stick around such a lonely and dark place. Lex loved it. He closed his eyes and leaned his hooded head against the stones, forcing down his bubbling nervousness.

The sucking sound of her shoes in the mud announced her approach. He wasn't sure how to greet her, so he kept his eyes closed and waited.

"Hey."

He pretended to wake up, rubbing his cheeks.

"Sorry. You must be tired because I kept you up last night."

"No, it's cool," he said after clearing his throat.

She sat next to him, keeping her back straight, and sighed. Pulling a bottle of pills from her pocket, she popped open the lid and slid two pills between her lips. Lex found himself glancing at those pursed lips and her slender throat as she swallowed them down dry.

When he tried to look at her eyes from under the hood, he saw she was staring at the dirt floor.

"I heard about the stairs. You sure you shouldn't be lying down or something?"

She shook her head, green tresses swaying. "No. It feels a little better today, and ibuprofen cures everything. What did you find out?"

His voice became more confident. "They weren't ever going to give you the story. It was all a setup. They kept talking about this guy named Wolf. Wolf, I think, persuaded this girl Lacie to tell you about those jerks from last night. Lacie doesn't like you much, I guess, so she was quick to agree to the fake story."

"Yeah," Penelope mumbled. She tapped her foot on the packed dirt floor. "That sounds about right."

"But they played Lacie because they used her just to pass the message. They want you to join them. It was never about the story. They want you to join their stupid club, and that kiddie quiz game last night was their little initiation."

The tapping foot stopped, and he looked up to find her wide dark eyes staring at him. "Me?" she asked. "Why?" Her eyes seemed to brighten.

He had expected her to sound revolted. Instead, she sounded hopeful.

"Why? You want into that masked henchmen brigade? Do you even know what they're all about yet?"

She frowned and resumed tapping. "No, I don't, but there's something about the way they see things and one another. I guess I'm not completely disgusted by them."

"Listen. There's more. The last step is meeting this Wolf guy. They are going to put you through another stupid test Friday night, but it's going to be at that abandoned mall in South County. That's where they will meet you and ask you to join them. Probably do a blood ritual or something. Sacrifice a kitten."

"This coming from the ghost hunter," she teased.

"That's different," he retorted stuffily. "That's science."

"Pseudoscience, maybe."

He sucked his teeth. "You sound like my mother."

She glanced at him from under a protective layer of bangs. "You're not going to like this, but I'm going Friday."

He shook his head. "I figured you'd say that. I want to come with you. May I?"

She grinned. A cute grin, a grin he wanted to see again. "So proper. And sure… but why?"

He stared into the woods in front of them. Slight breezes tickled the dead foliage, creating gentle rustling sounds. The air smelled like two seasons—the dried smells of winter and the rich, thick smells of spring. He tried to find the words.

"I've always just had a sense of things. Not seeing into the future or anything. It's a feeling I get. Sometimes it's in my gut. Sometimes it's right in the middle of my forehead. Sometimes it's like fire needles all over my body. I can just tell when things are going to go wrong or right. And when I saw you, I just got a feeling. I've learned to follow those feelings. Every time I don't, I regret it. For now, I want to come. And I think there might be something we can do to prevent them from having the upper hand, but I'll need your help."

"Yeah, I can help. What was the feeling?"

He glanced up and back down. "What do you mean?"

"Was it a wrong feeling or a right feeling?"

"Both."

She nodded, and they sat in silence for a few moments.

Lex laid his hands on the natural stones, running his long fingers along their surfaces, touching the gaps in between. "Why did you choose this place?"

"I thought you'd like it," she said.

"Well, you were right. I like it a lot. Bathhouses like this were built over springs. People, mostly rich people, traveled long distances to bathe in the spring waters. They believed the water could lengthen their lives, heal their injuries, and give them insights into the unknown. And spring water has been known to attract paranormal activity."

She ducked her head. "I didn't know all that, but it just seemed like a place you'd like. Do you think this place is haunted?"

"I don't use that word. And I don't say 'ghost' either. But, yes, I would conduct an investigation here."

"Would you?"

"Right now?"

She shrugged. "Why not?"

"Well, it's daylight. I mean, I've picked up a few things during daylight, but not many. And I usually don't do this with other—"

She was already nodding. "Oh. Oh, I see. You need to be alone. Sorry I asked."

"No, no. I mean, just because I haven't done it before doesn't mean I can't. And who knows when I'll get back here, right? Would you mind if I—"

"Not at all. I want to see. I'll be quiet. I promise."

He began to remove his items from his bag, including the EVP recorder that had been around her ankle less than twenty-four hours beforehand. "You aren't scared?"

She shook her head. "Nope. I was a little freaked out in the cemetery, but I've never done anything like that before. Now, I guess I should be, but I'm not. Maybe I've seen living people do too many terrible things to be afraid of what ghosts can do. I mean, paranormal entities."

He glanced up from his bag, but she turned away. He wanted to ask her what she meant by "terrible things," but as the EVP recorder reminded him, he had known her less than twenty-four hours. He couldn't ask. Not yet.

Once all the preparations were made, he began his recording.

"This is Alexander 'Lex' Sterling. The date is Wednesday, March ninth. Time is 16:22 Central Military Time or 4:22 p.m. Central Daylight Time. Location is Laumeier Sculpture Park, spring bathhouse. This is my first visit. And I'm accompanied by Penelope—"

"Penelope Pine," she piped in.

"Penelope Pine, probably the most intriguing female I've encountered during any investigation, ever."

Did I just say that? Seriously? He wanted to slap himself in the forehead. *What is wrong with me?*

But he saw her smile even wider. She scooted just a little bit closer.

"Now we will start the observation. I'll add notes to the journal and then attempt contact."

As he pulled out his journal to write, he felt her head rest on his shoulder.

8

VICTIMS OF THE SYSTEM

I've lost my damn mind, Penelope thought. *What is wrong with me?* In the last few days, she had wandered around a historic cemetery after visiting hours, followed a stranger, gotten in a car with more strangers (in masks, no less), and broken her rib while banging around an abandoned house.

Oh yeah, she reminded herself. *And lied to my parents.*

Yet she didn't want to call it quits. Even though Lex had proven the group members had been lying to her from the start, she felt compelled to learn more about them. Somehow, she felt connected to them already. Their philosophy intrigued her, and their obvious close bond made her heart ache. Friends her age who truly understood her—it was something she had always longed for.

The sight in front of her, however, filled her with doubt. She wondered if she was in over her head.

She and Lex stood outside the chain-link fence gate and scanned the sign attached to it.

"Could they arrest us?" Penelope asked.

"Sure," Lex said with a shrug. "But they would probably just call our parents."

That turned her pale skin even paler, which caused Lex to chuckle.

"What's so funny?" she asked.

"You're not used to trespassing, are you?"

"Not really," she said quietly. "The cemetery was supposed to be a one-time thing."

"You think the Broken has permission to use that farmhouse as its little test center? So technically, this is your third time trespassing. The only reason you're nervous now is because these guys put up a sign."

"True," she muttered.

The red-and-white sign read "Private Property. No Trespassing. Violators Will Be Prosecuted to the Fullest Extent of the Law." They had passed the mall on the road as they approached it. It was set lower than the road itself, so passersby could see the long stretch of its exterior. From the outside, it appeared to be in decent condition other than the untended planters overgrown with dead foliage.

The previous forty-eight hours had passed in a blur. Wednesday's hunt at Laumeier had turned up little to Penelope's untrained ears. Afterward, Penelope drove Lex home, but he asked to be dropped off a few blocks from his house. He said he didn't want his mom to ask her twenty questions.

When he told her to stop the car, they were still in a commercial area, not a neighborhood. She asked if he was sure this was close enough, and he mumbled something in reply about wanting to pick up some razors. He jumped out of the car and started walking.

Penelope was curious. Something was up. She tried circling the area. After passing the same strip mall four separate times, she accepted that she had lost him.

Did he intentionally disappear? she wondered.

They had spent most of Thursday and Friday texting each other. Penelope tried to hide her recent phone obsession from Mike. This proved easier than expected because he worked late Thursday and had been stuck at the airport all Friday afternoon waiting for Henry's delayed flight.

Earlier that day, Penelope had told Taylor with confidence that she wanted to be considered for the features editor spot. Taylor had seemed delighted. Lacie, however, slammed her story's first draft about the clown girl, and her syrupy, fake sweetness was replaced by sneers. Penelope could only guess Lacie was irritated that Elijah hadn't looked at her since she had passed on the message to Penelope. When Lacie asked Penelope how the story was turning out, Penelope surprised herself by looking Lacie in the eye and responding, "It's fantastic, actually. Thanks, Lacie."

Also, Penelope found she wasn't nearly as worried about Lacie's jeers as she had been before. Maybe it was the constant ache in her side, or maybe it was just that Lacie didn't seem all that threatening anymore. She hoped the story's final draft would be enough to prove her talent to Taylor. An actual story about the Broken would be a bonus, but she wouldn't count on it. No, her interest in the group had surpassed journalistic curiosity to something much more personal.

The first clues and instructions started popping on her phone at about 5 p.m., and Lex's recording was right. The cryptic clues led them directly to the mall. The final meeting place was inside the mall itself.

Its location was a riddle.

Broken app: *Its stories are over. But your story is just beginning.*

Lex had sneered when she showed him the message. "Wow, how cliché. But what can you expect from a group calling themselves 'the Broken'?"

Penelope had parked her car in a retail store's lot across the street. They noticed that the mall's front lot stood empty except for one vehicle—a security SUV without a driver.

With caution, the pair walked down a skinny driveway leading to the mall's underground parking. Dusk shadowed most of the road. Dead weeds had sprung up between the road's cracks.

The fence with its no trespassing sign served as the last barrier to the lot.

Lex leaned in closer. "Do you wanna go back? I saw a Mexican place on the way here, and that roadside graveyard—"

"That's your idea of a fun Friday night? Mexican food and a cemetery?"

He beamed a wolfish grin.

"No. No Mexican, and no ghosts," she said with a furrowed brow. "At least, not at that graveyard. Maybe we'll find some *paranormal entities* inside."

"Oh, this place isn't haunted," he said with nonchalance.

"Are you sure about that?"

"Come on. It's an old mall. What do you expect, the ghost of Suncoast? Some emo anime fan from the early two thousands who splatters you with black eyeliner?"

"Sounds terrifying."

"It is terrifying. I agree," he said in mock seriousness. "And don't forget about that rent-a-cop prowling around inside."

"God, I hope we don't find him," Penelope moaned.

"Good point. Let's go back. We could do something normal like a movie. I swear."

She didn't bother replying. Instead, she sucked in a breath and shimmied through the crack in the fence.

Lex groaned and joined her. In her peripheral vision, his hand reached hesitantly for hers. When she clasped her fingers around his, she felt a million tiny jolts where their skin met.

She was grateful for the contact. Even though she wouldn't admit it, the idea of a prowling, overzealous rent-a-cop scared her more than Lex's ghosts. Every dark space and corner seemed to be the perfect hiding spot. The underground parking lot stood deserted. Concrete pillars loomed ominously above their heads. There were no sounds other than their footsteps, and even they seemed muted, as if the darkness were creating a vacuum.

Penelope's anxiety caused her mind to cartwheel. Nothing could escape from a vacuum in space. Could she and Lex be sucked in? Where would they go? Would they be entrapped in one of the pillars for all eternity? Maybe the pillars were the coffins of teenage trespassers. If she and Lex were consumed by the darkness, what would be left of them?

Penelope broke into a jog, trying to outpace the thoughts she knew on one level were ludicrous but on another level felt all too real. Lex's hand slipped from hers as she sped ahead.

Lex guffawed. The sound escaped the vacuum and bounced around, seeming to grow louder before it grew fainter, turning into long, low moans.

Penelope picked up speed, sprinting toward the center of the parking lot. Lex's feet pounded the pavement behind her. He reached her just as she stopped outside a pair of glass doors.

Penelope let out little hisses of breath, side aching.

Lex watched her with his arms crossed. "I was gonna ask if you should be running with your rib, but you freaked out before I could say anything."

"Uhh, no," she wheezed. "Shouldn't have done that."

"I suppose there wouldn't be any point in me asking if you wanted to—"

"Nope," she said, forcing herself to face the mall entrance. Seeing the doors restored some of her confidence and chased away her crazy nightmares. This entrance was familiar to her.

She grasped her fingers around the handle and pulled. Nothing happened. She peered at the handles through the glass to discover a chain wrapped around them secured with a lock.

"You didn't think it would open, did you?"

"A little. Look. The lights are on."

"It's still clean in there. Not that messed up," Lex said. He leaned in to whisper in her ear. "Must mean they're still hoping to sell the place. Must mean they've spent a lot of money on security guards."

"Now you're just trying to scare me. Be quiet while I think." Penelope roamed the outside wall. Just as she suspected, there was another door on the opposite side with a sign reading "Employees Only." When she tugged on this handle, it opened. Inside a lighted staircase led to a hallway.

Lex asked, "How did you—"

"I used to come here with my dads," she said as she began climbing the stairs. "I remember seeing this door and wondering where it led."

"Well," Lex whispered, "you're about to find out."

At the top of the stairs, they peered around the corner. A narrow hallway extended in both directions. Evenly spaced, numbered doors lined one of the walls.

"Corridors run behind all the stores," Lex explained. "Each door leads into a different store. My sister worked at the mall back home."

"Well, only one thing to do." She tried the first door. Locked. "I'll start going this way. You go that way."

Penelope tried the second, third, and fourth doors. On the fifth, the latch released. "Lex!" she whispered and backed away.

He jogged over to her and pressed his body against the wall. Extending his arm, he gradually inched the door open, peeking around the widening gap. "I don't see anybody," he mumbled.

Her phone buzzed. Penelope glanced at its cracked screen.

Broken app: *Ten-Minute Warning.*

"Our friends are getting anxious," Lex said as he moved through the door. They had entered one of many mall stores. Its lights were still on, the rug was newly vacuumed, and the walls were free of spray paint. Some shelves still remained, as well. Only the canned music, products, and people were missing.

"This is weird," Penelope said.

"Like the long-awaited zombie apocalypse," Lex said with a grin. "I love it. When did this place close?"

Penelope advanced with caution, almost tiptoeing. "It completely closed last year. But it tried to stay open for a long time. It was a slow, painful mall death."

"Sounds tragic."

They reached the front of the store, where tarps covered the large display windows. A grated gate covered in a tarp blocked the exit to the mall's main thoroughfare, but there was a two-foot gap between the floor and the gate. Lex sprawled his long body on the floor and peeked his head into the mall, checking in both directions.

"I don't see anybody," he whispered. He shimmied under the gate, then reached his hand down to help Penelope do the same. The carpet of the store transitional to the tiles of the mall, which felt cool on her open palms. They both stood.

Lex looked down the long hallway, his eyebrows pinched together. "Do you know where you're going?"

Penelope held her breath. What she saw caused her eyes to mist over with tears. It was empty. All of it. She had expected it to be empty, but she hadn't expected to be emotionally influenced by the sight. Quickly, she wiped her eyes.

"Are you okay?" he asked.

"Yeah."

"Guess it really was a slow, painful mall death," he said with a little smile.

"It's super sad, right?" She chuckled as she wiped her face again. "Sorry. It's just that this is the first place I came with my dads after we became a family. It was before Christmas. They asked me to go through some stores and tell them what I wanted for gifts. I had never done that before."

"What? Faced a Christmas mall horde?"

"No," she said. "Received gifts. As in more than one."

He stood next to her, listening and still. After a few moments, he muttered, "I mean, if this is too much for you, some chips and salsa sound good right now."

She whacked him in the stomach.

He pretended to double over. "Oof!"

"Don't be a poop. Let's go."

"So, you do know where you're going?"

"Of course. 'Stories.' There's a movie theater all the way at the other end."

They left the store and started a quick walk. At every corner, they would hide long enough to scout out the next stretch. The other vacant stores contained a few shelves and forgotten signs but little else. The gleaming floors were free of footprints or scuffs. Overhead, the skylights filled with a darkening gray as night continued to settle. The planters underneath them contained skinny palm trees so tall they almost touched the ceiling.

Somehow, the lack of people made it easier for Penelope to recall memories with her family, as if the empty setting were providing the perfect stage for her mind's own private play.

She saw the toy store where she had picked out a giant stuffed frog. That jewelry store was where Henry had cried when she had her ears pierced. Down those stairs was the food court where she drank three sodas and went across the hall to play three rounds on an electronic dance pad. Of course, she still went shopping with her dads, but this mall had been the setting of so many family firsts.

She let out a shaky sigh. "You know, it is a little sad. All of this going to waste. Think about what could be done with a place like this."

"Yeah," Lex said. "Like a massive indoor paintball field."

"I was thinking sheltering the homeless."

"That too."

As they approached the last turn before the movie theater, Lex pulled her to a stop behind a corner. Ahead, Penelope could see the snack counter. Movie poster signs still remained, advertising some of the biggest box office hits from a few years ago.

"I'm not going in with you."

"What?" Penelope said. "Why?"

"Because they don't want me there. Uninvited guest crashing the party might be enough to scare them off or freak them out. If they make a bunch of noise, they'll invite other guests—adult guests with clubs."

"Where are you going?"

"I'm staying close. Don't worry. If things start looking sketchy, I'll come back to get you."

"But if you're not in there, how will you know?"

"I'll stay out here in the mall. We haven't seen one guard. Don't you think that's a little weird? Maybe your friends got caught already."

"Don't say that." She stared at the door leading into the theater. "They're not new to this stuff. I'm sure they took precautions. Everything is going to be..."

She trailed off when she realized he was no longer by her side. He had disappeared again. "Well, there's one guy who won't get caught," she said to herself as she approached a dusty velvet rope strung between two shiny metal poles in front of the theater entrance. She ducked under it and opened the door.

Unlike other places in the mall, darkness shrouded the corridor. She couldn't even see outlines of the doors ahead of her, but dim light seeped out from underneath one exception at the end of the corridor.

She hurried to it and pulled on the handle. It swung open to reveal an empty movie theater. It smelled of old popcorn and soda. Black stains from drinks and candy and who knows what else covered the worn red seats. The carpet leading up the aisles was in a similar condition. Outdated sconces lined the maroon wallpaper. They emitted a yellow, sickly glow. She inched to the front of the theater.

Clapping made her jump.

She turned around and realized she had walked right past them. In the back row, Drips, Garnet, Skin, and Nail rested their feet on the chairs in front of them.

A fifth figure, standing alone, clapped after the rest had stopped.

"Elijah," Penelope gasped. "What are you—?"

"Don't call him that," Garnet snapped. "No real names. Ever."

"Garnet, it's cool. It's expected, right?" He peered at her over the rims of his thick black glasses and ran a hand over his dark brown hair tied in a ponytail. "Right now, I'm Wolf."

Elijah looked the same as the photo editor she knew from journalism class, yet he wasn't the same at all. His posture, his speech patterns, his facial expression—everything she knew about him seemed the opposite of the goofy, talkative, talented boy she knew from class.

"Wolf Cub, actually," Drips said.

Garnet punched him on the shoulder, and he yelped.

"Please excuse my friends. They don't have any manners. Yes, I'm Wolf, or Wolf Cub. We are the Pack, part of the Broken, a society of like-minded youth who are devoted to dismantling society's concept of what is beautiful or broken." He turned for a moment. "Garnet, if you please."

"On it." She slid out her seat and left through the same door Penelope had entered.

"Garnet will make sure our elderly guard friend stays far away. We spotted him during our initial scout of the area. He is enjoying a probably well-deserved coffee and candy bar in what used to be a hair salon. Please, won't you sit with us?"

Penelope stepped forward so she could see their faces. This was the first time she had seen them without masks. Skin and Nail were so similar it was almost impossible to tell them apart. The exceptions were cosmetic. Skin had died his short, blond hair red, and Nail had piercings lining his ears and brows. They were nearly as pale as Penelope with striking blue eyes.

Beneath his Afro, Drips had a big, slanted smile, round cheeks, and honey brown skin. He had his thumbs jammed in his pockets. He was short, only a little taller than Penelope, and thin-framed. His eyes twinkled with amusement or bemusement. Penelope couldn't tell which.

She turned her attention back to her almost unrecognizable classmate. "Eli—Wolf, what are you doing here?"

"Lois, I'm here to invite you to join us. I'm afraid we can't give you a story to publish. Going public would welcome criticism and consequences."

"Society wouldn't get it," Drips added. "We'd just be a bunch of juvenile delinquents. Victims of the system. All that meaningless shit, and that's if we were lucky. Instead of pity, we'd probably get criminal records."

"On Monday, you passed our test. We would be honored if you—"

Garnet barged in, cutting off Wolf and banging the door on its hinges. "Look who I found snooping around."

Penelope turned to see Lex with his hands pinned behind his back. Garnet held him in place as he struggled.

"What are you, some kind of quarterback?" Lex shouted. "This crazy girl tackled me."

"Cornerback, junior women's league. Division champions for three years straight." She shoved him forward.

Penelope rushed over when she realized Garnet had strapped his wrists together with a zip tie. "Let him go!"

"No! He's a spy, Wolf. She was going to snitch on us."

"No, she wasn't," Lex yelled.

"Why are you here, freak?" Garnet jerked on Lex's arms so hard he winced. "He's the *freak* from the cemetery. I knew they were teamed up as soon as I saw him. She's been lying to us. This is all a setup. She'll call the cops."

"That's not what—" Lex said, but Wolf held up a hand to silence him.

Wolf stepped forward. He turned to Penelope, his eyes narrowed. "Is this true?"

"No," Penelope said. "Let him go, dammit!"

"Let me talk," Lex demanded.

"Your turn, intruder," Wolf said, turning to Lex.

"There are three squad cars in the front lot, and the cops are heading this way."

"Shit!" Drips exclaimed. "We gotta get out of here, guys."

"How do we know he's not just saying that to trick us?" Garnet asked.

Lex shrugged the best he could with his arms pinned. "Fine. Stay here. Watch what happens." He sneered.

"Caution first. Always," Wolf said. He thought for a moment and nodded. "We're leaving."

Lex thrashed his arms. "Cut these, you crazy b—"

"If you say it, I'll cut you instead," Garnet threatened.

Lex clenched his teeth together, but his eyes spoke volumes.

Garnet pulled a pocket knife from her jeans and sliced through the middle of the zip tie. Penelope rushed up to Lex and gripped his arm.

Wolf stared hard at both of them. "Lois, you are here due to our invitation. We will escort you to safety. Your friend, however, is a stranger to us."

"Well, we're not separating. You want me to join your group? He comes, too."

Lex rubbed his wrists. He gave Garnet a dirty look and said, "Yeah, and if you assholes try anything, I'll run right to the cops and tell them you guys are tying people up and torturing them. I have the zip tie cuts to prove it."

"Fine. We've wasted enough time. We'll leave together." Wolf approached Lex. Even though Lex was taller, Wolf seemed to tower over him. "And if you do anything to harm my Pack, I will make you regret it. That's a promise."

9

NEWEST WOLVES

The emergency exit doors on either side of the movie screen were locked from the outside.

"Some fire escape," Drips exclaimed. "How is this up to code?"

"Because, moron, we're not supposed to be in here. It doesn't have to be up to code," Nail said. "Back into the mall, right?"

Wolf made a steeple with his hands and fingers, resting the index fingers on his lip, as he thought. "Where did you see the cars, Lex?"

Lex pulled the drawstrings of his hoodie tight so the hood would stay up as he moved. "Outside. The main lot," he said. "Closer to the underground lot than the other end."

Garnet scoffed. "He could be lying to us to get us caught."

When Penelope turned to Garnet, she was startled by the other girl's beauty. Penelope hadn't seen it before, probably because Garnet hadn't wanted it to be seen.

Garnet kept her black-tipped hair in a messy bun on top of her head. The cartilage of each ear was pierced with four studs, and her lobes displayed small gauges. A hook hung from her nose's septum. Her beauty was evident in her eyes and facial structure. Underneath the anger, her irises shimmered with green and golden flecks. Her sweeping, cream-colored facial features made her appear strong yet delicate.

Wolf glanced at Garnet, Lex, and Penelope. "Until we escape, we have to trust one another. There is too much at stake. We can't waste time doubting everything someone else says and does. Agreed?"

Six voices consented.

"One of the main exits of the big department store at this end leads outside," Penelope said. "We could leave through those doors and run to the main street."

"Those doors could be locked, too," Nail said, shoving his hands in his pockets. "We'd be trapped."

"True, but the only other choice is to walk toward the officer's location, which doesn't seem logical. Penelope's plan is the best we have at the moment," Wolf said. "Garnet, take point. Lex, from what I've heard about you, you are more than capable. Take rear. Let's go."

As the Pack exited the theater, Penelope glanced around the mall. Everything felt different. It was still empty and silent, but it wasn't an eerie silence. This was the silence heard by the prey before the predator's strike.

The sky had changed from dark gray to the darkness of night, and the skylights overhead bowed down with the weight. Penelope's breath quickened as she fell in step near Nail and Skin. Garnet and Wolf led, and Drips followed behind her. Lex, meanwhile, had disappeared.

No one spoke, and everyone padded on silent feet. To reach the department store, the group had to move down a short corridor of empty stores and pass a large opening with a vaulted ceiling. Once they reached the end of the short corridor, Garnet signaled for them to wait as she crept forward to scout.

After a few moments, Garnet waved for them to join her. They dashed into the rotunda.

A large carousel remained. The faces of the animals seemed to be screaming in horror at some unseen terror. In their mania, they tossed their necks and rolled their eyes. Penelope had to tear her gaze away from them.

As they circled around it, Lex rushed up from the side. "They're coming," he whispered. "There must be a camera somewhere or something because they are coming right here. They're only a little bit behind me."

"Do we have enough time to run?" Wolf asked, keeping his voice level.

"You'd have to sprint. Penelope can't sprint because of *you* assholes and your stupid test," Lex growled.

"I refuse to argue with you right now. We split. Skin, Nail, and I will run ahead to secure a route. We will regroup with you in five minutes at the eastern exit doors inside the department store."

Garnet's face twisted in anger, but she didn't argue. "If we're not there in five minutes..." Garnet reached into one of her pockets and threw her keys at Wolf.

He caught them and reluctantly tucked them away.

They heard the grumblings of distant male voices as the beams of high-power flashlights flickered across the corridor.

"Go. Now," Wolf said.

The three of them sprang into action, dashing toward the department store. The four remaining wolves jumped on the carousel, maneuvered around the animals, and ducked into hiding positions off the platform and against the center panels covering its inner workings and painted with green hills and blue skies.

Penelope was on one end. Lex squeezed in between her and Drips. Garnet claimed the other end. Their knees were pinned to their chests.

"Hey," Drips whispered, "it's not always like this."

"Drips, shut up," Garnet hissed.

"No, man. I'm just saying. We don't always get into trouble like this."

"You're about to get into a lot *more* trouble if you don't *shut up*."

Even Drips stopped talking as the light beam reached the polished floor to the right of them. They were facing the department store, the furthest away from the direction of the officers' approach.

Panic rose in Penelope's chest. Lex glanced at her, his own face tightening. He reached for her hand and clung to her.

The approaching voices became distinguishable. "I'm so sick of these damn kids thinking they can just bust in here."

"Just another Friday night in paradise."

"You're a real comedian. Anyway, about your car. If it's your tranny, you might as well start shopping."

"Yeah, that piece of shit you drive wouldn't be worth the repair money."

"I still think it's the carburetor."

"You always think it's the carburetor."

"Doesn't mean it's not the carburetor."

"This guy. I swear."

Garnet had been counting on her fingers. She held up four, and everyone nodded. Four officers heading this way.

A scuffle. It came from under the platform. It sounded like tiny, rusty nails scraping across the floor. Probably a mouse or a rat. Penelope held her breath.

Go away, go away, go away, go away, she prayed to the sound.

But her prayers weren't heard. Drips's yelp pierced the silence. "My foot!" he screeched. "It's trying to eat my foot!" When Penelope looked down, light glinted off a rodent's beady eyes. She gasped.

Drips, in a complete panic, jumped onto the platform.

"Hey, you! Stop!" an officer shouted. Eight feet pounded the floor.

"*Damn you, Drips*!" Garnet screamed. "Run, run!" They scrambled out of their hiding spots, off the carousel, and toward the department store. The officers were still three stores behind them.

"Stop!" another yelled. "Damn kids!"

"We have to lose them," she said. "Somewhere inside. Come on."

The store extended back and back until nothing was visible but complete darkness. It was longer than it was wide, so Penelope could make out the store walls. A few makeup counters remained by the entrance. Garnet zigzagged in between them with the three of them trailing her. She veered to the left, moving toward a checkout counter.

Every time Penelope's feet hit the floor, the pain in her ribs reignited. Her run across the underground lot earlier that evening had not been a good idea. She gave up trying to breathe steadily as the stabs knocked all the air out of her lungs. Despite her difficulties, she managed to keep up and joined the other three as they pressed together behind the counter. *Thank you, Mike, for getting me to run*, she thought.

Garnet pulled her phone from her backpack and tapped with her thumbs. She waited a moment before the phone buzzed with a reply. "Once they pass us," Garnet whispered, "go to the wall closest to the street, to the left. They found something."

Although they were breathing heavily, none of the others were struggling as much as Penelope. She tried inhaling slowly, but that just seemed to strengthen the ache. Instead, she tried to take small, shallow breaths, blowing in and out through her mouth in tiny puffs. Her heaving sounded too loud to her.

The four of them stilled as they listened to the heavy footfalls of the officers entering the department store. Garnet shuffled to the end of the counter. She held one finger up to her lips as her eyes shifted to the ceiling, the floor, and the wall. She looked eager and ready to strike.

Who's the predator now? Penelope thought.

The thudding of their boots grew closer. Then, much to their relief, farther away. The guards had passed them. Still, the four teenagers waited until the footsteps faded completely.

"Are you ready?" Garnet whispered.

Penelope wanted to say no, but they all nodded their heads yes.

Garnet held up three fingers. Two. One. A fist. They jumped out from behind the counter, running as fast as they could.

"There they go!" one of them shouted. Four flashlight beams, like spotlights, fell on them. "Stop. Now!"

The light blinded Penelope, but she forced her body to keep moving. She locked her gaze on the bottom of Lex's legs. Nothing else mattered except keeping up and following him.

Very few obstacles blocked their dash to the opposite wall. Once her eyes had a moment to recover, Penelope found herself grateful for the flashlights at her back. Their light allowed her to sprint with no concern over running into some hidden box or shelf.

Penelope turned her neck. The officers were gaining.

From along the wall, they heard Wolf's voice. "Over here! Hurry!"

Skin, Nail, and Wolf had managed to pry open one of the sliding glass doors. Skin and Nail leaned their bodies into opposite door frames. "Come on, come on, come on, come on!" Skin begged as he strained.

When the four of them reached the doors, they ran sideways through the narrow opening created by the twins. Once all four were across, Skin and Nail dodged away from the door frame. The glass door slammed shut behind them. They didn't wait to see how quickly the officers would find a way through. Instead, all seven of them raced toward the main road.

"Wolf, tell me you found something," Garnet huffed, shouting over their pounding feet.

Wolf didn't answer verbally. He just held up his phone. In response, Garnet thrust her fist in the air.

To adjust for the sloped driveway, they leaned forward to maintain their pace. Streaks of light streamed along either side of them and under their feet. The officers had managed to open the door and were pointing their flashlights. Shouts in the distance commanded them to stop.

Penelope wondered if she should. Running would only get her in more trouble.

She forgot the thought almost as quickly as it formed. For some reason, she trusted the group. She believed Wolf when he said he had found a path to safety.

The group reached the top of the drive, the main entrance to the mall. It had been closed off from the main road with concrete road barriers. One, two, three, four, five of them jumped over the barriers as easily as if they were sidewalk gaps.

Lex, she realized, had moved toward the rear of the group so he could stay close to her. She had almost fallen behind. Now, she stopped running long enough to pull herself over the barriers. Everything above her waist hurt. She wanted to stop, but Lex grabbed her by the elbow and tugged.

"Come on. Almost there," he said. "And next time, I pick what we do."

Penelope nodded, but she was too tired to laugh. She forced herself to run until they reached the highway. Cars zipped by them. Some honked.

The cops continued to close in. The streaking lights surrounded them.

Penelope and Lex glanced around for the others. No one.

"Over here, guys!"

To their left, a music store faced the road at a higher elevation than the mall. Garnet waved at them from the front door. "Come on!"

They turned left and ran inside. With a huff, Garnet shut the door.

Penelope crumpled to the carpet, moaning and clutching her side.

"Come on, princess," Garnet hissed, grabbing her by the armpits. "Ghostboy, help me." The two of them dragged her across the carpet.

Penelope managed to turn her head toward the counter. A younger man stood behind it, shaking his head and smirking.

When they reached the back end of the store, she realized the rest of them were already crouched in the corner of a dark, small room. The space contained a few chairs, music stands, guitars, and amplifiers, but nothing else. Garnet, Lex, and Penelope closed the door and squeezed in next to the group members.

As they struggled to catch their breath, they heard the front door open again.

"Good evening, officers," the young man at the counter said. "May I help you?"

"Yes, you can, kiddo. Did a bunch of hoodlums run in here?"

A glass window was cut into the top half of the door, so Penelope could barely make out the shapes of the others around her. Drips put a hand to his chest and gasped, like the "hoodlum" remark had been a personal insult to his character. Wolf suppressed a chuckle.

"No, sir. It's been pretty quiet, but I did see some teens run across the street."

The shopkeeper's polite, professional tone didn't seem to lighten the officer's mood. "Bud, Gary, go check on that."

"I swear to Christ, Bill, you're buying the first round after this."

Bill, at least they figured it was Bill, just sucked his teeth as they exited. "We'll have a look around, if you don't mind."

"No, of course," the employee replied. "Be my guest."

"Shit," Nail murmured.

The five members of the Broken exchanged glances. Wolf, letting out the smallest sigh, nodded. As if on cue, all five of them leaned forward and put their fists in a circle. They began a frantic, soundless tournament of Rock, Paper, Scissors. Skin and Nail won the first round with rocks. As Garnet, Drips, and Wolf began the second round, Skin made frantic spinning motions with his hand, encouraging them to hurry. They could hear the officers' footsteps coming closer. The first try was a tie, the second was a draw.

"Screw it," Garnet said. She jumped up from her crouched position, threw open the door, and shouted, "My dad's a pastor! You'll go to hell for throwing me in jail!" The door slammed shut behind her. A moment later, they heard the front door bang open as the officers yelled for her to stop and ran in pursuit.

The remaining six stayed in place as they held their collective breath. One minute passed. Two. Three.

The wait gave Penelope the time to process what had just happened. The team had realized they were about to be discovered, and Garnet had sacrificed herself. Penelope frowned with worry.

They heard a slight, gentle rapping on the door. "They're gone," the shopkeeper said.

The team rose to their feet. Wolf moved to the front of the group and opened the door. Satisfied, he swung it wide and led the rest out. They formed a semicircle around the shopkeeper.

"Where did she go?" Wolf asked.

"She ran across the highway. There was a red light at that intersection, so she jumped over the hood of a car." He shook his head. "That's Garnet, right? I've heard about her. She's nuts."

Wolf ignored his commentary. "What about the officers?"

"In pursuit of a dangerous suspect, I guess. They chased her across the highway."

"Now what?" Drips asked. "We can't just leave her. She did that for us, Wolf."

"We'll head to the meeting point and wait for her word." Without waiting for anyone to agree, he moved forward.

The shopkeeper put his palm in the middle of Wolf's chest, stopping him mid-stride. "Hold on just a hot second there, Wolf Cub. We need to talk."

"There's nothing to discuss here, Haze."

"Wait," Lex cut in. "Is that his club name or whatever? Haze? Is he in this cult, too?"

Haze's eyes widened. "You mean you brought some random losers with you, and now they know my name?" He whipped out his phone as his lips curled into a cruel scowl. "I know a certain Alpha Wolf who needs to hear about this."

"Haze, just calm down a second and listen," Drips said. "No need to get Big A involved yet."

"Drips is right," Wolf said. "These two are the newest wolves of my Pack, replacing Zig and Zag."

Haze raised an eyebrow and brought his phone to his face. "I didn't see any notifications about new members in the Pack."

"They're just very, very new. It just happened."

Lex blurted, "Wait, I'm not—" but Penelope interrupted him with a gentle poke in his side.

Haze jerked his gaze over to Lex. "Not what?"

"I'm not—not *that* new. It's been a week already."

Haze blew air out from between his pursed lips. "Jeez, you really do have some young puppies, Wolf Cub. Just remember. You owe The Ozone a favor. A big one. You know how much I love collecting favors, especially from Alpha's baby brother."

Wolf gave Haze a solemn nod and walked toward the door with the five others following.

Haze added, "Next time, have the sense to *ask* another member about a location if somebody works right next to it. I would have warned you that the mall is crawling with security. And Cub," he called through the crack of the closing door. "If Garnet is single, send her this way."

Wolf pulled the handle to slam it.

"In your dreams," Drips scoffed.

A night breeze had picked up. Penelope leaned against Lex to keep warm and to remain standing.

"We're going over there," Wolf said, pointing to a building with a red-and-white sign across the street.

"That's your meeting point? A greasy diner?"

"Maybe ghostboys don't have to eat, but all that running got me hungry," Drips exclaimed. He came over the other side of Penelope and wrapped her arm across his shoulders. "Sorry about this, but you could use some help."

Lex grumbled as he took her other arm and helped her across the street, following the others.

BROKEN APP: MEMBER PROFILE

Name: Nail and Skin

"Legal" Name—SECRET: Nate (Nail) and Seth (Skin) Robinson

Membership: Two years

Allegiance: The Pack, led by Wolf Cub, ranked tenth of ten teams

Broken app: *Below is an audio recording of their responses.*

Wolf Cub: *What makes you one of the "broken"?*

Nail: *Jeez, do you have to be so damn blunt? Can't you give us some softball questions first, like what is your favorite color?*

Wolf Cub: *Everybody else had to answer in this order. I'm not giving you special treatment just because you're recording your responses.*

Skin: *He has a point, bro.*

Nail: *Fine. One of us has a learning disability in reading and writing, which is why we're not typing our answers.*

Skin: *One of us likes to get into fights. Wait, no. That's both of us. One of us gets* caught *getting into too many fights.*

Nail: *One of us was addicted to alcohol for a while, but he's sober now.*

Skin: *One of us is attracted to girls, and the other one is attracted to all of the above.*

Wolf Cub: *Really?*

Skin: *Yup. He isn't too public about it.*

Wolf Cub: *I can definitely sympathize there. Wait a second. Don't distract me. You two can't hide your problems behind each other. No one else got to do that.*

Nail: *Are you saying that because you want to know which one of us likes dudes?*

Wolf Cub: *I have a hunch, but, yes. Yes, I want to know.*

Nail: *Well, how about this? Both of us would rather fix cars or motorcycles than do homework.*

Skin: *Both of us grew up in a house where our parents expressed love with their fists.*

Nail: *Both of us have been in and out of so many relatives' homes that we've lost count of how many times we've moved.*

Skin: *Both of us have a really cool uncle, though. He's always given us a place to crash.*

Nail: *That's true.*

Wolf Cub: *You're both cheating. This was an awful idea.*

Drips: *I could have told you that before you even started, Wolf. They always pull twin crap like this.*

Nail: *Shut up, Drips. This is our interview.*

Drips: *Cool. Let me ask a question. Which one of you was putting the moves on Wolf just now?*

Skin: *Both of us would deny ever having the guts to flirt with Wolf.*

Drips: *Uh-huh. Sure. Smooth moves, there, Skin.*

Wolf Cub: *That's it. Interview over.*

Nail: *But we didn't get to answer the other two questions!*

Wolf Cub: *I think everybody gets the idea.*

10

YOU BELONG WITH US

"Large coffee. Black."

The waitress, a woman in her thirties, frowned at Lex. "It's a little late for coffee, isn't it?"

Lex stared at her.

Her frown deepened. "Well, fine. No sugar or cream, either?"

He continued to stare.

The waitress sighed in resignation. "One large black coffee. Got it. I have four cokes, one water, one double-chocolate-fudge milkshake, and one coffee. I'll be back for food orders in a minute."

The six of them sat in the diner's largest booth, which had a curved seat and a table in the center. Penelope, on one end, was next to Lex, followed by Drips, Skin, Nail, and Wolf, who was directly across from her.

Other than the words said to the waitress, none of them had spoken. Penelope was just relieved to be sitting. After taking their seats, she remembered she had tucked two packets of ibuprofen in the back pocket of her jeans. She gulped three pills and waited for them to take effect.

Exhaustion was catching up to her. She hadn't slept much since before her visit to the cemetery, thanks to anxiety, pain, and late-night text messages. That evening's narrow escape had drained her energy reserves.

"Where to begin?" Wolf muttered, breaking the silence. He pushed his thick glasses to the crown of his head as if they were blocking the flow of his thoughts.

"How about by telling that one to leave?" Nail's voice dropped low as he pointed to Lex. "Actually, tell both of them."

"We can't," Skin said.

"Why not?"

"Because, bro, Haze saw both of them with us. What happens if we don't add two new members in a couple of days?"

Nail shrugged. "We find two more new members."

Skin ruffled his red hair in annoyance. "And just hope we don't bump into Haze again for a long time? Find two clones of them or something?"

"Fine, she's legit." Nail twirled an eyebrow stud as he spoke, his gaze going cold. "But not him. He's not one of us."

Lex, hands folded and elbows planted on the table, snickered.

"Something funny?" Nail said. Penelope tensed. She didn't like that dangerous undertone in Nail's voice.

In response, Lex placed a mask of ignorance over his facial features. Nail's jaw tightened, and he began to stare Lex down. In an instant, the mockery was gone from Lex's face, and the two engaged in an eye-boring staring contest.

Wolf held up a hand at Nail. "After all the commotion, I don't think a public fight would be the best choice right now."

"You're right. Sorry," Nail muttered, breaking eye contact with Lex and staring at the table.

Lex snickered again.

"I swear I'm gonna beat his ass," Nail seethed.

"Stop it," Wolf said. He glanced around, making sure no one had heard. "Just stop. And *you*," he said, staring at Lex, "you might be treating this as a joke, but one of ours could be in the back of a police car right now. She did that for *all* of us. Remember that."

"I didn't ask for her to do that," Lex mumbled.

"I think," Penelope said, breaking the tension, "we all just need to figure out what to do next."

The waitress returned with the drinks. Wolf kept the extra coke next to him. The waitress gave Penelope the water and placed the steaming coffee in front of Lex.

Drips snatched up the milkshake and slurped down a good quarter of chocolate goodness in one long draw. Then he said, "Well, it's simple. Lois, you're eligible. Lex, you're not."

Lex lifted his mug and sipped. "I'm so offended."

Penelope shook her head. "If I'm joining, he's with me."

Skin bumped his brother with his elbow. "Lois and Lex—There's a scandal if I ever heard one."

"Dude, you're such a dork."

Wolf acknowledged their joke with an eyeroll. "Explain it to them, Drips," he said.

Drips took his lips off the straw to answer. "To be one of us, you have to have something broken inside of you. Usually outside forces cause the break. Family. The world's bullshit. Whatever. We're all a little messed up here. That's why we all trust one another. We're one busted up, dysfunctional little family."

"*If that which is bent never breaks, what happens to those who are already broken?*" Skin said, his voice quiet as if he was reciting a holy verse. Penelope remembered the phrase from her phone the night of the farmhouse test.

"We get pushed aside, that's what," Drips said, answering Skin's question. "In the eyes of everyone else, we've already become *that* next generation of teenagers. We are labeled as society's worst mistakes. Those labels—invented to describe our races, our genders, our orientations, our *conditions*—become parts of us. We lose our individuality under the weight of all the labels. Here, we reject all of that. We know we've been messed up and beaten down, but we also know those of us who get to the ground and get back up are stronger because of it. That's what unites us."

"So," Lex said, holding his coffee up to his lips, "you express all these beautiful sentiments by trespassing in abandoned malls?"

"Wolf, can I please beat his ass now?" Nail pleaded.

"Stop threatening him," Penelope said. Her eyes burned with anger.

"You're so confident you know the end conclusion. *Nails* usually get pounded, don't they?" Lex inquired as he sipped.

"Shut up, everybody. And you know stuff is getting stupid when I'm telling everybody else to shut up." Drips rotated his gaze around the table. "Listen man," he said, addressing Lex, "you don't get it because you're not one of us. We got your business card that night at the cemetery, remember? We checked you out. You're loaded, dude. Your mom is some super famous professor at Wash U. Your house is bigger than my house, Wolf's house, and Skin and Nail's house put *together*. And you go to that snooty private school with tuition costing more than all four years at most public colleges."

Penelope tried her best to hide her shock. It made sense to her why he hadn't wanted her to drop him off in his neighborhood. He always changed the subject every time she asked him about his school, too. She had just assumed he hated it there.

Drips shot her an inquisitive look, eyebrows raised. She hadn't hidden her surprise well enough, and he had spotted it.

When he opened his mouth to taunt her, the waitress returned for food orders. They each spoke in hushed voices. To her credit, the waitress didn't try to engage in small talk. She just wrote down the orders and hurried away from the morose youth.

Lex was a statue beside her, but his words didn't reveal his stress. "So, you think you know everything about me because of my mom's money, huh? You got me all figured out. Congratulations."

"No, but we know you haven't had to deal with some of the stuff the rest of us have gone through," Skin said.

Lex finished the last of the coffee and gestured to them with a final tip of the mug. "You don't know shit about me." He sneered. "Excuse me," he said to Penelope. She stood up so he could slide out of the booth.

After watching him exit, Penelope didn't sit back down. "You got a lot of nerve, all of you, saying his business like that. He's right. You don't know him, and you don't know me."

"We know enough about you, Lois," Drips said. "You're one of us, whether you like it or not. Wolf knows your real name, so we checked on you, too. We know about the adoption. We know about the events that led up to that adoption. And we know about the fire."

A boiling explosion of emotion burst from her stomach and left a scorching trail throughout her body. Her hands began to shake, and she felt her facial features bend with heat and tears. She reached into her pocket, pulled out two dollar bills, and threw them on the table. "Screw you! I'm out," she seethed, running for the door. "And my name is *not* Lois," she shouted behind her as she exited.

After running around the outside of the diner, she stood facing the highway, abandoned mall, and music store. She could hear her own pulse in her ears, could feel it in her rib, and her hands were balled into tight fists. Once she unclenched her hands, she brushed a few hot tears away from her face. The traffic zoomed along the highway, the bright headlights playing tricks on her already blurred vision.

"Hey," she heard behind her. Turning, she saw Lex standing in the grass, leaning against the diner's brick wall. He had nestled himself in a deep shadow between the beams of two floodlights.

She walked over to his spot and carefully sat in the grass. He did the same.

Lex pulled his hands into his sleeves. She struggled to regain control of her breathing and to stop the tears. He pretended not to notice, leaving her in peace while remaining close to her.

Once she had regained her composure, he bit his lip. "I owe you an explanation." He looked across the street as if the words would materialize in the distance.

When he finally spoke, it sounded as if each syllable caused him pain as it exited his throat. "We weren't always what we are now. We're rich, I guess. My mom worked hard for a long time before someone decided her research was worth publishing. But those first few checks went to my dad's medical bills. Cancer sucks, you know?"

Penelope pursed her lips in empathy. She and Lex had texted a lot, but it had all been superficial stuff. She had sort of just assumed he had a normal home life.

Lex paused to pull his hood lower across his face, shutting out her pity. "My dad was the only person who ever understood me. When he looked at me, he didn't see what I could be. He didn't see my *potential.* He accepted the current me." He let out a huff of air. "I haven't been the same, I guess, since he died. My sister is gone at school. And, suddenly, we live in a house four times the size of anything I remember from when I was a kid." He paused. "You think differently of me now?"

By protective habit, she started to pull her knees up to her chest, but sharp pain from her broken ribs stabbed her. She settled for a shrug. "Nope."

He sighed again, but it was deeper, more relieved. She felt him shift his gaze over to her. "I heard what they said to you," he murmured.

Penelope sniffed. Lex's words caused the raw emotions bubbling at the surface to boil over her internal walls and spill out of her lips. "My birth parents were never in my life. I was too young to remember them. Dad left us when I was still a baby, and Mom died from an overdose when I was two. My aunt and her boyfriend raised me, and they cooked the drugs that killed my mom in their basement. My room was down there. One day, there was an explosion. I was ten."

Penelope pulled the neckline of her T-shirt down, revealing white streaks on her skin. "I was hospitalized for, hmm, three months? Yeah, three. When I came out, I didn't have a family anymore. I mean, they're alive, I guess, but the state took me away from them. I was a foster kid. Then a few months later, my dads adopted me. They gave me all this stuff I didn't even know you were supposed to have in life. Drips is right. I'm broken, and I probably always will be."

She let out a sigh. "What about you? Do you think differently of me?"

He threw his arm over her shoulders in reply. She leaned into his warmth and relaxed, closing her eyes.

A few moments later, she felt him stiffen. She followed her eyes up a pair of black jeans to see Drips standing over both of them.

"What up, Mason?" Lex said, keeping his face buried in his hoodie.

Drips took a step back as if Lex had struck him. "What did you just call me?"

"Mason. Mason Morston. Is everybody else still waiting for food? Are *Nate* and *Seth* still sitting there with Elijah? I mean, shouldn't you be there with them in case your girl *Helena* shows back up?"

Mason sputtered, "How, how, how did you—"

Lex pulled his phone from the front pocket of his hoodie, made a few taps, and held his screen out to Mason. Penelope already knew what was on it—all the information they had collected on the Broken. Most of their late-night text messages had been exchanged working as partners to uncover everything they could about the organization. Combining his tech skills with Penelope's researching skills, they had found all the Pack's real names, the names of all ten Broken teams and their ranks, and their recent visits to abandoned properties across the St. Louis area.

Lex took advantage of Mason's silence. He tucked the phone away and said, "I see the Pack is number ten out of ten teams. I mean, it's not like there's a shortage of vacant houses in this city. What's the damn problem? Is it because Elijah's big brother Warren is the one who started all this? He's a crappy coder, by the way. It took me about five minutes to break through his security."

Mason opened his mouth, closed it, opened it again. "Hold on." A few moments later, he returned with Elijah. This time, Penelope held the phone up.

Elijah tried to snatch the phone, but Penelope jerked it away and handed it to Lex, who tucked it back in the hoodie pocket. They stood up, Lex supporting Penelope as they did so. "Rich mom, what can I say?" he said. "She paid for me to attend a coding camp when I was eleven. Biggest parenting mistake she ever made with me, she says." He shrugged.

Elijah pushed his glasses up the bridge of his nose. "We can't talk out here. The cops might still be searching for us," he said. "Come back inside."

"Nope," Lex replied. "We got more than enough to blackmail you into leaving us alone. Let us walk."

"Wait," Penelope said, putting an arm on Lex's sleeve. "Let's hear them out."

Lex raised an eyebrow at her, and Penelope could only shrug in response. After witnessing Garnet's sacrifice for the group, Penelope believed her initial instincts about the group had been correct. The members shared an unbreakable bond, a bond that appealed to Penelope in a powerful way. Even though they had exposed her darkest secrets, she wasn't ready to give up on them or the chance to share that sort of bond. Not yet. They knew about her, the bleakest parts of her, and they still wanted her to be one of them.

I could finally belong somewhere, she thought. *I just hope Lex forgives me for this.*

She glanced at him before focusing on Elijah. "No more surprises. No more threats." She waited until Elijah nodded before adding, "And I have some questions as well as some requests."

Elijah frowned. "No more surprises. No more threats."

Lex and Penelope followed Elijah and Mason into the diner. Their food hadn't arrived yet. "So which one is Nate, and which one is Seth?" Lex asked as he slid back into his seat.

Skin and Nail glanced at Wolf, who nodded in permission. "I'm Nate," Nail said reluctantly. "My brother is Seth."

Penelope spotted Mason going for his phone. "Don't bother contacting Garnet—I mean, Helena." Penelope retrieved her two dollars from the table and tucked them back into her pocket. "We can message her ourselves from the app. We can access your internal messaging system just fine."

Elijah took a moment to process the situation. "What do you want, exactly?"

Lex gestured to Penelope with his thumbs. "We came back inside because she wanted to, and that's it. So do everything she says, or we will go public."

Elijah pinched the bridge of his nose under his glasses. "Fine."

She pulled up the names of all the members of the Pack. "First of all, no more nicknames. They're stupid. I get it. They protect your anonymity when you're out together. But we already know who you are. No more of that crap with us."

"Whatever. Next."

Penelope jumped into her next point. "Zig and Zag are listed as team members, and their true identities are Xavier and Yuma from our newspaper staff. Is that right?"

"Correct," Elijah said. "They quit because Xavier is going to college. We needed people to replace them."

"So you scouted me out?" Penelope asked, half disgusted and half flattered.

"Yes, I did," he replied.

Mason held up a hand. "Hold up. Wait. Can I ask a question? Why did you act surprised when you saw Wolf? Sorry. Elijah. Whatever. You knew before you even walked in the theater that he would be there."

"It was surprising to me," Penelope muttered. "This person, this Wolf, isn't the Elijah I know from school. Explain yourself, Elijah. You barely know me from journalism class, and you suddenly think I want into your secret club? Why?"

"No, I'm not the same *Elijah* from school. That flippant, oh-so-talented photo editor is the person I could be if society was set up for my success. All day at school, we hear lies. 'Follow your passion. You can be anything you want to be.'. Bullshit. Society doesn't want us to succeed. Journalism, as much as I love it, is the biggest lie of the school day. Have you seen the career prospects for photographers? Come on. A profession devoted to the truth and objectivity? Turn on any of the cable news networks. Nobody gives a shit about that stuff anymore. Elijah is more of the character, not Wolf. Wolf knows a thing or two about reality."

His gaze on Penelope hardened. "You asked why we recruited you. Isn't it obvious, Lo—I mean, Penelope? Anyone who meets you can tell you're like us. Long before we researched you, we knew you would understand us. The way you mastered the test was also incredible. You belong with us."

With hesitation, Penelope asked, "To do what?"

"If all you see is us breaking into abandoned places, then you don't get it," Elijah said, mostly to Lex. "We are attracted to the decayed, crumbling, and forgotten places because *we* are forgotten. We see these places as beautiful, just as we see one another as beautiful. It's true. We have teams, and those teams have ranks based on how many new places you discover and explore. But nobody cares about that."

"I do," Mason cut in.

"Shut up, Drips," Elijah said. "It's more about being with one another in these places that match *our* place in society. When we are visiting a decrepit factory or whatever, we are allowed to be ourselves. We can be broken. Before we enter a location, we all say our labels to one another. Then we leave them outside. When we are in those broken places, they can no longer define us. It's cleansing. It's empowering. For some of us, it's also the difference between life and death."

They were the most beautiful words Penelope had ever heard. The idea of leaving the categories society had given her was liberating. But could she be so open about her past with these people, these *kids*? A glance at Lex revealed a skeptical eyebrow raised. She turned to Elijah. "If we join, we would have to do that? Put it all out there to you?"

"Yes," Seth said without hesitation. "That's what brings us together."

The waitress arrived with their food, depositing plates with quiet thuds on the plastic table cloth. Each nodded or muttered in gratitude, but no one touched their meals.

"What's in it for us?" Lex asked when the waitress bustled away.

Elijah centered his gaze on Penelope. "I think what he's asking here is what's in it for *him*, correct? Penelope, you're with us. Aren't you?"

Penelope looked at Lex, then down at her lap. "Yes. Yes, I am. I want in." She already felt empowered, even as Lex's jaw tightened. *Elijah is trying to corner Lex by using me*, Penelope thought.

"Don't do anything you don't want to do," she murmured to Lex. "This is my mess, not yours."

Elijah, however, turned to Lex and said, "What's in it for you is this—We need someone with your skills on our team. Paranormal activity has always been a *concern* during some of our visits to locations with certain histories. And if we can document any activity, it will propel our scores. We could be placed in the top three. And, of course, anything you collect could be published on your own sites and social media as long as you do not record us."

"I do better on my own," Lex grumbled.

"Do you?" Elijah inquired, glancing meaningfully at Penelope and back to him.

He sighed. "Fine. One time. I go one time, and then we see what happens after that."

There was a collective sigh of relief.

"So," Mason said excitedly, "where are we going next? We need new locations if we are going to get to the top three."

"I know somewhere," Lex said. Penelope turned to him in surprise. "But I don't know if any of you could handle it."

BROKEN APP: MESSAGES

Saturday, 2:42 a.m.

Drips: *Hey. Are you up?*

Wolf Cub: *Of course. Is Garnet home yet?*

Drips: *Yeah. I just finished texting her everything.*

Wolf Cub: *I'll add her.*

Drips: *Uh, that might not be a good idea. She's really, really pissed right now.*

Wolf Cub: *I'm aware, Drips. I'm getting her.*

Broken app: *Wolf Cub added Garnet to the message thread.*

Garnet: *This is bullshit. BULLSHIT!*

Wolf Cub: *I know.*

Garnet: *If I had been there, I would have flipped that damn table!*

Drips: *Babe, come on.*

Garnet: *Lois lied to us. Definitely once, maybe twice. I still don't buy this whole RANDOMLY bumped into each other at the cemetery thing. And her freak boy is not even one of us. How do we know he isn't the one who called the cops? They're not Pack. Neither of them.*

Wolf Cub: *I agree with you.*

Garnet: *You do?*

Drips: *You do?*

Wolf Cub: *Of course I do. I told them as much. But we're stuck. We have no other options.*

Garnet: *I say we call Lois's bluff. She wouldn't rat us out.*

Wolf Cub: *You would risk the secrecy of the entire Broken organization?*

Garnet: *No. We can't do that. Fine. We hit her where it hurts. She's obviously got a crush on that freak. Tell her if she goes public, we'll get her Ghostboy.*

Wolf Cub: *What are you implying by GET her Ghostboy?*

Garnet: *We don't have to actually DO anything to him. Just threaten him. Scare him a little.*

Drips: *This dude runs around cemeteries for fun. You think he's going to scare easily?*

Wolf Cub: *Irrelevant. We're not threatening anybody, at least not yet. His location suggestion for tomorrow is incredible. And when we see these two in action, we'll be able to determine if they should be ours or not. If not, we'll figure out how to stop her from going public.*

Garnet: *We're not still doing the circle tomorrow, are we?*

Wolf Cub: *Yes.*

Garnet: *WHAT?! In front of OUTSIDERS?! No way. No WAY.*

Wolf Cub: *Lois needs it. Maybe her freak doesn't, but she does. Remember, she was recruited. She understands who we are. And I don't think her friend will cause new problems while she's around.*

Garnet: *Well, if he does, leave him to me.*

Wolf Cub: *Of course.*

Drips: *Garnet, just try to play nice tomorrow. Don't make everything worse than it already is. And go to sleep. Please, babe?*

Garnet: *Shut up, Drips.*

Drips: *Love you too. You see what I deal with?*

11

THE LEAST MORALLY CORRUPT

"Did you get my last text?" Penelope asked.

Lex reached into his pocket and held the screen out to her. "Yes, but did you get mine?"

They sat together with his arms around her shoulders in the back of a red, lumbering Dodge Ram van.

Penelope had texted him late Saturday morning, after Lex had finally managed to shuffle out of bed and pour some coffee down his throat. He was so tired he could barely keep his eyes open. He never felt like this after an all-night investigation. Maybe caring about someone other than himself was more exhausting than he realized.

As he was munching on toast, his phone buzzed.

Penelope: *Hey.*

Since when did one word as bland as "Hey" make his heart lurch? *I'm pathetic*, he thought.

Lex: *Hey.*

Penelope: *I can go tonight. My dads asked who I knew there. I said a couple of people, including my new friend. I also asked to reschedule my birthday dinner to tomorrow so I could go. So, they decided they should analyze my use of the word "friend."*

Lex felt little pinpricks in his fingertips and in the pit of his stomach.

Lex: *Oh, so, they figured out I'm a special friend?*

Penelope: *After hours of torture, I confessed to having a boyfriend.*

He stared at that word for at least thirty seconds before formulating a reply. He opted to play it cool. Playing it cool protected him from embarrassing himself.

Lex: *Information obtained during torture is unreliable.*

Penelope: *True. But either way, I promised them I would bring you to the dinner. That was the only way they would agree to let me out again tonight.*

Lex: *I'm meeting your parents tomorrow. Is that what you're telling me?*

Penelope: *Yes?*

Lex reached behind him and pulled his hood over his bed hair, which was cut low on the sides and longer on top.

Lex: *Ugh.*

In the van, Penelope examined Lex's phone screen and rolled her eyes. She was cute even when mock irritated. "Yes, I saw the *ugh.*"

The van rumbled along Interstate 44 at a steady pace. Nate drove, and Seth sat in the passenger seat. Lex's investigation backpack was wedged between his feet. Mason, Helena, and Elijah occupied the seats directly in front of them. "Does that mean you're coming?"

Lex pouted. "I feel like you keep dragging me to all these places I don't wanna go, and then everything turns out badly."

"That happened once," she said. "And tonight is your idea."

"What? Now it's your turn?"

"Oh my *God,*" Helena groaned. "You two are making me *sick.* I swear if you start making out, I'm going to throw up. Just like, all up in your laps."

"Ignore her," Mason said. "She's grumpy because her parents had to pick her up at the police station last night. She'll be fine."

"Shut up, Drips," she said. "But hey. Lois, you gotta tell me. Is Ghostboy a freak in the cemetery *and* in the sheets?"

"Nobody is getting freaky in this van," Seth shouted before anyone else could reply. "If I leave one speck of anything in here, my uncle will slaughter me."

"And me," Nate added. As the only person who could drive a stick shift, he was the chauffeur.

Garnet was undeterred. "I just wanna know, that's all! Is he? He's a freak, right?"

Lex opened his mouth to retort, but Penelope put a hand on his leg to stop him. She leaned forward. "This coming from the girl dating a guy named Drips…"

"Oh!" Mason shouted, bouncing up and down in his chair. "Shots fired. Seriously, that's not how I got that name. Let's not start any rumors. I'm clean and healthy down below, thank you."

"You're such a moron," Helena muttered to Mason as she elbowed him in the side.

"Everybody stop arguing for the next forty-five minutes," Elijah said, projecting his voice. "I didn't get to bed until five. I want some sleep. Give us some peace and quiet until we get there."

"That's *if* there's anything there," Helena said.

"Oh, there will be," Lex reassured her with a mysterious smile. "Don't you worry."

The van's bouncing jostled Lex awake. Beside him, Penelope opened her eyes and gingerly stretched when the van decelerated at the exit. There was little to see other than two gas stations, an old fast-food place, and a huge antique shop. Darkness had already claimed the sky.

"Where do I go, Lex?" Nate asked.

"Turn right at this fork," he said, "then left at the light. You'll see it."

Nate stopped the van on the shoulder so they could check out their destination. Lex had been mentally preparing himself for this, but actually seeing it made him pause longer than expected.

The building sat away from the highway due to the large parking lot that accommodated semitrucks. The long squat structure had disjointed pieces stuck together on the sides and on top. There were no lights, so all they could see was a darker shadow against the fields and trees surrounding them. As he stared at it, he realized the rest of the group had also gone quiet.

"We're going in *there*?" Mason said.

No one answered. They just kept staring at the building.

"It's weird, isn't it?" Elijah said. "I mean, it's just an old truck stop. But you look at it, and you just know there's something—"

"Wrong," Lex finished for him. He let the word sit with them for a moment. "If you pull around the side, you can park behind it so nobody will see the van."

The van turned onto the parking lot, and it bumped and jumped so much that Lex almost hit his head on the ceiling. Nate put the van in park next to a dumpster, and all seven of them piled out. A few of them stretched and shook their legs, but they all kept their eyes on the building.

"I seriously got the willies," Seth said. "I've been in factories, hospitals, apartment complexes—every type of broken building you can imagine. Where the hell did you bring us, Ghostboy?"

Lex felt all their eyes shift from the building to him. He folded his arms across his chest. "That road over there used to be Route Sixty-Six, the Mother Road. And this building was one of those places everybody knew. If you drove past it, you stopped. It was a truck stop, but it also had a full-service restaurant and a motel. It was iconic. Still is for many people."

He felt himself gaining confidence as he continued reciting the story. "Time passes, right? The interstate was built, then the gas stations. This place became outdated. It shut down, but the people working down there," he said, gesturing to the gas stations, "said they kept seeing lights on as well as darting, dark figures. It got so bad that people wouldn't drive through here at night, so they called in my dad's team."

Lex pulled out his investigation notebook and showed them an earlier page with his dad's handwriting. "My dad and two friends stayed here overnight and captured some of the most intense video and audio in his history as an investigator. It's what made him famous in the paranormal circles."

He tucked the journal back in his backpack and pulled a key from his pocket. It was on a key chain with a rubber State of Missouri hanging from it. "After my dad's video and audio went big, other paranormal groups started calling the owner of the property. It had been sitting vacant for years. But after that he had people willing to pay to spend the night in the place. The owner was so grateful, he gave my dad a key and told him to come back any time. He never got to use it."

"Why not?" Nate asked.

"The rest of his guys didn't want anything to do with this place, and my dad didn't want to come alone." He smiled as he remembered his father. "He was a fearless man, but he also knew when to be cautious. When things started to look bad for him, he gave me all his investigation equipment. He also showed me places in his journal he wished he could visit again. This was one of them. I've been to all of them, actually, except this one."

"Why haven't you come here before now?" Elijah narrowed his eyes.

"He made me promise not to go alone," he said. "And I don't have a car to drive this far." When the silence settled in again, Penelope's hands grasped his arm.

"Well, a couple of things are certain," Elijah said, his voice as confident as he could manage. "We won't get caught like at the mall. Yes, that was my fault. I should have known there was a problem considering no other group had been in there yet. But check it out. No one is here. We are in the middle of nowhere. I don't think any other group has driven out this far for a location. If we do this, we will make top five or higher."

"What are we waiting for?" Helena asked. "You can't tell me you guys believe in this crap. Ghosts? Come on."

"I don't know, babe," Mason said. "My grandma always said not to mess with this stuff. It's like, imagine somebody says there's a killer snake in your closet. Is it unlikely? Well, yeah. But still. Why open the damned door if you don't have to?"

"We do this like any other location," Elijah said, trying to reassure them. "We use our Broken names. We keep our phones out. We use the zip ties. We move in pairs. If anything feels unsafe, we move out."

Mason ruffled his Afro as he thought. "Fine," he acquiesced. "But if I get possessed, you do my exorcism, Lois. You're the least morally corrupt out of all of us. I can tell."

"Aww, thanks, Drips." She winked at him.

"It's decided. Let's begin." Elijah reached out his hands, but Helena backed away.

"No, no, no," she said, shaking her head. "No way. They aren't even with us officially. I'm not doing this with them here."

"Well, I don't want to do it anyway," Lex huffed, pulling at his hood.

"Garnet," Elijah said. "No one will judge you. That's not what we do. Not us. Not here." He stared at Lex and Penelope. "What is shared here stays between us. Does that make sense?

And, for you two, for tonight only, your participation is optional."

They both nodded, and Elijah extended his hands again. Helena clasped his left hand, and Mason grasped his right. Nate and Seth joined by holding Helena. Penelope grabbed Mason and gave Lex a pleading look. He smacked his face with his palm and groaned. But he stepped forward and held hands with Penelope and Seth. They all shut their eyes—a human circle in the middle of cracked concrete.

"This is stupid," Lex whispered.

"Shut up," Helena said.

Elijah ignored them. "*If that which is bent never breaks, what happens to those who are already broken?*"

They were quiet for a few moments. Mason exhaled. "I'm forgotten," Mason answered. "I'm defiant. Disrespectful. I'm gifted and talented. ADHD. I'm wasted intelligence. I'm an empty future that hasn't even begun. I'm nothing."

Nate said, "I'm forgotten. I'm poor white trash. I'm a verbal and physical abuse case with anger management issues. I'm a twin, so I'm exchangeable. I'm a punk, a troublemaker, and a scourge on society. I'm nothing."

Seth picked up where his brother left off. "I'm forgotten. I'm dyslexic. I'm learning disabled. I'm an abuse victim. I'm just another name on the counselor's and special educator's caseloads. I'm the twin with all the extra problems. I'm nothing."

Elijah's voice joined the others. "I'm forgotten. I'm a gay. I'm sick in the head. I'm in the closet at school because I'm a coward. I'm wasted talent. I'm a disgrace for a son. I'm not worthy of love or affection. I'm a displaced teen couch surfing with friends and relatives. I'm nothing."

Garnet grumbled something about how this was not right, but once she began, she adopted the same open, reflective tone as everyone else. "I'm forgotten. I'm a pastor's daughter. I'm the youngest of three kids with two older brothers in drug rehab.

I'm the next in line to fall prey to sin and temptation. I'm a ticking time bomb. I'm a loser drug addict without using even once. Without being given the chance to be something more. I'm nothing."

Lex realized they were the only two left. Their participation was optional, Lex reminded himself.

Penelope, however, didn't hesitate. "I'm forgotten. I'm a foster kid. An adopted kid. I'm a burn victim. I'm the girl with the dead parents and the drug-cooking relatives. I'm the child of two gay dads. I'm the girl everyone pities. I'm nothing."

He felt his face contort. He wanted to grab her and hold her. How dare she call herself nothing?

But she and the others were waiting to see if he would join them. Penelope had shared, so he knew he had to do the same.

"I'm forgotten," he muttered. "I'm—well, I'm a paranormal investigator, which doesn't exactly get me a lot of friends. And I'm too smart for my own good." Once the words started, he found them easier to say. They came at a steady pace, and he allowed them to continue to flow out of him. "I'm the younger sibling, chasing my big sister's shadow. I'm too much like my dad. I'm depressed. I'm that kid everybody assumes will bring a gun to school someday. I'm alone. I'm a freak. I'm nothing."

After a few seconds of silence, Elijah said, "*Forgotten finds forgotten. Nothing finds nothing. Broken finds broken. We are forgotten. We are nothing. We are the Broken.*"

Before Seth could even let him go all the way, Penelope swung around their clasped hands and grasped Lex around the middle. Her face pressed against his chest and her arms around him. She was the warmest thing he had ever felt. His own arms, without him realizing it, had circled around her back as well, and he rested his head on top of hers. They pulled in a few deep breaths before pulling apart.

She wiped her cheeks with her hands. "Don't ever talk like that. I can't stand it."

The others were still close, he realized.

Mason reached a hand out and put it on Penelope's shoulder. He said, "You've got it wrong, Lois," he told her gently. "It's not that what he said isn't true. It is true for most people who don't get him or see him. So, yeah, it's true. But that's not all there is to him, right? To any of us. We're messed up, but we're a pretty mess when you swirl us all together."

"My boyfriend, the poet," Helena scoffed, but there was no hostility in her words. Her tone was almost playful.

"Hey, I gotta know," Mason said. "Did you two just meet Tuesday, or were you working together the whole time?"

Lex shoved his hands in his hoodie pocket and stared at the ground. "Um."

Penelope's hands clasped his arm again and buried her face in the fabric of his sleeve.

Mason couldn't hide his shock. "So, you guys have only known each other four days?"

"You embarrassed them," Elijah chided. "There's nothing to be ashamed of. It's more typical than you'd expect when two broken people meet. Bonds form quickly, and they can be intense, too. Even the Bard knew that in the 1590s."

"Wait. If we're Romeo and Juliet, I want to be Mercutio," Lex shot back. "Romeo was a moron."

"And Juliet should have gone for him first, anyway," Penelope said.

Elijah, smirking defiantly, gestured to Mason and Helena. "I couldn't keep these two off each other for the first three weeks after they met."

"Watch it, Wolf," Helena said. "Let's get this party started."

"As you wish," Elijah said. He reached into his pocket and pulled out a handful of zip ties. "We use these to keep track of the rooms we have already explored and searched. Put one around the doorknob as you leave."

"They also double as a convenient restraining device," Lex said under his breath.

"Let it go, Ghostboy."

"Let it go? It happened yesterday." He pulled up his sleeves, displaying the cuts to illustrate his point.

"Thanks for volunteering, you two," Elijah exclaimed. "You'll be partners tonight."

"No!" they shouted in unison.

"Trust. You'll need to trust one another if we're going to be one Pack. That includes the person who grates on your nerves the worst."

"I want to stay with Lex," Penelope said.

"No." Elijah shook his head. "We can't risk you getting more hurt than you already are."

"I'm fine," she said.

"Well, we can't have two non-members wandering around by themselves, either," Helena said. "They don't know the first thing to watch for. So, if you want to be inside with Ghostboy, you'll have to scout with Wolf."

"Fine."

"It's decided," Elijah said. "Nail, stay with Drips to keep watch. Skin, Lois, and I will scout. Garnet, you follow Ghost wherever he decides to conduct his investigation."

"Is that my code name? Ghost?"

"Yeah. Seemed fitting," Elijah said. "Do you approve?"

"Better than Ghostboy."

"The phones stay close. Except for you, Nail. I know your phone is busted. Ghost, Lois, keep the Broken app open at all times. Now that the version on your phones is for members, it won't make weird noises or block use of other phone functions. Instead, we use it to message one another and view one another's feeds. Are there any questions?"

No one spoke. Elijah nodded and faced the truck stop.

"Let's begin."

BROKEN APP: MEMBER PROFILE

Name: Wolf Cub

"Legal" Name—SECRET: Elijah Atkinson

Membership: Three years

Allegiance: The Pack, led by Wolf Cub, ranked tenth of ten teams

What makes you one of the "broken"?

When we started this organization, the idea was to create an app to help homeless teens survive. We thought we could create a ranking system of abandoned locations all over the city. Download the app, and bang. Here are all these places. No one would have to hunt for a safe spot to sleep for the night ever again.

But, about three years ago, the focus shifted. The concept of "urban exploration" took off, and we found ourselves—the truly homeless and rejected—facing all these other teens invading our locations.

At first, I hated them. My brother and I were homeless because we had no other choice. We ran away from my mom and stepdad because he thought an effective way to stop someone from being gay was violence.

Alpha took so many beatings for me. I was the one who decided he couldn't take any more. We left, and we slept where we could. And then these "urb ex" kids start barging into our sleeping spots. It was poverty porn to them. "Wow! Check it out. Busted toilets! Take a video of me talking about the damn toilet for my channel!" That is who most urb ex'ers were and still are.

But every once in a while, someone different would find us. These were the truly broken. They gravitated to the most broken spaces because they were the only spaces that made sense. Soci-

ety is governed by these norms, expectations, and requirements. You have to fit into this mold before the world will allow you to exist. Well, maybe it's not us with the problem. Maybe it's the world. Maybe we need to make an app for not just the broken spaces, but the broken people who need them. That's how all of this started.

Why is the Pack at the bottom of all ten teams?

I could care less. Next question.

What was your favorite location you ever visited?

We took a road trip down to that abandoned Renaissance Festival theme park. Its crown jewel was supposed to be an authentic medieval castle. The castle was still under construction when the park owners went bankrupt, but enough of it was there that we were able to immerse ourselves in this fantasy world. I stood on the ramparts while two Pack members fought one another with sticks on the footbridge. Two more used the keep as a tower of secrecy for private *matters. The day ended in a battle for control of the drawbridge. Juvenile, perhaps, but I'll never forget it.*

12

DEATH BY THE PARANORMAL

As Lex turned the key, Penelope realized she was holding her breath. What did she expect to happen when the door opened? Would an apparition rush out and howl in their faces? It was everyone else's anticipation and excitement that had her worked up, she reassured herself. There was no way she was scared.

She found herself looking at her shoes as she tried to calm her racing heart. At least she had worn sneakers this time, not her flats. She had learned her lesson.

The old metal door wailed as Lex opened it. Lex turned on his flashlight, allowing the others gathered around him to see inside. The first room was a kitchen, dank and dusty from neglect. Old food stains encrusted the dated appliances, and canned goods lined the shelves.

"My dad wrote that this entrance was only used by the workers." Lex struggled for a moment to grab his journal while holding the flashlight, but Elijah plucked it out of his backpack and held it up for him to read.

"Thanks. After you walk through the kitchen, there will be a set of double doors leading into the main restaurant. The booths extend to your left, and there is a bar area and pool tables on the right. Another door opens onto stairs that lead to the second floor, where the rooms for rent are. Room Two has an emergency exit leading to the roof. Don't use that exit unless you're out of other options because there isn't a ladder. You'd have to jump down." Lex signaled to Elijah he was finished reading, and Elijah put the journal away. "You guys do what you have to do. I'll be in Room Three."

"Why there?" Mason asked.

"That's where the murder happened," he said before bursting through the door.

"Hey, wait!" Helena said, shoving past the twins and Elijah. "We move in pairs, Ghostboy, like it or not."

"Whatever. You guys go in and have fun with the bloodthirsty undead," Mason muttered, sitting on the stoop. "I'm going to sit right here with my buddy Nail, mind my own business, and keep the van safe."

Reluctantly, Nate bent his legs and sat next to Mason. "I wanna see the bloodthirsty undead." He moped as Penelope, Seth, and Elijah walked in.

The door shut with a shiver.

Silence.

Three flashlight beams searched the area. All Penelope could hear was their breathing and the slight shuffling of their clothing.

Suddenly, something changed. Everything in the beams of light shimmered. The flashlight bounced on various objects—the oven, the ripped curtain, the can of peaches. They vibrated, pulsated with life. Everything was in technicolor.

Those objects not in the harsh beams seemed to breathe. She didn't want to look, but she couldn't turn away.

I'm terrified, she realized. *Did a murder actually happen here? And what could be left? Can hate stain a place or leave some mark that can't be removed?*

Elijah leaned over. "I think we should take our time in here. Check out the ceilings." His own flashlight beam danced along the lines in the ceiling. "Those tiles are sagging. There must be some water damage. The whole thing could cave in if we're not careful."

"What about Ghost and Garnet upstairs? Could they cause a cave-in if they're walking around up there?" Seth asked.

"Maybe," he said. "That's why I said to be careful."

They exited the kitchen, which opened to the actual restaurant. Standing among the booths, Penelope wondered what the place would have been like all those years ago, feeding weary travelers. Now, the tables were caked in layers of dust. Spider webs dangled in the spaces between the tables and the benches. The long counter, lined with stools, was cracked and faded.

"Anybody hungry?" Elijah asked, pointing his beam at a saucer plate with a half-eaten, moldy piece of cherry pie.

"Gross," Penelope whispered back.

They moved around the empty booths and past what had been the front entrance. With the door and windows boarded up, they couldn't see the highway. It made the place feel like a bunker—or a tomb.

Elijah pointed his flashlight at a dusty, coin-operated fortune teller machine. A woman's torso and head were inside. She held her plastic hands over a crystal ball as if warming them. She wore no smile, only grim determination.

"Holy shit, that's creepy," Seth whispered. Elijah handed his flashlight to Seth and started rummaging through his photography equipment. Once he had assembled the camera, lens, and flash, he began popping the flash in the machine's direction. With each picture, the woman's skin turned white, and dark shadows formed under her eyes—a human skull on a clothed, living body.

Brrrt. Brrrt. A buzzing sound. Penelope's heart leaped, and she let out a gasp.

Elijah exhaled and jumped back but let out a bark of laughter. "It's my phone," he said, grabbing it from his back pocket. By its third vibration, he answered, the camera hanging from the strap around his neck. It was a video call from within the Broken app.

"We're set up in the third room," Helena whispered. "You'll see the room numbers when you sweep up here. He used this stick thing to help him figure out the right one. He said it's called a dowsing rod. He's got all this weird equipment running. Now, he's in like, a trance. I don't even know how else to describe it. Wolf, how long are we staying here?"

"Garnet, you aren't scared, are you?" he asked her with a quirked eyebrow.

"Screw you, asshole," she said before she disconnected.

A side room featured a bar as well as space for pool tables. Although there were marks on the floor left by three tables, only one remained, its felt playfield slashed diagonally from end to end. None of the pool balls remained except for a lone eight ball perched in the middle.

Penelope stayed close to Elijah as he wandered around all the areas on that floor—the restaurant, pool table, kitchen, and bar. She told him she was trying to improve her own photography skills for the day when she became a professional journalist. He gave her an "I don't buy that line" type of smile, but he let her tag along, whispering to her tips about technique and form. He snapped photo after photo, his camera whooshing and clicking with each picture. Seth wandered on his own.

After five minutes, Elijah signaled for Seth to regroup. "Let's head upstairs and walk through the rooms for rent. Just don't disturb them in Room Three."

They nodded, and Elijah opened a small door across from the main entrance. He slipped a zip tie on it before closing it behind them. The thin staircase, covered in cheap brown carpet, forced them to walk single file—Elijah in front, then Penelope, and Seth last.

The top of the stairs was blocked by another door, this one with a sign that read, "For Renting Tenants Only." They ascended the stairs one step at a time. Penelope couldn't shake the feeling that the air had become thinner. The silence played tricks on her ears, as well. They were buzzing a little, a high-pitched keening.

Halfway up, they heard a sound. Downstairs. Something rolling.

One second, two seconds, three.

Plop.

"What was that?" Seth whispered.

"The eight ball," Penelope said, eyes wide.

"Bullshit."

"Skin, go check," Elijah said.

"Bullshit!" he said, louder this time.

Elijah didn't protest. "Whatever. Let's just get up there." After taking few more steps up, the phone buzzed again. When Elijah picked up, he snarled, "What?"

"Hey, dude! What the hell? What did I do?" It was Mason.

"This better be important, Mason. I mean, Drips."

"It is. Man, you're not going to believe this, but I swear, I saw like, lights or something in the woods over there. And I'm telling you, I'm telling you, man, I saw a person. Maybe people. But it's so dark, all I can see are shapes."

"Quit screwing with us, Drips," Seth shouted, his voice frantic. "Put my brother on. Where's Nail?"

"I can't," Mason said. "He went to go check it out."

"By himself?" Elijah said, his disapproval audible.

"What else were we supposed to do? Both leave the van? And he volunteered, anyway. Is my girl all right?"

"We're heading that way now," Elijah said. "She's still with Lex. Keep us updated."

"You got it, Wolf Cub," he said, and Elijah disconnected it.

Silence again. Elijah let out a long sigh. "Come on, guys. This is crazy. How many times have we done this stuff, Skin? That noise, of *course* there's an explanation. We hear weird noises in places like these all the time. We're just worked up.

Lex, I mean, *Ghost* got us all freaked out when he mentioned the murder and—"

Slam! The door at the bottom of the stairs shut behind them.

All three of them burst into a run.

Elijah rushed through the door at the top and held it open for the other two. Once Penelope and Seth were near, Elijah shut the door behind him and leaned on it as if trying to prevent something else from following.

"What the natural *shit*?" Seth exclaimed.

"Shh," Elijah said, gesturing at the rooms on the right side.

"Don't tell me to *shh*!" he hissed back as loudly as he dared. "What was that? Seriously?"

Rooms One and Two had zip ties around their handles, letting them know either Helena or Lex had already explored them. Room Three, the last one, was at the end of the hall. The left wall was empty except for a few black-and-white photos of Route 66 landmarks.

Penelope pressed against the wall next to Elijah. Stabbing pains traveled around and up her side, but she wasn't about to admit Elijah had been right. She just sucked it up.

She felt something else against her back. A shaking. A tremor in the wall.

"Guys, listen," she breathed.

They all held their breaths, staring at one another, afraid of what they would hear or not hear.

Rattling, clanging. Pots banging together in the kitchen. And footsteps, stomping beneath them like heavy boots.

Thud, thud, thud.

"I'm done, man," Seth said at full volume. "Let's pack up and get the fuck out of here."

Elijah opened his mouth to reply, but Helena interrupted him by bursting out of Room Three, eyes huge and panicked. "Guys, come here!" she begged, gesturing for them to follow.

Seth, Elijah, and Penelope followed her into Room Three. The room was completely empty except for the same thin carpeting covering the stairs and hallway. Darker spots showed where the bed, television, and chest of drawers had been placed.

Helena pointed her flashlight at Lex, who was sitting cross-legged in the corner. He was still, eyes closed, EVP recorder around the wrist holding the flashlight and EMF meter in the other hand. His open journal and pen rested in his lap. Penelope recognized the equipment as well as his position, but something seemed wrong. He didn't flinch when the flashlight hit his face, and his skin glistened with moisture.

"I heard you guys freaking out, and I figured we were leaving. I went to snap him out of it. Just shake his shoulder, you know? But he won't wake up!"

Penelope pushed past the others and knelt in front of him. "Lex, Lex!" she called. He didn't respond. She reached forward and touched his face, running her fingers down her cheek. "He's ice cold, but he's sweating. Lex!"

The others stood around her, dumbstruck, when Elijah's phone buzzed again. Numbly, he answered it.

Mason pleaded, "Wolf, we gotta go. Now. I don't know what's happening, but I keep hearing all these noises on the ground floor. There, there! Did you hear that?"

They went quiet again, with Penelope keeping her hand on Lex's cheek as they listened. Something plummeting downward with a crash. Another. Another.

"It's the ceiling tiles," Elijah said. "The ceiling tiles are buckling and falling." As he said the words, at least three more plunged to the floor. They continued, one after another.

"All of them at once? We've seen a couple at a time, but like this? And there's a rhythm to it, like something is down there doing it. I told you this was a bad idea," Mason squawked.

"Where's Nail?" Elijah asked, ignoring his last jab.

"He still hasn't come back. I'll let you know."

"You're right. We need to leave, but we have a problem with Ghost," Elijah said. "Not like, a ghost, but *the* Ghost. We're coming."

Lex opened his eyes. Penelope leaned toward him. "Hey! You scared us, are you…" She trailed off when she realized his eyes weren't focused on her. He was locked onto something behind her or elsewhere. "Lex?"

He blinked a few times and tried to stumble to his feet. Unable to remain upright, he swayed. Penelope put her hand out to steady him, but his knees buckled. All of his weight came down on her.

For a moment, Penelope tried to brace her legs to hold him up, but she crumpled. They both fell to the ground with him on top and Penelope landing on her broken rib. Her face contorted in agony.

Seth went for Lex, and Helena knelt down for Penelope.

"Penelope, are you all right?" Lex asked, his voice thick as if he had just awakened from a long sleep. "I'm so, so sorry."

Seth pulled Lex to his feet, wrapping his hand around his waist. "Jeez, you're skinny, but you're tall! Don't do that falling crap again, or we'll both go down."

Helena put her face close to Penelope's. "Dude, your boyfriend just got on top of you for the first time. That's pretty awesome."

Penelope managed to smile. "You're crazy, Garnet."

"I know, right?" she said, smiling back. "Hey, are you ready to try to get up? We need to get the hell out of here."

"Are you going to help me?"

"No, I'm just gonna watch," she mocked. "Yes, of course I'll help you. Come on." Helena pushed one hand under Penelope's neck and the other at the small of her back. She lifted her into a sitting position, then hoisted her to her feet. Once Penelope was standing, Garnet threw her arm around her waist.

Penelope nodded to her in gratitude but moved Garnet's arm away. "I got this." *One person unable to walk is enough to deal with.*

She walked gingerly to Lex, who was slumped against Seth. "Lex, can you talk?"

Lex's head lolled, slipping from Seth's head. He mumbled something Penelope couldn't understand.

"He keeps coming in and out," Seth said, straining under the weight of the taller teen. "He's trying to snap out of it but can't. I don't think being in here is helping."

"Let's go!" Helena said. "I'm pretty much done with Room Three for the rest of my life."

"We have two choices," Elijah said. As he spoke, Penelope gathered Lex's equipment and stuffed it into his backpack. "The emergency exit is in Room Two, but we'd have to jump down and land on concrete. The other option is back through the main level."

"Oh, great," Helena exclaimed. "Physical injury or death by the paranormal. This is perfect."

"She has a point," Seth said. "Jumping onto concrete is probably going to get a few of us hurt. But downstairs, I mean, there's no way something could actually hurt us, right?"

Bang! Bang!

Something underneath them shook the floor right under their feet, like an angry neighbor with a broom handle.

"Emergency exit it is," Seth shouted.

They all dashed around the corner to Room Two. Just like Room Three, it was empty, but this one had a door in the back corner. When they opened it, a flat roof spread out before them with the parking lot at least fifteen feet below them. The van stood in its spot by the dumpster.

Mason appeared in the parking lot beneath them, shaking his head. "That's too high. Let me bring the van around." He dashed over to the van. When he got there, he moaned loudly and grabbed at his Afro with both hands. "Shit! Nail has the keys."

"Right here!" they heard. It was Nate, dashing toward them from the right by the gas station. "You guys, there are a lot of cars at that fast food place, but not many people inside."

"That means there are other people here," Elijah said. "Playing tricks. How many cars?"

"At least five."

"I'm going in," Seth said, cracking his knuckles. "I won't be made to look the fool like this."

"No," Elijah said. "Five cars is too many. We are separated, and two of us can't fight."

"And I don't want to fight," Mason hollered. "I'm too pretty to fight."

Elijah resolved, "We're leaving. Alpha Wolf needs to hear about this. Nail! Get the van."

"But—"

"Now, dammit!" Helena barked.

Yelling in frustration, Nate sprinted to the van, started it, and pulled it around the side of the building.

One by one, they lowered themselves onto its roof and slid to the ground. Nail stayed in the front seat with his foot on the brake. Elijah, Seth, and Mason all had to help Lex down, and they did the same for Penelope to spare her rib as much as possible. Once they were in the van, Nate turned around one last time.

"Please, please, please, please? Seth and I can take them by ourselves. You know we can. Please?"

Elijah didn't reply. He just stared. Nate didn't bother asking again. He peeled out of the parking lot.

13

DON'T SLIP AWAY FROM ME

Seth and Nate's uncle owned property near a creek. After getting on the interstate and traveling westbound for four exits, Nate pulled off and drove the van down a skinny highway, a gravel road, and finally a dirt road. He parked in the middle of the woods.

"We'll be safe here," Nate said. "Uncle Harold put that dusk-to-dawn light in a few weeks ago, so it's not pitch black. The creek is down the path."

Hearing the word "safe" put Penelope at ease. She sensed her body releasing some of its tension and her muscles relaxing. Even though the thought of spending the night in a cramped van didn't thrill her, anything was an improvement from the truck stop.

Then, a thought struck her like a baseball bat to the side of the head. *My parents are going to kill me. I told them I'd be home by midnight.* Biting her lip, she sent Henry a quick text.

Penelope: *Hi, Dad. I need to stay over. The person who was supposed to drive me home is drunk (not my boyfriend, he doesn't drive), and I want to be safe. I'll be back first thing in the morning. Love you.*

More lies, Penelope thought as she swallowed down a thick wad of guilt. *I hate doing this to them.*

Mason's voice shook her from her sullenness. "Let me out. I need to pee." He climbed over Elijah and slid open the side door. Helena piled out after him.

"Ten minutes, you two," Elijah yelled after them.

"Yeah, yeah," Helena called back dismissively.

Penelope turned to Lex. "How are you?"

During the ride, he bent his large frame and let his head hang between his knees while Penelope ran her fingers along his back. He straightened and turned to her. "I'm fine. I just need some air."

After Lex put on his backpack, the two of them exited the van. For the first time, Penelope could appreciate the night—cool and clear with stars dusting the sky. She wrapped her fingers around his, and the pair wandered down the tree-lined trail.

"Can you tell me what happened?"

"Uh," he stalled, pulling at his hood, "I don't know if I'm ready to talk about it. I mean, I want to. Don't think I'm keeping anything from you. It's hard to explain. My dad always warned me not to do meditative mind without someone else who knew what they're doing. He said you can slip away. If someone isn't there to fish you out, it can get dangerous. I don't know if that makes any sense. And thank you."

"For what?"

"For fishing me out." He did everything he could to avoid her eyes, staring at the overhanging tree branches, the dirt clods his sneakers sent bouncing into the grass, and the overgrown foliage on either side of the path. "I'm so sorry for hurting you."

"I'm fine. Really," she reassured him. "I ate like five pain pills before we left. I'll just need to rest this week. No more haunted truck stops for a while."

"What about malls crawling with security?"

"No."

"Graveyards and related scavenger hunts?"

"Nope."

"Dinner with your parents tomorrow?"

She looked at him hopefully. If she wasn't grounded for not coming home, she would need to repair some damage with Mike and Henry. She didn't want them thinking Lex was the cause of her new rebelliousness. For some reason, it mattered to her what they thought of him. "Really?" she asked.

"I owe you that much."

They came to the end of the trail. A gravel bar dipped into a rushing, bubbling creek. A slim moon shone overhead, and its light covered the water's surface in a sugary glaze. She grasped his other hand in hers, forcing him to face her.

He tried to hide again, turning away from her, but she dropped one of her hands and reached for his chin, directing his face with her index finger and thumb. "Don't slip away from me," she whispered. "I think I need you too much to let you do that."

His expression seemed to soften. "I think I need you, too."

As he leaned in, he wrapped his arms around her waist, and her own arms folded around his neck. He tried to kiss her cheek, but Penelope turned her head so her lips would meet his. His grip around her tightened, pulling her closer, and she felt him inhale as the kiss deepened.

They walked slowly back to the van holding hands. She wore his hoodie, and her zip-up sweatshirt hung over his shoulder. Under the hoodie, Lex wore a gray V-neck T-shirt. He looked longer and leaner in it but also more vulnerable.

They could see blue phone lights in the van, but all other interior lights had been shut off. Just as they approached, they saw Mason and Helena also coming out of the brush. Helena was trailing Mason, picking bits of leaves and sticks from his hair.

"How'd you get Ghostboy's hoodie, Lois?" Helena goaded, flicking away another twig.

"How'd you get that crap in your hair, Drips?" Lex fired back.

Helena cackled.

All four of them climbed back into the van. Elijah tapped at his phone screen, displaying the time. "I said ten minutes. You're fortunate I didn't come after you."

"No, you're *un*fortunate," Mason said good-naturedly. "I have the body of an African slash Greek god."

"Shut up, Drips," Elijah muttered and yawned. "You aren't my type."

The twins' uncle kept a few blankets in the back of the van for overnight hunting excursions. Mason and Helena shared one. Seth snatched another one before his brother could grab it, and Elijah said he'd be fine with just his coat. Lex wrapped the last one around the two of them. It smelled like campfire smoke, an earthy and comforting smell. Unlike the odors of other, more life-threatening fires.

"I keep texting my brother, but no answer. We'll have to figure all this out in the morning. Let's just sleep for tonight."

For once, no one argued.

When Penelope stirred awake, she realized the van was moving. Gentle, blue morning light filtered through the trees.

"Wakey, wakey, eggs and bakey!" Nate shouted just before he blasted a classic rock station.

"Does that mean you have food?" Seth said. "Tell me you have food or something to drink."

"Nope, just good old American Southern rock. Yeehaw! Buckle up, ladies and gents. We're blowing this popsicle stand."

When Lex grumbled something about rednecks, Penelope chuckled into his chest.

Within minutes, they were picking up speed on the interstate. The sun rose in front of them, and the cold morning air made her want to snuggle as deeply into the sleeping bag and his body heat as possible. She was still wearing his hoodie, so she reached up to pull the hood over her head, more to wrap herself in his smell than to keep warm.

.His right arm wrapped around her neck, while her left hand rested on his jeans under the sleeping bag. Her side hurt, her head hurt, and her mouth tasted like dry steel wool, but she couldn't stop smiling.

Nate saw it first and swore. Penelope jerked up, looked in the direction of Nate's focus, and gasped at the sight of thin black smoke. It slithered like a mamba snake, rising from the trees.

Drips said, "Isn't that right by where the—"

"Holy shit. The truck stop," Elijah said.

Nate turned off the radio, veered out of the fast lane, and prepared to exit. They waited in tense silence.

A cold stone of dread formed in the pit of Penelope's stomach. The van passed the same gas stations and fast-food restaurant, but this time the businesses were crowded with cars filled with gawkers. The smoke had grown thicker, and it churned and heaved in the still morning air.

The highway, formerly Route 66, had been closed off, and the pavement past the barriers was packed with fire trucks, police cars, and St. Louis City news station vans.

The truck stop itself was nothing but a pile of burning cinders.

Nate pulled the van into the gas station and slowly rolled through the parking lot.

"Drips," Elijah called out.

"Already got it," Mason said, his voice the most serious Penelope had heard it. He was holding his phone, scanning over a news article. "'Historic Route Sixty-Six Truck Stop Burns to the Ground,'" he read. "It says the fire started last night shortly after midnight. Witnesses say, before the fire started, they saw a red van and—"

"Read it," Elijah demanded.

"A group of teenagers, climbing off the roof and getting into the van."

Elijah leaned forward and put his hand on Nate's shoulder. "Nail, you have to listen to me. Do not speed. Do not do anything suspicious. Get back on the interstate. Nice and easy."

"We've been set up!" Nate screamed, pounding his fists into the steering wheel.

"Hold it together. We'll get them, but not right now. Right now, we are less than fifty feet from the scene of the crime, and we are the number one suspects. Drive."

"Come on, bro," Seth said, grabbing his brother's arm. "Come on, you're the only one who can drive a stick. Don't lose it on us now. You got this."

"Yeah," he replied, taking a deep breath. "Yeah, I got this." Nate crunched over the steering wheel and maneuvered the van around the lot. At one point, they were perfectly parallel with a police car, and all of them ducked into their seats.

Penelope had the strange sense she had lost all control, and she felt detached from everything happening outside the window. Surely that mound of ashes surrounded by vehicles wasn't the same place they had just been last night. Was it?

They pulled onto the interstate without incident, and Elijah instructed Nate to drive for at least fifteen minutes before trying to find a spot to pull over. He also told them to stay quiet, to keep their heads low, and not to touch their phones.

With nothing better to do, Penelope gripped Lex's hands under the sleeping bag as tightly as she could, and he squeezed back.

When Nate found a shoulder wide enough, he put the van in park and turned off the engine. They sat in stunned silence for a few seconds.

"Ghost," Elijah said without glancing behind him. "Give us your backpack."

Lex lurched. "Excuse me?"

"Give us the backpack. Now."

His reply seethed out from between his clenched teeth. "No."

Penelope put her hand on Lex's chest to hold him back, even though he hadn't made any threatening movements—yet. "Why? Why do you want it?"

"Think about it," Elijah said, eyes hard. "You're the journalist."

Penelope's face melted in resignation. "Lex was the only one who knew our location last night. It's either the coincidence of the century, or you think he leaked where we were going."

"Let me get this straight," Lex snarled. "You think I set all of you up? Including myself? Including her?" He gestured to Penelope. "Falling on—*hurting* her, you think that was part of some act? That's revolting and ridiculous. Do you have any idea what *was* in that place? No, of course you don't. You're too focused on the physical and obvious. I know what happened to me last night. That backpack contains all of my data—data that could at last confirm the existence of the paranormal. You expect me to just hand it over?"

"Lex, dude," Mason muttered, "it doesn't matter what's on those files. It could be Casper singing show tunes. We all have to delete any data from our devices indicating we were ever there. For the record, I don't think you tried to sabotage us. I bet it was some mistake. But somebody is out to get us. Somebody is trying to frame us. Whoever wants to frame us made most of those noises last night. They wanted to scare us out so they could start the fire. We gotta be careful. We have to destroy any evidence we were there, including anything in your backpack."

Lex leaned back in the van chair and folded his arms. The backpack, Penelope noticed, was still wedged between his feet. "Over my dead body."

Elijah lunged. He twisted his torso and dived over the back of the seat. His fingers wrapped around the backpack's handle and pulled. Lex bent over to squeeze his arms around the backpack. A tugging match ensued, but Elijah's grip proved the stronger. The backpack flew over the seat, and Mason tossed it up to Nate.

Seth and Nate opened both front doors and ran out of the van. Elijah and Helena threw open the sliding door to dash out, and Penelope and Lex followed them. Mason stayed by the van, shouting at them, but no one could hear his words over the roar of the interstate. Standing in a field of mushy dead grass, they formed two groups—Seth, Elijah, Helena, and Nate with the backpack on one side and Penelope and Lex on the other.

Lex went still. "You have one chance to give it back."

"We will give it back," Elijah said, "after we go through the files."

Lex didn't hesitate. He charged them, sprinting at full speed and barreling toward Nate. Nate, in a panic, hurled the backpack to Mason. Mason jumped, reaching high, but the backpack soared over his head as well as the van.

It landed in the middle of the interstate with a *plop*.

A semitruck sounded its horn, but it couldn't veer in time. Eight wheels of the eighteen-wheeler rolled over the backpack.

Next, a car.

Another. Another.

With each wheel, the noises changed from sharp popping to duller and duller cracking and crumbling.

Lex yelled in rage and hysteria. He ran to the side of the interstate, waited until he had a few moments between cars, and dashed in the middle of the road. An approaching SUV blared its horn at him as he grabbed the bag and ran back into the field.

His legs folded under him, and he unzipped the bag. Slowly, he turned the backpack upside down, and shards of black and gray plastic tumbled out. The only intact item was the leather cover of the journal. When Lex opened it, all the ripped pages floated into the grass.

Lex stood up and glared at Nate, who had run up to the side of the shoulder.

Penelope, still standing in the wet grass of the field, held out a hand, opened her mouth to call to Lex—Lex whose dreams had literally been destroyed before his eyes. Before Penelope could say anything, Lex's fists were in Nate's face.

Lex punched him, again and again, pounding into his nose, forehead, and eye sockets. Elijah, Helena, and Seth tried to grab one of his long limbs, but he kept pulling free.

Elijah changed tactics. He threw an arm around Lex's neck in a headlock, and Helena swung her own fist directly into Lex's right eye. Seth, meanwhile, began kicking him in the side. Lex refused to release his grip on Nate, even as his knuckles split and his lip broke open.

Penelope, horrified at the violence, the blood, looked at Mason, who was also frozen in terror. He nodded to her, and the two of them ran toward the brawl. Penelope dived in front of the prone Nate to block Lex, and Mason grabbed Helena's fists before she could strike Lex again.

"Stop it! Enough!" Penelope begged. For a moment, she thought Lex couldn't see her through his rage, thought Lex's fist would come down into her face.

But Lex halted. Unsteadily, he found his footing. Mason grabbed his arm to hold him up as he spat a wad of bile into the grass. Penelope turned to Nate beside her. His face a mask of dripping red, he didn't move from his spot on the stained ground. Penelope couldn't discern any of his facial features under all the blood. Two of his earrings and one of his eyebrow rings had been ripped out and were lying in the grass.

Behind them, Penelope heard tires crunching gravel. She turned around and saw a small car parking behind them. A middle-aged woman in the passenger seat rolled her window down. "Are you kids all right?" she called out. "Should we call somebody?"

Mason helped Lex turn his face away, and Helena pulled Nate into a sitting position pivoted away from the voices.

Elijah put on his own mask of innocence and confusion. Penelope knew that mask. It was the same Elijah he pretended to be at school. He quickly smoothed his ponytail and readjusted his thick-framed glasses.

"Oh, wow! You guys are just the sweetest for stopping and checking on us. Yeah, we're totally fine. We're getting in the van now. Just a little argument."

The man next to the woman leaned over her. "It looks like somebody got hurt."

"A little roughed up, but nothing to worry about. You know how teenagers are," he called out with a shrug. "Always fighting about something. We're fine. You guys have a great Sunday morning."

The driver and the woman nodded, but Penelope could see they still looked tense and unsure. As soon as their car was out of sight, Elijah said, "We need to get in the van and drive. Those two are probably calling the cops right now."

Mason helped Lex, and Helena and Seth both had to carry Nate. Penelope did her best to gather the few salvageable journal papers and tucked them in the leather cover.

"Lex and Penelope, take the middle seat. Bring Nate to the back with me."

"He needs a hospital," Penelope said. Her voice sounded flat, and some distant part of her brain registered that she was in shock.

"No, he needs me," Elijah corrected her. "I know what I'm doing. Five years living with a stepdad who wanted to beat the gay out of you will teach you a thing or two about emergency aid." He had already pulled a medical kit from the back of the van. "Can anybody else drive a stick?"

"I used to change gears for my dad when I was little," Helena said. "That was years ago."

"It will have to do. Just stay in the slow lane and try to keep it in first or second. Hopefully, we won't grind the gears too badly." Elijah pulled the keys from Nate's pocket and handed them to her. Nate lay in the backseat on top of Penelope and Lex's sleeping bag. "It's best if we drive slowly anyway."

Lex barely stirred as the van pulled back on the highway. His lip was swollen and wet where Helena had landed a blow, and his shirt was caked in mud. Blood poured from his split knuckles. Wordlessly, Penelope helped him out of his T-shirt so he could use it as a wrap for his hand, which he pressed against his mouth.

The side where he had been kicked was already a mottled red color. Each of his exhales came out with a shudder, and his fingers holding the shirt to his mouth quivered.

Behind her, Nate moaned, desperate and animal-like. She couldn't bring herself to turn around to see him, but she heard the gurgling of a bottle just before a pungent smell filled the car.

Rubbing alcohol, she realized.

"Nate, this is gonna suck. Cuss and yell as much as you want."

He did. He cussed and yelled through the alcohol swabbing and through every stitch, but Elijah displayed the infallible concentration of a surgeon. As he worked, he spoke in between Nate's exclamations. "No hospitals. No parents. No one can say anything. Do you understand? Anything. This wouldn't be just a slap on the wrist. This would be juvy court and then juvy hall."

The sharp snip of a scissors indicated he had finished stitching one of the cuts. "We have to get rid of the van," Elijah said.

"I can dump it somewhere," Helena volunteered, "after I drop you guys off. I think I'm getting the hang of this."

"Until you hear from me, everybody lie low. And check through all your social media posts, blogs, whatever. See if you wrote anything that could have given someone a tip."

The scissors snapped again as he said, "We're all in this together. Lois and Ghost, you're a part of us now."

Too numb to speak, Penelope leaned against Lex and cried.

14

DON'T THANK ME YET

Parasites. Once the word formed in her brain, she couldn't shake it out. The word had burrowed in deep, and every time she tried to take a bite, her stomach heaved in revulsion.

"Penny," Mike said, "sweetie, you've hardly touched your food."

Out of the corner of her eye, she saw Mike give Henry a concerned glance, his brow furrowed. Both of her parents had already finished their meals and were on their second glasses of wine.

Mike had tanned Caucasian skin, a thick brown beard, and a head of hair with tight curls. Henry, home from his lecture series, was slightly lighter skinned than Lex and shaved his head. They sat together on one side of the booth, and Penelope sat on the other, alone. They had taken her to The Hill, a section of St. Louis City known for its Italian heritage. Its restaurants served the best pasta in the city, including crab alfredo.

But those noodles looked too much like intestinal worms.

"I guess I'm just not hungry." She didn't sound convincing, even to herself.

"Is this about that boy who was supposed to join us, Penny?" Henry asked with narrowed eyes.

"No." The need to protect him caused a tightening in her chest. "It's not his fault I stayed overnight. Please don't blame him."

"We don't." The wine forgotten, Mike leaned toward Penelope. "We're proud of you for making that decision. We know teenage drinking happens. We were young once, remember?"

"A long time ago," Henry mumbled.

"Longer for you," Mike quipped.

Henry raised an eyebrow. "By a year, Michael. Hardly worth bragging over."

As they bantered, Penelope continued to sulk, twirling a noodle with her fork.

"It's not about you staying over, but we can tell something is wrong. And it's hard for us not to assume it has something to do with the new boy." Henry clenched a fist. "If he did anything to you, just tell me, and I'll—"

"It's not him," she insisted, trying to keep the heat out of her tone. "His mom is a professor like you, Dad. And it's not him. I promise."

Mike laid his hand on Henry's arm and spoke to his daughter. "Honey, listen. Tell us when you're ready. We're here to help if you need it."

Penelope forced herself to nod, and she begged the stinging in her eyes to subside. Crying all over the table would be mortifying. And if she cried, her dads would never leave her alone until she told them what was going on.

No matter what, she couldn't tell them about anything. That was hard when the secrets were so plentiful. The incriminating fire. The brutal fight. The mangled face stitched together in the backseat of a van.

It didn't feel like the same day. Shortly before noon, Helena had stopped the van a few blocks from her house. Lex was already gone. He had slipped out of the van the first chance he got to find a bus.

Penelope had managed to jog the rest of the distance and slip into the house unnoticed. After jamming Lex's hoodie under her bed, she showered and changed clothes. Right on time, she appeared downstairs ready for the family birthday outing, wearing a short purple dress, black tights, her paint-splattered flats, and a gray knit hat over her green hair.

She felt as if she were barely holding herself together, as if she were a doll losing all its stitches.

"Let's change the subject. Presents," Mike said, jamming some cheerfulness into his tone. He sipped from his wine glass again and pulled a single envelope from his back pocket.

Henry grumbled something about "beating little boys down" into his wine glass before draining it.

"You're an anthropologist, and you're shocked by teen melodrama?" Mike asked.

"When my baby is involved, yes."

Mike directed his attention back to her. "Penelope, before you open this, you should know we got a call from Mr. Jaeger on Friday night. He told us the good news about your applying for the open features editor position." Mike reached across the table to squeeze her hand. "We are so proud of you for taking this step. He told us how talented you are and how we need to do everything we can to push your writing ability to the next level." Mike gestured to the envelope.

Penelope, feeling more confused than before, slowly opened the envelope. It was a brochure from a university in New York City. It read "Six-Week Journalism Summer Intensive Program for Teens! Live the NYC life. Hone your skills. Write and publish your work." The program began in late May, after school let out. She glanced through the information inside and gasped when she saw the price, which didn't even include airfare. "I mean, this looks incredible, but—"

Henry smiled. "Penelope, that's your present."

"The brochure?"

"Yes, the brochure," Henry said with a playful, mocking tone. "No, silly! The program. If you tell us you want to apply, we will make it work. There's a colleague up there who owes me a favor, so we can send you for a discount. It's a rare opportunity, Penny."

"Wow, I—" A riot of emotion roiled through Penelope. Journalism jobs—ones that paid a living wage, anyway—were rare. Elijah had been right about that. Opportunities like this one could open doors for her. However, leaving the city seemed like the last thing she wanted to do in the near future. It wasn't just about Lex. The thought of leaving any of her Pack behind made her eyes sting again.

Her dads watched her, and she realized she wasn't concealing her dismay very well.

"All right, that's it." Henry pushed his chair back on the hardwood floor with a screech. "Tell me his address. I'm gonna show this little boy what happens when he messes with my girl."

"No. No. I'm just overwhelmed. It's such a wonderful present. I don't know what to say. Six weeks away from home is a long time, though. Can I think about it?"

Mike gave Henry another reproachful look. He tilted his head at Penny and shot her a slight smile. "Sure, honey. Just make sure you let us know before registration is due. Everything must be submitted by the end of the month. If you don't want it, we can use the money to do something else this summer."

She tried a smile. "Got it. Thank you. Really. I love you both so much."

"We love you, too."

About thirty minutes later in her room, she kicked her flats off and reached under the bed for Lex's hoodie. She threw it on over her dress and climbed into bed.

Lex had no phone now, she knew. It had been crushed along with everything else in his backpack. Even if he did, she wasn't supposed to contact him on it. There was nothing left to do but wait for word. Giving up, she slipped away into the dreamless, empty sleep that only comes from total exhaustion.

She slept undisturbed until her phone buzzed. Behind her curtains, the neighborhood was dark, and the rest of the house beneath her was silent. The world rested with a quietness reserved for after midnight and before dawn. Struggling to focus her eyes, she gripped the phone tightly and examined the cracked screen.

The message awaiting her looked exactly like those first few ominous texts she received last Monday.

Broken app: *I'm alone. I'm a freak. I'm nothing. I feel like you keep dragging me to all these places I don't wanna go. And then everything turns out badly.*

After a few moments, a reply appeared. And another, and another.

Avriel: *Hey, cowboy, you must have balls the size of a bull hacking into whole-group messaging like this.*

Essence: *What kind of an emo message is that, anyway?*

Symmetry: *It's music to slit your wrists to, isn't it?*

Avriel: *Identify yourself, buckaroo, before I come over there and make you.*

Mumble: *Come over where, exactly? Avi, quit being an idiot.*

Avriel: *Hey! That's* Mister *Idiot to you.*

The app remained silent for a few moments. She hadn't realized members could group message everyone in the app. She scrolled back through the messages, rereading the first cryptic message. Then, it dawned on her. She knew those words. They were some of the exact same phrases Lex had said to the Pack.

If she recognized the phrases, Elijah would surely do the same.

Her phone buzzed with another message.

Wolf Cub: *Ghost, that better not be you. Did you hack into the app again?*

Penelope covered her lips with the tips of her fingers as she understood what had just happened. Trouble for the Pack had started as soon as she and Lex had joined them—but only Lex had been persistently hostile. Elijah probably understood the terrible circumstances surrounding everything that had happened to his group the last few days, but he had no reason to defend Lex. Instead, he had every reason to blame the person who was putting him and his group at risk.

The hacker didn't reply, but the other leaders seemed more than eager to eviscerate their number one suspect.

Haze: *Wow, Cub, you let a hacker stay in the group after he already hacked us once?*

Griffin: *Isn't Ghost the same one who beat the shit out of Nail?*

Anax: *Oh, so the dude isn't just a hacker, he's a violent hacker. Perfect. This is a mess. The Pack is a mess. Cub, how could you be so damn stupid?*

Wolf Cub: *I was trying to keep everything under control.*

Haze: *Well, you screwed that up, didn't you? And now, this other thing happened last night. We all saw that the Pack was scheduled to go out there, and then the situation went up in smoke, if you know what I mean.*

Wolf Cub: *Let's not be hasty.*

Avriel: *Shut up, Cub. You've caused us enough headaches. If we've found the skunk, let's smoke him out. Kick him out of the app. Block him.*

Griffin: *We need to do more than just block him if he's put us all at risk. He needs to pay for this.*

Rhapsody: *Where are you hiding your little ghost friend, Cub? Conjure him. Now.*

At last, the mysterious hacker replied.

Broken app: *You're so confident you know the end conclusion.*

The app closed. When she scrolled over to reopen it, the app itself was gone, as if it had never existed at all. She tried to turn her phone on and off three separate times, hoping the app would reappear. No luck. The hacker had destroyed the app, most likely.

The other teams—her own team, even—would continue blaming Lex. He had hacked into the program once. Elijah knew Lex had never wanted to join them. It wouldn't be a stretch for them to believe he had done it again just to tear them down. They would decide he had also somehow managed to delete the app completely. At least, that's how it appeared to her on her phone. After all of Lex's reluctance and insults as well as Nate's beating that morning, everyone would be more than eager to declare him guilty of setting up the Pack last night.

But it wasn't Lex. That much she knew. *Who else could pull off something like this?*

Elijah was the Wolf of their Pack. He was their leader, but she had seen no indication he could code. He was in as much trouble as the rest of them. He didn't make sense.

But Elijah's whole code name wasn't actually *Wolf.* Mason had used *Wolf Cub* more than once. Elijah, after all, wasn't the only Wolf. There was an Alpha Wolf, she remembered, and that Alpha started the Broken and developed the app.

She had changed out of her dress and into jeans before she had formulated a plan. The hoodie slid over her slim frame, too. It was close to midnight on Sunday, making it a school night. That didn't matter. Keys and wallet in hand, she rushed downstairs, shut the door as softly as she could, and jumped into her car.

Mason. She had to get to Mason. Out of all the members of the Pack, he was the most reasonable and caring. He was the only other person who had wanted to break up that day's fight with love instead of more violence.

He would believe her when none of the others would.

She headed toward the apartment building where the group had picked Mason up on Saturday night. The high-rise complex was in the Grand Center Arts District, which was popular with dancers, studio artists, musicians, and other performers. She parked on a side street and jogged to the main entrance facing Grand Boulevard. The front door to the building was locked, but there was a buzzer allowing guests to call to specific apartment numbers.

A week ago, she would have scurried off and tried again tomorrow after school. Now she randomly started punching combinations of four numbers. About one out of every four resulted in ringing tones. No one seemed to be answering that late at night, though. On her sixth attempt, a groggy voice answered.

It hollered, "Who the hell is this trying to get into my house right now?"

"Oh, my gosh! I'm so sorry," she sputtered, trying to sound as helpless and silly as possible. "I'm trying to reach my boyfriend. It's important. Do you know the combination of the Morston Family?"

"Ugh. Two seven four five. Leave me alone." With a final curse, the resident hung up.

She punched in the numbers. No one picked up, so she called again. And again. And again. After five minutes, a young girl's voice said, "Late is the hour. The nightingales are singing. Yet over and over, my phone keeps ringing."

"Huh?" Penelope said.

"Sasha!" she heard Mason call out in the background. "Knock it off. Who is it?"

"Some white girl, I think! And, no, it's not your hellcat warrior queen."

"Give me the damn phone and go to bed," he said. There was a shuffling, then Mason voice. "Hello? Who is this?"

"Mason, it's me."

"Penelope? Oh. You got that little message too, huh?"

"Yeah."

"Hold up. I'll come down."

A few minutes later, Mason appeared wearing sweats and a T-shirt, a comb stuck in his Afro. "Come on, I know where we can talk."

"You didn't bring your phone with you, did you?"

"No?"

"Good."

Mason didn't ask for an explanation. They strolled down Washington Boulevard until they reached Spring Avenue. Penelope knew where they were going as soon as she caught sight of it. A church of white brick and stone with nothing left but the walls themselves stood guard on the empty block. Two supports held up the back wall. There was no roof, door, or windows: just the walls covered in dead vines.

"After you," Mason said, gesturing to the entrance. Penelope walked in and sat against the back wall.

"A bunch of kids at my school got caught in here once," he said, pretending to pinch something between his thumb and forefinger and smoke it. "That was funny."

"Morons. Who picked up the phone earlier?"

"My little sister. She's in seventh grade. She thinks she's a poet, and she loves weirding out strangers." He paused and exhaled. "So, is this when you convince me Ghostboy didn't do it?"

"Yup."

"I'm listening. I'm not saying I'm going to believe you, but I'm listening."

"I think it was Elijah's big brother, the Alpha Wolf. He's the one who set us up."

Mason laughed. "What makes you say that?"

Penelope sensed she was already losing her opening and laid her theory out in a rush. "Warren's the one who started this. He developed the app and formed the Broken. Lex and Warren are the only two people, at least that I'm aware of, who can both code and knew where we were going Saturday. It must be one of them.

"I suspect Warren has been using the app to listen to everything we say and track our locations. If he's good enough to make apps that can take over your phone, I'm sure he can use the same programming to spy on us. And I think Warren intentionally used all of those phrases he heard Lex say before shutting the app down so we would assume it was Lex."

Mason was shocked. "What would motivate Warren to do such a thing? Elijah leads one of the groups in the Broken. Yeah, the Pack is the lowest ranking, but Warren is the only reason Elijah is alive right now. Who do you think took all of those beatings Elijah mentioned today? It was Warren. Elijah patched him up, over and over. They were homeless together, too, finding abandoned places all over the city to sleep. That's how they came up with the idea in the first place."

He picked out his hair as he spoke, keeping his hands busy as his frustration mounted. "You don't know that story because you just joined us, but they're family. All of us are. Seth, Nate, my Helena, Elijah. They're as thick as blood to me. You're going to tell me the guy who brought us together framed us?"

Penelope asked in a hushed tone, "Have you ever met Warren?"

Mason sputtered. "No. He got a full-ride scholarship to the University of Missouri-Rolla to become an electrical engineer. He manages the app during his down time from his dorm room. That's what Elijah told us, anyway." He paused to stare at her. "Why isn't it Lex? I never heard that part."

"Because," she said with stubbornness, chucking a loose pebble across the dirt and stone floor. "I know."

"Because you love him."

"Yup."

He smirked. "Everybody calls bullshit on me when I say I love Helena. They say I'm too young to have any idea what that word means."

"Well, I'm not."

"I know you're not." He groaned, the sound echoing slightly off the white stone walls. "Listen. I'm going to check into this. But you gotta go to school tomorrow, and Elijah is in your journalism class. Fake it. Act. Be the meek Penelope they expect you to be, not this new out-after-curfew Lois. Don't confront my Wolf Cub—my *brother*—about anything, and don't say shit to him about Alpha. He would completely lose it. I promise I'll investigate. I'll contact you by Wednesday night. Deal?"

Mason nudged her to ensure he had her attention. "You have to lie low until then. No visiting Lex, either. I mean it. Don't. If you're anything close to correct, he's the target. You going over might result in more attention."

She reached over and hugged him. "Thank you." He groaned again and hugged her back.

"Don't thank me yet." His voice sounded more like a grumble than words. "I didn't say I believe you."

"I know, but I knew you'd listen. How's Nate?"

"Awful. Lex could have killed him, Penelope. Seth keeps waking him every thirty minutes to check his bandages and his pupils. He's got a nasty concussion."

"But Lex—"

"I know. I saw what happened. I'm not blaming anybody. None of it was fair. That's why I'm doing this for you. Do you understand? Not everything has an easy answer." He stood up and brushed the dirt off his pants. "Come on. Let's get to bed. We have school tomorrow."

Monday. Tuesday. Wednesday. Penelope willed for them to pass like any other day. Wake, shower, eat, class, class, eat, class, home, eat, sleep. Repeat, repeat. Her body moved through the routines, but half of her brain space was devoted to replaying every moment from the week before.

The amazing, the heart wrenching, the peaceful, the scary—all of them.

She devoted as much of that energy to her schoolwork and writing as she could. It paid off. The second draft of her profile on the hospital clown went straight to Taylor, who loved it. As for Elijah, Penelope followed Mason's advice and ignored the leader. She even avoided any contact with Yuma and Xavier, who had been a part of the Pack only a few weeks earlier.

During a few free hours, she visited her local hardware store and spent too much money on a flashlight. Somehow, she had a feeling she'd be needing it in the near future. Anything would be an upgrade to her dollar store one, which provided a beam only slightly better than her phone, but her new purchase boasted drop protection and a twist focusing optic, whatever that meant.

Lex would be proud, she thought.

On Wednesday in Advanced Painting, she painted him. Her depiction included a low hood and obscured facial features. In the background, she included the memorial grave to Kate along with other gravestones. The sky burned.

"Who is that?" Lacie said with repugnance as Penelope prepared to carry the canvas home at the end of the day.

"Someone I met thanks to you," she said. Lacie scoffed and turned away. Penelope whispered at her back, "He's alone. He's a freak. He's nothing. But he's mine."

When she reached home, she checked the mailbox as she always did. Inside, she found an envelope with *LOIS* scrawled on it in black marker. When she opened it, a thumb drive and a handwritten note fell out.

Tucking the thumb drive in her pocket, she read the sloppy handwriting.

I believe you. Look through the files. But we have a problem. Many of the group leaders are getting together Friday night to figure out what to do with Ghost. I think that's just a cover. We have to get to that meeting without Elijah knowing.

For his safety, you have to break up with Ghost.

Make it believable.

15

LET ME BE PUT TO DEATH

After examining the pictures on the drive, Penelope was convinced. She had to keep Lex away. For twenty-four hours, she tried to figure out how to orchestrate the breakup. She couldn't hurt him, yet she had to hurt him. That lone contradiction prevented her from sleeping more than a few minutes at a time and kept her stomach from holding down food. Thursday passed in a blur as she stumbled through the motions.

When she got home, she threw down her things, kept the lights off, flopped on her bed, and covered her eyes with her arms. She was running out of time, and she was no closer to coming up with a plan. It had to be tonight. But how?

All the agonizing, however, had been pointless. Lex appeared outside her window.

He rapped on the glass, ever so gently, his Chucks standing on the slanted garage roof. It seemed years since she had sat out there on the night of her birthday. For a mortifying second, she thought she had left her painting from school on her bed. But no, she had put it in her closet.

Quietly, she slid up the window. He shimmied through, bending his long limbs around the window frame. Once he was inside, he stared at the floor.

He was wearing a different hoodie, dark gray this time, and kept one side of his face away from her. "I climbed up from the deck. I'm sorry. I should have knocked at the front door. I didn't want to be a creep, but I didn't think your parents should see me like this."

She reached up to touch his cheek. Reluctantly, he turned toward her. Penelope couldn't help but gasp. The right side of his face was a swollen mass of black-and-purple flesh. He could only open his eye enough to form a thin slit. His split lip had scabbed over, but it was still swollen.

He chuckled at her response to his injuries. "It's been fun at school. The teachers won't look at me. The counselor bugs me every day. The other kids—well, they never liked me, anyway. Home sucks, too. Mom says I'm falling into a 'dangerous spiral' or something, and she won't talk to me until I tell her what happened." He paused and asked hesitantly, "How's Nate?"

Penelope grabbed him, hugging him as tightly as she could. "I don't know. I haven't talked to anybody since Sunday night. That doesn't matter right now."

He squeezed back. "I just couldn't take it anymore," he choked out. "I had to see you."

This is it, she thought. *This is when I should pull away and tell him to get lost.* But that thought passed over her with the same force as a gentle whisper trying to push down an ancient tree. In his arms, she couldn't do it.

His hands touched her neck and pulled her in for a kiss. Penelope felt the world sway underneath her. Everything was different this time. Saturday night, they shared reluctant, nervous touches as if they were afraid of being scolded or discovered. This time, he executed his focus with his hands, his lips, and his breath. He moved away from the kiss and began running his mouth down her jawline.

She shared that focus as her own fingers crawled under his hoodie and around his sides. When her fingers accidently brushed his scrapes, he let out a gasp of pain. Quickly, she moved her fingers to caress the velvet skin of his back, and the gasp changed to a soft exclamation deep in his throat.

Refusing to be outdone, he buried his mouth into the curve of her neck. Letting out her own gasp of surrender, Penelope arched her back and leaned into him. His lips moved up from her neck to her ear. "Let me stay tonight," he whispered. "Please. I'll be gone in the morning before anyone knows I was here."

The thought of him staying until the morning hours finally woke her up enough to murmur, "If they do see thee, they will murder thee."

"Are you quoting Shakespeare to turn me on?" he asked slyly, his words muffled by her own skin under his lips. "Because it's working."

"Shh," she hissed, pulling out from his grasp. "Let me think. Clear my head."

Like Mason said, Lex is the target, she reminded herself. *He can't be anywhere near me.* Letting him stay could be his doom. Her heart threatened to burst out of her chest as she realized the necessity of the task awaiting her.

She reached around him and put her hands in his back pockets. His eyebrows rose in pleased surprise, but he realized she was only searching for a new cell phone. He didn't have one, thankfully. He gestured away from the window, and she led him to sit down by the closet.

"Lex," she said, swallowing a lump in her throat, "you have to go."

He studied her and asked with suspicion, "What happened? Did they put you up to this?"

She held his hand to her lips and kissed it, mostly to give her lips something to do other than quiver. "I can't tell you. I can't. But it's really, really bad. You're in danger. I know that sounds stupid, but you are. You have to let us take care of it."

"What? They still think the fire was my fault?"

"Yeah, and they want payback. There were a couple of texts made to look like you had sent them. And they weren't just sent to our group, but all the groups in the Broken. There's so much more to it, and I can't tell you." She covered her face with his hand as well as her own. Her next words came out as a bleating request, not a command. "Please stay away."

"Let me be ta'en," he recited, pulling his hand down so he could look into her eyes. "Let me be put to death. I am content, so thou wilt have it so."

"Are you listening at all?" she rebuked, sniffing back tears and trying not to look impressed at the quotation. "This is serious. Get out. Now."

"You think they followed me, don't you?"

"Yes."

Lex raised an eyebrow. "Nobody follows me. Ever."

"Helena did at the mall," Penelope pointed out. Her resolve strengthened as she shielded herself with facts. "She tackled you, remember? You're good, but they've been doing this urban exploration crap for a long time. Now they want you."

Lex's mirth vanished, and the hard statue that replaced it cut a piece from her heart. He rubbed the good side of his face. "I'm going to respect your wishes, but I want you to understand you're hurting me more than any of them can."

"Fine," she said, feeling the tears form and then run down her cheeks. She didn't wipe them away. "Fine. I'm hurting you. Better than what could happen to you."

He glanced outside. "It's dark. Your lights are off. If someone is tracking me, they couldn't see in here. Let me guess. Was this the plan all along? Are you supposed to break up with me to protect me?"

"Yes," she said, wiping her eyes.

She watched him wrestle with the situation for a moment before his shoulders slumped. He was going to acquiesce, she realized. A part of her wanted him to fight her more, but another part was relieved it was almost over.

"How long does it usually take to break up with someone?" he asked, fighting back his own tears.

"I don't know," she replied, confused. "At least another five minutes, I guess?"

He took her into his embrace. "Then let's make these five minutes count."

The next night, she ran out of her house and into Mason's beat-up sedan. Leaving her dads on another weekend evening, even though they hadn't yet met the mysterious boyfriend allegedly causing her all this grief, had been tricky.

When she couldn't come up with a good enough story, she lied. Yes, she was going out with Lex, but they would meet him soon. She peppered them with false promises of a Sunday dinner at home with Lex as the honored guest.

Her parents also inquired about her spring break plans next week. *Not getting arrested*, she had thought. But she said she wanted to mostly stay at home and relax. She might enjoy some painting and writing, too.

Throughout the conversation, she had to be careful to hide the right half of her neck, which was covered in rose-shaped, blue-tinged bruises.

Mason was driving. Helena had claimed shotgun next to her boyfriend, and Seth sat in the backseat behind the driver. Penelope, once again wearing her more practical sneakers, slid into the back behind Helena.

Mason glared at her before he started the car. "Did you break up with him? Oh, wait. Never mind. Judging by the fact you're wearing his hoodie and your neck looks like it's been attacked by an overly aggressive octopus, I'm going to assume the answer is no."

"For all intents and purposes, we are broken up," she said in hushed undertones. "It might not have gone down how you pictured it, but the end result is the same. He's not coming, and he'll stay away."

"Fair enough." Mason turned the engine.

Penelope realized Seth had been glaring at her since she climbed into the car.

"What?" she asked. "Why are you looking at me like that?"

"Your Ghostboy gave my brother a concussion." He bared his teeth in challenge.

"Well, your brother destroyed the one thing that meant something to my Ghostboy. And he isn't in great shape, either." She blew air out from between her lips. "How is he?"

He glanced at her, trying to maintain his anger. "Are you actually asking?"

"Yeah. I'm asking."

His gruff reply came out from the back of his throat. "Better. He's slowly getting there."

"Well, I'm glad to hear it. But still." Penelope crossed her arms in front of her. "You shouldn't be so damn rude. I'm the one who could be saving Elijah right now."

"Don't act so noble," Seth said. "You aren't in this for him. It's for that freak."

"Think what you want. I couldn't care less." She averted her gaze out the window and tugged at her black hat. "I'm here. That's what matters."

"Lois got a mouth all of a sudden," Helena snapped.

Penelope considered shooting her own barb, but now wasn't the time. Too much was at stake tonight. "Where are we going?"

"Elijah told me where the meeting would be," Helena said. "It's in the dry sewer tunnel in Forest Park. Elijah has been taking us there since a few years ago. That was back when there were only three teams. Elijah and Warren stayed in those sewers after they left home."

"So, so, so, so… does this mean what I think it means?" Mason asked, bouncing up and down in his seat.

"Don't you dare, Drips," Helena warned.

"We're going down that manhole, aren't we?" Mason asked the question, but it was obvious he already knew the answer.

"Yes." She face-palmed.

"There are four of us, aren't there? It's basically fate."

"Oh my God. Not again, Drips!" Seth yelled from the backseat. "Don't you think tonight's a little bit too serious for this shit?"

But Mason wasn't listening. He plugged an antique MP3 player into the car, scrolled through his music, and pulled up a theme song to an early 1990s cartoon. He blasted the volume. "I'm the orange one, obviously," he shouted over the chipper tune. "Helena, babe, I'm sorry, but you're the red one. Seth is purple. Lois, I guess that makes you blue."

Despite everything, Penelope laughed. Seth was shaking his head, hiding a smile under his hand. Even though Helena had punched Mason in the shoulder for it, she was grinning, too. Mason played the song on repeat the entire route to the park.

Driving through Forest Park at night under such tense circumstances was a surreal experience for Penelope. Typically, she rode through the urban green space during the daytime with her dads for all sorts of family outings. The city's zoo, science center, history museum, art museum, and outdoor theater were all located within the park's thirteen hundred acres. She had spent many fun weekends visiting all of them since her adoption six years ago. Since it was a Friday night in March, there were a few cars driving along, but the streets seemed unusually quiet.

They passed the zoo's empty parking lot and turned down a slim drive leading deeper into the park's interior. Mason parked the car, and all four of them piled out.

"Everybody comes here for like, you know, the animals or whatever," Helena said as she tied her black-tipped hair back into the bun. "This park is more than that to us. It has some of the oldest dry sewers in the city and some of the easiest access points."

"We have to be careful." Mason tucked his flashlight in his pants. "We don't want anyone else to see us approach, so no flashlights for now. Luckily, there aren't any clouds."

They formed a line along the shoulder of the drive until they came upon a walking path cutting into the woods. Mason veered off the road and led them down the path.

Oak and hickory trees surrounded them on both sides. A few of them had the beginnings of buds, but most were still empty of new growth. Without flashlights, they had to rely on the natural light of the stars and the waxing moon. The sky itself was a murky navy thanks to the light pollution of the city surrounding the park. The branches created black outlines overhead.

When they came to a boardwalk extending over a low-lying area, Mason jumped off the paved trail and started down a footpath cut through the dirt and foliage. Its only footing was compacted dead leaves. Since this trail was narrower, Penelope was careful to avoid sticker bushes. Twice, she had to pull the sleeve of Lex's black hoodie from a snarling, outstretched vine.

"There it is," Mason said. Ahead, she could see a low, curved stone bridge reaching over a ravine. Mason picked up a jog. The others matched his speed, until the four of them skidded down the slant in the terrain. The jolt from running and the controlled fall down the slope reawakened the rib pain that was slowly getting better, despite Penelope's lack of rest. She still had to swallow ibuprofen to prepare for whatever awaited her that night, but the pain she felt now was a shadow to what she had felt on their other expeditions. She could handle it.

They reached the bottom of the ravine, and the walls were so steep she couldn't see the level ground above her. Under the bridge, a manhole in the middle of a concrete patch gaped open. Penelope spotted its lid a few feet away, compressing a scrubby bush.

One by one, they climbed down the ladder leading into the tunnel. Penelope was the last to descend. Her fingers clung to the wrought iron bars driven into the concrete, and she forced her feet down one step at a time. Above, she watched as the circle of bridge underbelly—the outside world—grow smaller and smaller.

Gradually, the sounds and air around her shifted from the chirping, rustling, living forest to the echoing, dripping, hollow underground. When she reached the bottom step, she jumped down the last few feet. The grinding pain in her ribcage caused her to crumple against the wall, but she waved Mason away when he rushed to her side. After a few deep breaths, she straightened. The three of them had already switched on their flashlights, so she reached into her pocket and pulled out her new, upgraded instrument.

They stood on a walkway that bordered what used to be the waterway. Above, the ceiling curved. Everything appeared aged and ancient. She had expected foul human odors and wet conditions. Instead, everything was still and almost clean, like an old sanctuary boarded up hundreds of years ago. The sweeping arches that formed the tunnels rose about ten feet over her head at their highest point. The beauty of the place stunned her speechless and trapped her gaze.

Helena grinned. "You're one of us, Lois. I know it wasn't under the best circumstances, but you are."

Seth nodded. "She's right."

"Come on. We can love on how awesome she is later," Mason said. "We have to save our Wolf."

"If he *wants* to be saved," Helena said in a dark tone.

The four of them picked up a jog down the long tunnel. Their footfalls created a cacophony of echoes that reached behind them, above them, and far into the tunnels ahead of them. Mason led the way, his flashlight bouncing around corners.

Penelope judged he could probably find his way in complete darkness if necessary. Every time they came to a juncture that opened into a fork or even multiple tunnel passageways, he didn't hesitate to consider the next turn. The others seemed equally confident in his ability to navigate the winding labyrinth.

Penelope tried to keep track of their route, but she quickly gave up. "How does he know his way?" Penelope asked Helena as they ran. "Do you come here every week?"

"Nope. Photographic memory," she replied, the pride audible in her voice. "You aren't the only one with a smart boy toy, Lois."

Mason stopped. "Wait, wait, wait," he panted. "Wait. Listen."

The four of them went quiet, gathering in a tight cluster.

"There," Seth said.

"Footsteps," Mason said.

"Here?" Helena said.

Seth explained to Penelope, "We came in the back way because we didn't think anyone would be over here. This isn't good."

"I'll check it out," Mason said.

"No," Seth insisted. "You know your way through here better than anybody. You have to lead. I'll go."

Before any of them could argue, he rushed around the corner. Penelope craned her head around long enough to see him vanish down another tunnel.

"What do we do now? Wait?" Helena asked with a grumble. "I'm no good at waiting."

Mason pulled in a few more deep breaths, and Penelope did the same to calm her beating heart as well as the ache in her ribs. Helena, who hadn't even worked up a sweat, just watched them with a smirk on her face.

"Five minutes," Mason managed to say. "We wait five minutes. Give him time to figure it out. We have to trust one another. If he's not here in five minutes, we'll search for him."

"Actually, no." The voice came from the tunnel they had just passed through. As one, they turned. Penelope gasped.

Haze from the music store stood before them, a pistol in his hand, barrel leveled at Mason. He grinned wildly.

"Pardon the pun, but I think I'll be calling the *shots* from here. Sound good, Pack puppies? I'd hate to have to put one of you down."

16

THE MOST BROKEN OF PEOPLE

"All three of you get against the wall," Haze said, gesturing with the barrel of the gun. The three of them sat down and squeezed together. Haze leaned in to take their flashlights and throw them far down the tunnel ahead. Penelope hadn't seen—or even thought of—Haze since the night of the mall chase. Now he was holding a weapon in her face.

"Alpha Wolf needs to have a chat with his younger brother," Haze explained as casually as if they were all dear friends. He flicked his ginger bangs. "It's best if you stay put until he's done."

Holding the gun with one hand, he removed his own flashlight from his pocket and adjusted it so it functioned as a lantern. After setting the lantern on the ground, he held the gun with both hands again.

"Alpha is here?" Mason asked.

"Of course," he said. "Who do you think sent me here?"

"You're acting on Alpha's orders?" Helena prodded.

Penelope glanced at her, amazed. Her own heart was pounding so hard in her ears she could barely hear the words being spoken, and she had to keep her lips pinned shut to stop her teeth from chattering. Never in her life had she been more afraid, but Helena was trying to dig out as many details as possible.

"Ah, Garnet," Haze purred as he stroked his freckled chin. "I'm thrilled to see you and that hot body again. If only we could spend time together *alone*. Yes, I'm acting on his orders. And, Lois," he continued, turning his eyes to her, "Alpha was right. You are a little babe, even if you are too skinny for my tastes. It's such a shame your creepy tagalong shadow isn't with you. Wolf Cub was supposed to bring Ghost to us. I don't see him. Is that your fault, cutie?"

Penelope asked, "Me? Never."

Haze spat. "Make your jokes. It's fine. This will all be over soon."

"Dude, don't you even know what's happening?" Mason asked, putting his hands out in a plea. "I was at Elijah's house early this week, and he let me use his computer. I found all these old pictures of Alpha and Elijah, and they're burning stuff. In the oldest photos, Elijah is still in grade school. They started small. Papers. Trash. But the stuff kept getting bigger. An entire garbage can. The dog house in the backyard. An old car. They tried to light somebody's trailer on fire. Then, I found pictures of little skeletons. I think they were animals. Shit, I don't even know. I just know they're both messed up and need help."

Penelope's respect for Mason reached new heights. He was appealing to Haze's sense of logic, something Penelope would have never even considered attempting. As Mason explained the pictures to Haze, Penelope could see all of them in her mind's eye. They were the same images Mason had placed on the thumb drive for her. For some reason, Elijah had been compelled to save those photos to his computer many years ago. It was all the proof the rest of them needed to show Warren was involved at the truck stop.

"Wait, wait, wait," Haze said, waving his hand at Mason to stop his talking while holding the gun with the other hand. "You knew all this time, and you're still trying to stop us? Don't you get it? This is the answer! This has always been the answer! The Broken? Are you kidding me? How long have we been living this lie? I've been leading Ozone for three years now, and for what? Some stains on my clothes, rips on my pants, and a place among the top three Broken teams. Stupid! It's all stupid." He slammed his scrawny fist into his chest and pounded it. "I'm still as messed up as I was the day Elijah recruited me. I'm not any better."

The gun bobbed in his hand as his anger increased. "We hide in these dirty, smelly, abandoned places, but what are we hiding from? Reality. We come out, and all that's waiting for us are the same judgments, accusations, and rejections of the outside world." He was getting louder and louder, waving both his arms now. "Alpha gets that. He's my Alpha because he knows how to finally set us free."

"How is that?" Helena asked, her tone unimpressed.

"Burn it away. All of it," he answered. "*All that is broken must burn.*"

"Become a damn arsonist? That's your answer?" Helena sneered.

"Don't worry. You'll soon understand, Garnet," Haze consoled her. "When you're the one setting the world aflame, you'll feel the power. You'll be cleansed. It will all make sense, I promise. Soon, Elijah will feel that power. Since you didn't bring us Ghost, another Pack member must pay for your transgressions."

"Seth!" Penelope cried out, finding her voice through the fear.

"*Skin* will have to pay the debt," Haze said, correcting her.

"He didn't do anything wrong, and neither did Lex. You just said yourself that you're the lunatics who are responsible for the truck stop fire," Penelope shouted.

"Wrong again, Lois," he spat. "Your Ghost hacked into the Broken app. He knows too much. If you insist on hiding him, another Pack member will have to do."

"Where's our dude? Where's Skin?" Mason yelled.

"He's been tied up and dropped in a sinkhole far from here. Wolf Cub will hear Alpha Wolf's words. He will understand. And then, he will light the gasoline trails we've poured through the tunnels leading directly to Skin's holding place."

Penelope didn't have to imagine being confined in a dark, small hole—alone, scared, and feeling the blasting heat of flame. Fire had almost killed her before. Now, one of her Pack members would suffer that same fate.

She forced her mind to figure out a plan, not get caught up in the swirl of memories. Elijah wouldn't light the fire if he knew it would harm Seth. She was confident of that fact. How could they communicate with Elijah? None of them had brought their phones to avoid being tracked, and they had all been locked out of the Broken app anyway.

But there was someone who had hacked into the app before. He could do it again.

Penelope leaned over to Helena. "I need a distraction," she whispered.

"What did she just say?" Haze barked. He approached both of them and aimed the gun directly over Penelope's head. "Answer me!"

Helena didn't answer with her words. Instead, she snapped her right leg out into a perfect sidekick. Haze tumbled to the floor. Helena shoved the gun away, jumped on top of him, and began a flurry of blows to his face. Mason and Penelope leaped to their feet, and Mason prepared to join the fight.

Penelope grabbed his arm. "Mason, you have to find anyone with a phone and message Lex. Tell him to hack into the app and tell Elijah not to set the fire or he'll burn Seth. Hurry!"

She shouted Lex's number at him as Mason took off running, scooping up his flashlight and dashing down the tunnel.

Penelope turned back to Helena and Haze and froze. Haze and Helena wrestled for control of her pocket knife. The knife point, directed at Haze's chest, inched closer and closer.

"Helena, stop!" Penelope exclaimed. "Don't do it!"

Helena hesitated, only for a second, but it was long enough for Haze to knee her in the back and roll out from under her.

"Grab it!" Helena said, pointing at the gun.

Penelope dived, but so did Haze. Penelope was closer. She picked it up, her arms shivering, and directed it at Haze. It felt cold and heavy in her palms. Adrenaline made her rib feel like a distant ache.

"Hands behind your back, ginger," Helena said, jerking his elbows. A zip tie from her pocket bound his wrists.

After Haze was secured, Penelope handed the gun to Helena. Her pupils dilated and forehead beaded in sweat, Helena accepted the weapon in a sure grip. She might be as scared as Penelope, but Helena's walls were so high she wasn't letting any emotion through.

Helena gulped and stared at Haze. "Don't move. Don't talk."

Haze, his nose bleeding from Helena's punches, obeyed without question or objection. With the tables turned and the lethal weapon in his face, all bravado melted out of him. Helena leaned over to pick up her pocket knife, fold it, and slide it into her front pocket.

Penelope said, "What now?"

"We wait for Drips and Ghost to pull through." Helena exuded a quaking breath. Another.

Penelope attempted to calm herself a little, too.

A few minutes passed before Helena said, "I know I've been rude to you and Ghost. When you go to church every Sunday and you're around all these nicely dressed people who are the biggest damn liars in the world, you never know who to trust. But you're both Pack now. Drips says you're good, so you're good with me, too. I just wanted you to know that no matter what happens tonight."

She's apologizing, Penelope thought in awe. *Even here, even now, she's thinking of us. Of her Pack.*

"Garnet, I—"

But Penelope was cut off. Four people approached. In the front was Elijah, wrists bound and hair out of its tie. Two others walked alongside him—guards, Penelope realized. One was male, amber skinned, built, and a little taller than Helena. The other, a young woman, had spiky black hair and a harsh gaze. Both of them carried guns.

Another figure trailed behind those three. He resembled Elijah, but his hair was almost black instead of Elijah's dark brown. It was straighter and longer, and his low ponytail reached between his shoulder blades.

In the dim light, Penelope noticed faded white and pink scars all over his face. A fresh red slash cut across the length of his neck. The two guards wore the same frantic, overzealous expression as Haze. The man in the center, however, showed no emotion. His features were blank, as if he were sleeping or staring at something so far in the distance it could never reach him.

Helena kept the gun on Haze, but the other two pointed them at Penelope.

"Drop it," the woman said.

Helena must have heard the eagerness in the guard's voice, as if the woman were hoping she wouldn't comply. Helena let the gun clatter to the concrete floor. The woman cut Haze free, who retrieved the fallen gun.

Haze stood nearly toe to toe with Helena, boring his hatred into her. Helena glared back at him, not flinching and refusing to back down.

He reared his arm back, rotated his body, and slammed the gun into her jawline. Helena gasped and stumbled. Again, the gun came down on her head, this time on the top of her skull. She slumped over. Before she fell, he slapped her across the face with the pistol, the blow landing right on her temple. Finally, she was allowed to fall in a motionless heap on the ground.

For the first time in her life, Penelope saw only red. She needed to hurt this man. Arms outstretched, she launched herself at him, trying to wrap herself around his arm and wrestle the gun away. A blinding pain in her side made her drop to the ground next to Helena, and in a daze, Penelope remembered the other two guards. She forced herself to breathe and at least keep her eyes open. The woman guard, who must have kicked her, stood above her with a smile.

Elijah cried out and rushed up to them, dodging around the guards with his hands bound. He stood in front of them, a protective stance, legs apart and trying to stand tall. "Stop hurting them. They're mine. The Broken falls apart if we don't at least honor the system."

"He's right," the woman admitted. "Haze, no more."

"Fine," Haze said, spitting a wad of saliva in their general direction. It landed on Helena's leg. "I just wanted to make it even. That's what this is all about. Right, Alpha?"

Impassive and unimpressed, Warren had observed the violence. He strolled forward and looked down at Penelope and Helena. "Anyone who commits a crime against the Broken will be punished." His voice was raspy and barely rose above the level of a whisper. "Again and again, the Pack commits crimes. We are here to punish you and reform you."

"Warren, stop," Elijah pleaded, gazing into his older brother's face. "Just stop it. You already know I got the message from Lex. I know Seth is stuck somewhere. I'm not going to hurt him. I'm not going to hurt these two, either. The Pack is family, like you. You'll never persuade me to hurt them, just like I could never hurt you."

Penelope continued to force wheezing breaths through her mouth. Through her agony, she was able to feel something that resembled hope. Elijah was not ready to follow his brother's orders blindly. Even now, he was fighting for his Pack.

"The Pack is yours, but all of the Broken is mine." Warren's voice dropped even lower. Each word carried a threat, like spear-shaped icicles. "I made the app. I made all of this. Haze of The Ozone, Titan of The Void, and Griffin of The Riot." He gestured to each of his gun-wielding guards. "They are my top team leaders, and they now understand. The Broken was only a tool to bring us together—the forgotten, abused youth. And now, we rise up. We fight back. We tear down and burn away the world that would be just as pleased to make us nothing."

As her pain became manageable, Penelope pulled Helena's head onto her lap. As blood trickled out the corner of Helena's mouth, Penelope gently ran her fingers over her face, hoping somehow she could feel she wasn't alone.

"Elijah," Warren said, using his brother's real name with careful pronunciation, "I love you. I thought you'd understand."

"Warren," Elijah said, choking on emotion. "I love you too. I believed you were better. I believed you were at school this whole time with that scholarship. Did you drop out? Did you even go at all?" He shook his head. "Whatever. It doesn't matter. I still love you. But I love my Pack. No, I will never understand. Maybe that's what the Broken always was to you. It's more than that for us."

And it's more than that for me, Penelope thought. She felt compelled to speak, to make sure her voice was heard. She couldn't let the Broken be destroyed, not when she had finally found what she had been aching for her entire life.

"It means everything," Penelope said, her voice quiet as she continued to cradle Helena's head. "It's given me everything I was missing. Friends I love. A sense of belonging. And I've learned to see beauty in the most unexpected places. Even in the most broken of people." Each word grew in strength until the final sentence echoed throughout the still cavern.

Warren hesitated for a moment, watching Penelope's tender care of Helena. For a second, Penelope thought she saw some reaction in his face. But it was gone before she could even make sense of it.

"Lois, your Ghost is why we are here. I had hoped to persuade the Pack gradually. Haze was instructed to call the police the night of your mall exploration. We wanted you to see how society treasures the pointless while neglecting true needs. The fire at the truck stop was meant to impress you with our capabilities and power."

"All you did was make us wanted criminals," Penelope said with narrowed eyes.

Turning to his brother, Warren ignored her. "As you yourself have said, Elijah, Ghost is not one of us. You have forced him into your Pack because Lois would not allow it otherwise." He turned his empty, black eyes on her. "You think you need him, correct?"

Penelope felt sick. Her words to Lex by the creek were coming back to her from the mouth of this foul human being. He had been listening the entire time.

"Shut up! Shut the fuck up!" she screamed. Helena stirred beneath her hand, then went still again. Penelope looked down at her. Tears were falling from her cheeks onto Helena's face. She hadn't realized she was crying.

Warren continued, ignoring her. "Yet, time and time again, Ghost hacks into the Broken. Perhaps worse, he dismisses and slanders everything we do. I heard him at the diner as well as outside the truck stop. He continually proves he doesn't understand. He's not one of us, yet due to Lois's interventions, he knows our secrets. Thus, he will be punished. When he hacked into the app to contact my brother, he was sloppy. We have his location now. Members of Ozone, Riot, and Void are tracking him as we speak."

"No! No, no, no! Don't touch him. Don't hurt him," Penelope begged. "Whatever you think the punishment is, I'll take it. Please!"

Again, Warren continued as if she had never made a noise. "The Pack is out of time. You must come to understand. You must join us, or—"

"Or what?" Elijah asked, incredulous. "What are you going to do? Kill us? Come on. Seriously? Are you even thinking? You're just gonna throw away everything? Griffin, Titan! You're seniors this year! Don't you care?"

"No," Griffin said. "Not at all."

"No," Titan said. "No, I don't care. Everyone else stopped caring about me a long time ago. It's time to make them care." He made a threatening fist.

"So, here we are." Warren reached into his back pocket and pulled out a book of matches. He pulled two of them free and held them out to Elijah. "Two matches, each representing a choice. Members of my top three teams have poured two lines of gasoline. One, which begins farther down that tunnel, leads into the pit holding Skin. The second, which starts back the way we came, leads to a pavilion located in the heart of Forest Park. We've also strapped a few explosives to the pavilion's pillars."

Warren let the matches dance across his fingers. "Your choice is simple. Pay the debt that is owed by lighting the path leading to Skin or blow up the pavilion. If you choose the second option, you will still have to free Skin. We will call the police and tell them two of the teenagers who burned down the truck stop just destroyed something else and can be found in the dry sewers. You will be arrested. Your future and life as you know it will be over. If you choose Skin, you can still run directly to him to free him. He will be harmed, but he will not die." He held the matches out. "Make your choice."

Elijah swallowed. He let out a shaky breath. "I already did. I'm not harming my Pack."

Again, a flicker of emotion flashed across Warren's face. But he regained control and said in his rattling voice, "Fine. So be it. The Pack is dead to us. My brother is dead to me. May you rot in the justice system for the rest of your life."

He extended the right match out to Elijah as Haze cut his wrists free. Elijah stumbled forward, as if he were sleepwalking, and snatched the match from Warren.

"I'll always love you, man," Elijah said, reaching out for his brother's shoulder. "I'll never forget what you did for me. I'm sorry all those years protecting me turned you into this. Years ago, I saved those pictures so I would never forget the mistakes I had made. But I thought we had moved beyond it. I thought you were better. I see now that was never true, and I failed to realize it. I won't ever be able to forgive myself."

Warren didn't move, just stared at Elijah's outstretched arm. Wounded, Elijah yanked his arm away and padded down the tunnel. Within seconds, the darkness enveloped him.

That left Penelope and the unconscious Helena alone with Warren and his zealots.

Haze prodded Helena then Penelope with the toe of his sneaker. "How long should we give them until we hunt them down like the stray dogs they are?" he asked hungrily.

Warren flicked the question away with his wrist. "Five minutes."

"Fantastic." Haze glanced at his watch. "I suggest you get moving."

"Huh?" Penelope asked. The guards surrounded her and Helena, faces pitiless. She didn't know what they would do to them when the time ran out, but she couldn't just lie there and wait. She managed to stumble to her feet, but the pain took her strength and she fell. Just thinking about trying to drag Helena made her so hopeless she couldn't find the energy to even try to stand again.

The seconds ticked down.

"Penelope! Helena! Get away from them, you crazy ass hats!" Mason followed his voice a second later, sprinting down the tunnel.

Penelope cried out, joy and exhaustion and agony warring in her voice. "Drips, hurry! We have to go!"

He closed the distance, shoved past the guards, and knelt next to them.

"They'll let us leave if we go right now, but we have to hurry," Penelope wheezed.

Mason nodded and wrapped his arm around Helena. She managed to wake herself enough to begin hobbling alongside him, and Penelope plodded behind. Mason led them down a tunnel, moving slowly but making progress.

"Shit," Penelope heard Titan grumble. "With Drips leading, we'll never find them."

"Doesn't matter," Warren said. "We'll have Ghost soon. They'll have to resurface."

17

YOU'RE THE BAIT

Lex had nothing left, so there was nothing to bring. Maybe a thermos of black coffee, he decided. His favorite mug, dented from overuse, never spilled or leaked—a miracle of modern science. He could run with it when the time came.

Not *if* he ran. *When.*

He hurried down the steps two at a time and ran into the kitchen. He pulled the mug from the dishwasher and silently thanked his over-caffeinated mother. She had brewed a pot before leaving for some weekend conference. After setting the coffee mug on the island, he spotted a little box with a hastily attached sticky note.

Lex, your sister sent this for you. —Mom

He screwed on the mug's lid and tore into the box. It was a package sent with two-day shipping. The receipt included a note from Nadine, his sister taking premed at Mizzou.

Little brother, I don't know what you're up to, but you got Mom worried sick. She said you don't even have a phone right now and you broke all of Dad's stuff. Get your act together before I drive down there and beat your ass myself! Seriously, I'm worried about you too. I'll be home for spring break. We'll talk then. Don't do anything stupid before I get there. Have fun with the present. Love you a lot.

Inside, there was a new EVP recorder, one that snapped around his wrist. She had even remembered the right brand. "Love you, too," he said with a smile as he set it up and put it on.

Holding the coffee mug with one hand, he hustled out the door and into the cold Friday night. No skateboard—too noisy, too bulky. He would travel on foot.

With his free hand, he pulled up his hood. Already, he felt a little safer, at least more in control. He knew how to do this. He knew how to hide, how to avoid, how to keep someone guessing until they grew tired of the chase.

His neighborhood was one of the oldest in the area, one that had represented wealth and class for many generations. The houses weren't as large as mansions he had seen in other places, but they were grand in their historical significance. Most of them were brick with large yards, full of mature, overhanging trees and meticulous landscaping, separated them from the road.

Lex had always felt like an outsider here. Not only were there few African-American families on the block, he also didn't know how to live like these other families. He hoped he would never know.

It had been an eventful afternoon, to put it mildly. When school let out, he grabbed the bus to Bellefontaine. If anyone had been watching him, there was no way they could follow him from his school. He doubted any other members of the Broken could afford to go there, and the security surrounding school grounds was always tight.

He wasn't visiting Bellefontaine for an investigation. His backpack, a spare one from the basement, included only books and notebooks, but he needed to go somewhere to just think. When he arrived, he beelined to Kate. She was still sleeping, a recumbent marble beauty who had been lying there long before he was born and would be there long after he died.

The place where he and Penelope had first met and where everything started seemed like the perfect spot to collect his thoughts.

He leaned against the monument and closed his eyes, trying to make sense of everything that had happened in the last two weeks. His knuckles were finally scabbing over (picking at them hadn't helped the healing process), but his face still ached, and his side where he had been kicked was turning different colors daily. Those sensations paled in comparison to his memories of her hands running up his back.

"You're here early," he heard. When he opened his eyes, he saw a familiar face looking at him from a golf cart. "I don't know if I've ever seen you here with the sun still up."

"Hi, Gladys," he said.

"Lord, look at your face! What happened to you?" she called out over the idling engine and patted the spot next to her. "Come for a ride with me, young man."

Frowning, he stood. He wasn't going to be able to shake her. But maybe she was exactly what he needed right now.

Pretending to reluctantly drag himself over to her, he threw his book bag in the back of the golf cart, slumped into the passenger seat, and pulled his hood low. "It's a long story, ma'am."

Gladys had a rare gift among adults—she knew when to pry and when to let something be. Turning around the tight corners, the two of them puttered around the cemetery's paths. During the ride, Lex admired the diversity among the tombstones as well as the soaring canopies of the trees. He let the landscape pass by as he continued to mull over everything. Gladys left him in silence.

When they reached a lake, she pulled over and turned off the engine.

The whispering water, the chattering birds, the rustling breeze—he soaked it all in, closing his eyes. It was rare for him to enjoy a cemetery's eternal, desolate beauty in the daytime. He let out a long sigh he hadn't realized he had been holding in.

Finally, Gladys said, "I've always believed that natural places can heal."

"Yeah," Lex replied. "Yeah, I get that."

Somehow, the quiet began to force all the emotion churning deep inside of him up and out. He had been trying to think his way out of feeling. Here, he couldn't do that. All of it hurt. Refusing to cry in front of her, he turned his head away.

He felt her hand squeeze his shoulder. That was all it took for him to start talking. "Have you ever felt like you don't deserve somebody, so you let them push you away?"

Gladys didn't hesitate long. "Yes. I think most people have done that."

"So, how do you know? How do you know if you're good enough for someone? What if it's not a normal someone, but someone who is really good? I mean, down to the core a good person?"

"Honey, you never know. It's not like there's a measuring stick somewhere to determine goodness. That's not the point, though. Who do you think has to decide if you're good enough?"

He blew air out from between his lips. "I do."

"Yes. And, if she's pushing you away, it sounds like she needs to decide for herself, too."

"I never said it was a she," he said.

"Well, I just figured. Had to be a female to cause a cute young thing like you this much hurt."

Lex chuckled lightly. They were quiet again for a few minutes before he said, "I don't know if I'll ever think I'm good enough."

"Then you better stay away from the living," she said with a look of reproach. "Real people don't want you comparing yourself to them all the time. There's nothing I can say to convince you that you're a worthy person. It doesn't matter how much stuff you've done or gone through or what other people say about you. You have to make peace with you. And that's really, really hard."

"Yeah, it is."

They didn't share any other words after that. Gladys dropped him off at the cemetery gates with a nod and a wave.

After taking the bus back home, he didn't know what to do with himself. He was too frustrated and rattled to do anything productive, so he sat at his computer and booted up a video game. It didn't take long for his screen to blip. Even though he didn't have a phone, he could receive text messages through the computer.

Unknown number: *Ghost, it's Drips. Everything's gone to shit. We need your help. Get into the Broken app and tell Elijah DON'T DO IT, or he'll hurt Skin. Penelope is fine for now. We're counting on you, man.*

Lex: *WHERE ARE YOU? WHERE IS SHE?*

But Mason never answered. Lex broke into a cold sweat.

He should have been there. Instead, he let her protect him. He could have stopped her. He could have done so much more to convince her that the only place he was supposed to be was with them. Instead, he had closed Penelope's window and disappeared into the night, letting his misery and doubt overtake him.

Now, the consequences of his inaction were right in front of him.

"Dammit, dammit, dammit!" he swore, pounding the computer desk with his clenched fists.

Lex allowed himself one moment to feel sorry for himself before he began his work. He knew this was his only chance to make it right. When he hacked into the app, he intentionally left a trail for them to follow back to his home address. He wanted them to come for him. The more crazy people who followed him instead of Penelope, the better. He would lead them on a chase all night to give her the time she needed to get to safety.

After he gained access to the Broken app, he kept his message to Elijah as direct as possible.

Lex*: It's Ghost. Whatever you've been asked to do, don't do it. Skin will get hurt. And if Lois is harmed in any way tonight, this Ghost will haunt you for the rest of your life.*

Less than fifteen minutes later, as he tried to blend into the darkness, he kept reminding himself he didn't want to be too good. He didn't want to completely disappear. He wanted to give them something to follow.

The Central West End district of St. Louis was a blend of high-rise apartments, overpriced homes, restaurants, bars, and medical buildings, all squished together. Weekend patrons of the district included college kids and aging hipsters willing to spend too much on Americanized sushi. A few of the most popular locations were located along a three-block strip.

At this time on a Friday night, he thought, *it will be packed.*

He decided that would be his destination. He could dip in and out of the crowds until the early hours of the morning. What could they do to him with people everywhere?

As he reached the end of his neighborhood's drive, he spotted his first enemy. Lex had expected darting shadows, but this person stood still in the middle of the street five houses behind him.

He could barely discern any features, but he recognized it was a woman. In her hands, she gripped something long and metallic. *A chain*, he realized. He hadn't expected weapons. *All the more reason to get into a crowd.*

Yet he couldn't understand why she wasn't moving. No point in trying to figure it out, though.

He needed to travel down one more block before reaching one of the busier streets that would lead him to the business district. His neighborhood's drive ended in a four-way intersection, and he needed to go right to reach it the fastest.

But in that direction about five houses away, two other women materialized from the darkness to stand under the yellow pools from the streetlights. One held a bat, and the other one gripped a broken bottle. Straight ahead, there were three more, but they were too covered in shadow to see anything but the outlines of their bodies.

Again, he looked behind him, in front of him, and to the right of him. They were herding him to the left.

He was never good at following orders.

Carefully, he sipped long on his coffee. If he was going to outrun them, he would need to use all his body. He'd have to leave his mug. With a touch of remorse, he set it down in the middle of the street.

Quickly, he slipped his index and middle fingers in the sleeve of his hoodie and switched on the EVP recorder. He burst into motion. He ran in between the roads leading right and straight ahead, cutting through the yards of his neighbors. His sneakers slipped on the wet grass, but he regained his footing and continued straight ahead.

The attackers in the road still didn't move, he saw out of the corner of his eye. As he approached one of the homes, he glanced up.

On the roof, one person crouched low and watched him pass.

He spotted two more on the next house.

Those were only the ones he could see. How many were waiting for him? How many were lurking in the shadows? How had they gotten to him so fast?

Sweat. He ran a finger across his forehead and flicked away the moisture. The run hadn't exerted him enough to sweat. His heart raced. He couldn't remember the last time he had felt this afraid. Maybe he had underestimated them.

It was his last coherent thought before they made their move.

When he tried to dash in between a house and a garage, a hidden figure leaped on top of him. He fell to the ground but pulled his legs into a crouch, ready to kick and spring back to his feet. But he never had time to even see the faces of those surrounding him.

A cloth smelling of cleaning solvent covered his nose. He thrashed at his attackers, but they pinned his shoulders and craned his neck back.

"Breathe deep, Ghost," one of them hissed.

He tried to resist, holding his breath until his lungs burned and spots appeared in front of his eyes. When he couldn't hold it any longer, he inhaled. A thick cloud penetrated his skull and body. It spread through his limbs, slowing his thoughts and freezing his movements. They removed the cloth and let him flop into the grass, shivering and gasping.

"Don't hurt her. Just me," he muttered before he lost the ability to move his lips.

"Oh, sweetie," another purred, "that's so valiant. But you're the bait to *get* her and the rest of the Pack puppies."

"Skinny emo guy like this caused us all the trouble?" another person muttered. "He was easy."

Another person next to him kicked him in his sore side, but he could barely feel it through the fog. "Love makes you predictable. You played right into our trap."

Somewhere far away, he heard a rumble and a boom.

The fog smothered him, and his eyes closed.

A stinging in his nose brought him back to consciousness. They had pinned him. He tried to thrash, but he was still constrained. But it wasn't human hands holding him down. He was tied to a post, hands behind his back and ropes around his midsection and thighs. Tape covered his mouth. A blindfold pinned his eyelids shut.

And they had taken his hoodie. Somehow, that one detail particularly irritated to Lex.

Although his neck ached, he forced himself to continue to hang limply against the ropes so he could listen to the conversation happening next to him.

"He should join Riot," a female voice said. "Did you hear what he did to Nail? Imagine him after *we* train him. Put a baseball bat or a Molotov cocktail in his hand."

"Riot is for women only," a male pointed out.

"All the better," she said. "My ladies and I will make him forget that green-haired twerp in a day."

"No, he belongs in Ozone," another male said. Lex recognized the voice from the music store after the mall incident. *Haze*, he recalled. "He's a hacker. We specialize in disappearing, and he can disappear in the digital world. And he's fast. With those long legs, he could leap between buildings."

A second male replied to both of them. "Griffin, Haze, you present reasonable arguments. However, we know reality is more than the physical in Void. Ghost, as his name suggests, belongs with us. We can teach him to bend reality with chemicals, explosives, and anything else we get our hands on."

Gasoline. That was what he smelled. The tips of his sneakers were soaked with it.

They had drenched everything around him in gasoline.

Footsteps approached. "Enough, all three of you," a raspy voice commanded. "You're not rivals. We are one army against everything, and you are my generals. The teams of Void, Riot, and Ozone all have critical roles to play, as does this troublesome young man."

"Alpha, what if the girl refuses?" Griffin asked.

"I'll light it myself. Lois will be one of us. We will burn away that which first broke her, and she will see why we cleanse with fire."

Lex heard shuffling footsteps as the surrounding people moved away from him. A door opened, letting in a blast of cold air. Once his nose had grown accustomed to the gasoline, he could smell the sharp aroma of dry hay.

"I'll search him and check his knots to make sure he's not going anywhere," said the deep voice who had identified himself as the Void leader.

"Secure the lock and bring me the key when you're finished," Alpha said. "Wait down the road. I'll be in the house. She can't be far behind us, and I want to speak to her alone."

When the door shut, the Void leader ran his hands over Lex's clothing. He knew it was only a matter of moments before this man found the EVP recorder. He patted across his shoulders, down his sleeves, and over his wrists.

But he didn't respond in any way. It was as if he had never felt it, but that was impossible. It was too thick and bulky. The stranger continued his search down Lex's legs. As he made his way up Lex's back, he slipped something into Lex's palm. A pocket knife, he realized. Lex wrapped his fingers around it.

"Find the loose bricks and dig out by the base," he whispered. Lex barely caught the words.

He was gone. The door slammed behind him, and Lex heard the lock click into place, bolting him inside.

Gingerly, he freed the tiny knife from the case and set to work.

18

SCARS GO DEEPER THAN THE SKIN

A light, drizzling rain couldn't erase the message from the grass. The flames refused to die out before the camera crews got to them, as if they knew they served a purpose. Even if they had, the word would have been scorched into the earth.

Sitting around the television at Mason's place, the same images appeared on every channel.

On the screen, firefighters surrounded a charred and crumbling pavilion in the center of Forest Park. The news report kept cutting from the pavilion's current state, nothing but black rubble, to its recent past state, a towering inferno that reportedly could be viewed from Interstate 64/40. In the grass, letters as large as the pavilion itself spelled out *SILO*.

The news scroll at the bottom included the headline "FOREST PARK BURNS—ARSON SUSPECTED."

A local news station personality appeared in the lower right corner. "We still don't know the identities of the two people taken into custody, but witnesses say they appeared to be male as well as 'young enough to still be in high school.' Although not confirmed, inside sources claim these two young men could be connected to the suspected arson that destroyed a historic truck stop last Saturday evening."

The camera zoomed into the reporter, perfectly coiffed and camera ready.

"As details of this horrific crime continue to emerge," the reporter said, "we will be the first to bring you the latest news. Stay tuned right here for the most updated information."

Mason flicked off the screen and dropped the remote on the carpet. "At least we know Seth and Elijah are safe. But now the media personalities have their villains. Nobody is going to listen to them if they try to explain the real story. Troubled, degenerate youth destroying our city and all that crap."

He paused long enough to hang his head, his hands clasped out in front of him. Somehow, seeing Mason this upset made Penelope even more so. Helena sprawled out on his couch. Her hair had escaped its bun, and Mason, sitting next to her, was running his fingers through it, from the top of her head down to the black tips.

Penelope stood and pulled her keys from her pocket.

Mason glanced up at her, then at Helena. "I can't go with you, Lois," Mason said reluctantly. "I'm sorry. I have to wake her every thirty minutes. I can't leave her."

"I know you can't leave her," Penelope replied, already off the couch and grabbing her keys. "It's fine. I think I need to do this one alone, anyway."

"Lois, don't you get it? We're Pack. We don't do anything alone. We need one another. We're stronger together. That's why I'm so pissed you have to go by yourself. Can you at least tell me what the word means?"

One hand on the doorknob, she turned her face in his direction as she said, "My old house from before I was adopted had a silo. That's where I was trapped when I was burned."

"Oh my God. Penelope, you can't go alone."

"No," she said. "That's why I have to face this by myself. I'm going to get Ghost. We're Pack, so trust me."

Before Mason could protest, she ran out the door.

It would take almost three hours to drive there, so her attention and awareness were critical for her survival. Even though Penelope had never been back since that day, she had always kept track of how to return, as if the old farm was the true north of her internal compass. Part of her would always direct her back.

It wasn't the route that kept both hands gripped on the wheels and eyes straining on the road. Thinking back, she couldn't remember the last time she had truly slept. Maybe last Wednesday? She hadn't been able to keep down food since Thursday night, either.

She focused on what had happened in the sewers. Due to Mason's guidance, they had exited the Forest Park sewer safely. While still navigating its turns, they heard the explosion above them. It shook the ground so intensely that dust fell on their heads and hair.

"See? That's why they call me Drips," Mason had said, shaking out his Afro. He was trying to keep her smiling. "Every time we visit somewhere, I get stuff in it."

Standing in the middle of Forest Park, they realized they were now in the center of a massive crime scene. Mason managed to lift Helena over his shoulder so they could hurry to his car. They would dash and hide, dash and hide, much as they had traveled through the mall. That chase felt like ages ago already.

Once they reached a gas station far enough away, Penelope had asked a stranger to borrow a phone. The man agreed, probably because Penelope was struggling to even stand upright after being kicked.

Penelope: *Lex, tell me you're safe. Please. Where are you?*

A few minutes passed. No reply. The stranger finished filling up his car and was staring at her with growing irritation.

Penelope: *Please. Please. Please.*

Still nothing. She deleted the texts from the phone's history, handed the phone back, and thanked the man again.

She had assumed they were too late. They had him.

Mason drove back to his apartment once he ensured his mother and sister were out for the night at a performance. But he drove Penelope by her house first so she could follow him in her own car. Even before seeing the news report, Penelope had known something was going to happen that would prevent her from staying.

An hour into her drive, she left the well-lit roads of the city and suburbs behind. Country roads in Missouri were thin, windy, and hilly. One wrong slip and a driver could plummet into a ditch. The danger of wildlife on the road was also a concern.

She cracked the window, letting the cold night air assail her face. Somehow, the smell of the outside kept her more centered in the task in front of her. Thinking of Lex in that place with those horrid people who didn't bat an eye at pistol-whipping Helena or burning down buildings scared her so much that she could barely wrap her fingers around the steering wheel.

It took everything in her power to maintain a safe speed. They couldn't be far in front of her, and they wouldn't know the way like she did. *They must have obtained the address from the old police reports*, she realized. They knew so much about her, yet she knew nothing other than the disturbing contents of a handful of old images.

None of it was fair. None of it was right. But none of that mattered.

Saving him was all that mattered.

From a distance, nothing had changed. Under the light of the stars and moon, the old farm silhouetted a slightly lighter, shaded sky. The house, barn, and silo sat alone in the center of the property with a gravel path leading from the winding road. Much like the abandoned farmhouse from her night of the test, the buildings were in the middle of a hay field. Penelope remembered playing in the long hay for hours just so she could avoid going inside the house.

As she pulled into the driveway, the difference between this house and her Broken initiation became obvious. These structures had been gutted and destroyed by fire, leaving only the husks of the buildings. She could see ash and soot staining the bricks on the house and silo, and the wooden barn leaned precariously.

Emotion tore at her insides and made her nauseated, despite the lack of food in her stomach. The last time she had seen this place, she was being carried out on a stretcher. She hadn't been in any pain. Third degree burns get down to the nerve cells, giving burn victims false hope. She had gone into shock.

Parking the car, she forced the memories all away.

None of that matters. None of that matters. None of that matters.

Before she could search for Lex, Alpha came strolling out the gaping front door frame as if she were a dinner guest. Even without his sidekicks, his presence was enough to make Penelope shiver.

Much like the surrounding buildings, he seemed to her a shell of a human being, lacking emotion, feeling, or reaction. His nearly black hair hung in the same low ponytail, and his black eyes stared at her as she climbed out of the car and approached him.

"I would welcome you," he rasped, "but I'm realizing now it would be more appropriate for you to welcome me."

"Where is he? Where's Lex?" Penelope demanded.

He crossed his arms. "Did you think I would have you drive out here just to hand him to you? Surely you must realize that isn't the case."

"What do you want?" she asked, her tone becoming more frantic.

"Your time," he said. "A little bit of your time. Please, follow me."

He walked back through the door frame, and Penelope followed. Six years ago, this had been the living room. The front windows were all broken out, and the front door was nowhere to be seen. Vulgar graffiti coated every wall. The cheap wallpaper hung in shreds, and holes gaped in the disintegrating drywall. As she stepped, glass shards and decaying wooden flooring crunched. Anything that could be pawned, traded, or reused had been stripped. This building was not a home, and it was too gone to ever be a home again.

Alpha didn't pause in the room. He cut through the kitchen and thudded down the stairs into the basement. Penelope stayed close behind him.

The basement. Penelope's childhood room. Where the fire had started.

All around, the debris of her past dragged suppressed memories to the forefront. In the corner, her moldy bedframe. On the wall, her one poster of a pink pony, the edges curled and blackened from the heat. In another corner, dirty clothes covered in a gray, wet film.

Two stained kitchen chairs faced opposite each other in the center of the basement. The dancing flames of at least a dozen candles created snaking, swaying streams of light. The entire space smelled of mildew and other living things that shouldn't grow inside a home.

"Have a seat," he said from the back of his throat as he claimed one of the chairs.

Penelope shook her head. "I'd rather stand."

"Why?"

"Because I don't trust you."

Alpha leaned his head to the side. "Odd choice of word, don't you think? Trust. You are the one I trusted enough to welcome into the Broken. I trusted you when you said Ghost was one of us. However, you tore my own brother away from me. Your Ghost destroyed my app. All of this is your doing, yet you claim *you* don't trust *me*?"

"You have an interesting way of seeing things."

He opened his hands a little. "I don't want to argue. We will never agree on who is to blame. We should focus on the here and now."

"I couldn't agree more. Where's Ghost?"

"I will tell you after we talk. You will know where he is. I swear it."

"Like your word means anything."

"Yet it's all I have. And do you have a choice?" Again, he gestured to the chair.

When she sat, she moved the chair back three more feet away from him.

Alpha chuckled. "As you wish. Now, tell me about this place."

"Obviously you already know," she said with a sneer, "or you wouldn't have brought me here."

"Yes, I know the facts. I don't know what you're thinking or feeling right now."

"Why do you give a crap about my feelings?"

"Because they are relevant to me and what we are trying to accomplish."

"How so?"

"You're messed up, and you always will be. That is what you told Ghost. You're one of us because you're broken. You are the way you are due to this place."

"Yes."

"Your skin is scarred, but the scars go deeper than the skin. Because of the people who lived here. Because of the decisions they made regarding your welfare."

She hesitated a moment before admitting, "Yes."

"Do you resent them?"

Again she paused, but she said, "Yes."

"Why?"

"I mean, they were cooking drugs in the same basement that was my bedroom. I think it's pretty normal to feel a little resentment about that, don't you?" She felt her anger rising faster than she would have expected. It was almost too fast to control.

Being in this place was affecting her. She tried to keep all of her focus on saving Lex, but she found herself being drawn into his questioning.

Alpha mulled over her words for a moment. "Normal, yes. I suppose it is normal. Just as it is normal that the tragedy changed you and made you *not* normal. Elijah spotted that in you long before we researched you. He said you had no friends. He said you could barely maintain a conversation without falling apart. He said you walked through the halls like a shadow, barely present and floating through your classes like a passive observer of your own life. Did you know you appeared that way to others?"

Her reply floated to her lips, almost outside of her control. "No, no, I didn't."

"Lois—*Penelope*—do you want to be this way for the rest of your life?"

"No. I don't."

"You can't just mend something that's as broken as you are. As I am. But you know that, don't you?"

"Yes."

"So you agree. You will never be normal—at least, society's definition of normal?"

"Yes."

"You acknowledge your brokenness will always separate you from being understood or accepted by the world?"

"Yes. I, I mean, no. No!" She shook her head to realign her thoughts. "There are people who accept me and understand me. Maybe the Broken was always meant as a tool to build your firebug army, but the Pack is strong with or without the app. We are strong because we accept one another for who we are."

"Strength? Acceptance?" he mocked. "Are you so sure? After Garnet tackled and tied up Ghost? After Ghost tried to goad everyone into a fight at the diner? After what Nail did to Ghost's backpack? After Ghost almost beat Nail to death?"

"It's different now," she said. "We are past all that."

"Are you sure? It's been less than a week since Nail was left bleeding on the grass. Is it possible, perhaps, that broken people in this society are always doomed to repeat cycles of violence and failure? Maybe the world isn't built for people like us. Maybe these bonds you think you feel are temporary salves. Hastily applied bandages."

"If this is where you try to persuade me to give up looking for Ghost because he actually doesn't mean anything to me, forget it."

"No," he said. "No, I'm not. I'm simply asking you to consider reality. Observe."

He lifted one of the lit candles off the ground. "This flame is real. This flame, in this moment and on that wick, contains all the power of an inferno. But it is small. Do you see? Eventually, it will die out. Maybe it runs out of wax. Maybe I take it outside where the elements are too much for it. The flames resemble the friendships and love you feel for the Pack and for Ghost. I'm not suggesting they are not genuine. I'm asking how long you can preserve them. How long before this flame dies?"

"Fine. Yeah, whatever. I agree. The real world sucks. Is that what you want me to say? I'm sixteen. Ghost is seventeen. I sound stupid when I say I love him. I don't care. I've known the Pack for two weeks, but I trust them. All of that is true to me right now, and I'm here to save him."

"What if I brought you here to save yourself as well as him, Penelope?"

"I would say I don't want anything to do with you, or any of the rest of them." She started ticking off on her fingers. "You snooped on us. You called the cops on us. You set us up. You could have killed Helena. Elijah and Seth are in jail, and I have no idea how to ever get them out. And you kidnapped my boyfriend."

He played with his ponytail for a moment as he regarded her. "You make it all sound so sinister when you list it like that." He closed his long lashes over his black eyes, once again gathering his thoughts. "I was only trying to build and preserve that which I have worked so hard to attain. Even now, that's all I'm trying to do. And regarding Ghost, you wouldn't even know him if it weren't for me. Do you think it was by chance that you ran into him at Bellefontaine? Does it make sense for an urban exploration network to begin a test at a public graveyard? I had been following Paranormal Lex for weeks, and I wanted him to join us. I wrote the test that way because I wanted you *and* Ghost to join me. Somehow, I knew he would follow you. He did, and here we are. You wouldn't have this love that you think makes you so special and superior if it weren't for me."

Penelope folded her arms across her stomach and turned her body away from him. "Congratulations. So what?"

"You put a burden on your new friends and your new love if they are the only glue holding your broken pieces together." He gestured to his neck and its slash, which looked bright pink even in the candlelight. "When my brother left me for reasons that were just, I tried to end my life. But I survived, and I realized it wasn't my brother with the problem. It wasn't me. It was everything else, refusing to provide me with any chance to heal, to live, or to grow."

Penelope shook her head. "I don't understand why you're telling me all this."

"Fine. Play ignorant. I'll be brief. I brought Ghost to you, so I'm asking for one thing in return. Burn this place to the ground."

"No. I'm not setting any fires."

"Why?" he pressed. "No one will be harmed if you set the fire yourself. You could destroy these monuments to your broken past. We have already taken the necessary preparations. All you would have to do is light one match, and it would be gone.

Think about it for a moment, Penelope. Think about it." He flicked in the air in front of him. "One drop of your fingers, one release of a pinch, and everything this place symbolizes could be destroyed."

Penelope muttered, "You're pretty dumb if you think burning down some old buildings is going to fix me."

"No, not fix," he said, strolling away from her. "But it could be a beginning of something new. A forest fire is healthy because it burns away the brambles and the dead trees, turning them into fertilizer, making way for new growth. You could do that now. The broken parts of you would still be there, but they would be the foundation for the new woman you could become. The cracks would be sealed by the heat."

Standing at the base of the stairs, he turned toward her. "At least follow me. Come look at this place. Come hold the match. If you tell me no, I will still tell you Ghost's location."

He extended his hand out to her.

I don't want him to think I'm giving in, Penelope thought. *But if I follow him, maybe we can end this sooner.*

Once she was on her feet, the two of them walked back through the house and yard. When they were far enough away to view all three buildings, Alpha reached into his pocket. He extracted one match from the book. With a flick of his wrist, he struck the match against the box, and a fingernail-sized flame came to life.

Holding it up to the moonlight, he said, "Just hold it. Tell me there isn't a part of you that doesn't want this place gone forever. No one will be hurt. No one will tell the authorities. Nothing bad will happen by destroying this place. Even if there is a chance of this one tiny act healing some part of you, why wouldn't you seize the opportunity?"

Penelope accepted the burning match from him, still expecting some sort of trap. But as she stared at the property through the flame, her jaw tightened, and her free hand curled into a fist.

That house was where her aunt and her aunt's boyfriend had entrapped her. They allowed drug users into their home so they could make a quick buck. They handed her opened boxes of sugary cereal in the morning to serve as her food for the entire day. They kept poisonous chemicals feet away from where she slept. They never hugged her, told her they loved her, expressed any affection at all.

Every terrible memory from her childhood, every dark secret of her past, was contained in that house.

Everything that made her a freak, a loser, *nothing* lingered in that house.

She hated it. She hated everything about it.

"Light it, Penelope," Warren urged. "Light it. Burn it down."

19

LAST SCREAMS OF AGONY

Lex moaned and tried to curse, but only strangled grunts emerged from the duct tape smothering his mouth. He planted his elbows in the hay, elevated his midsection, and gave himself five seconds to breathe. After he had managed to saw through the ropes around his wrists, he had lost his balance and tumbled forward. At least the hay had somewhat cushioned his face-first fall, though his stiff and groggy muscles screamed at the movement. The rope tying his ankles to the pole pulled at his skin viciously.

Trying his best not to pull anything else, he reached up and lifted off the blindfold. With his cheek pressed into the ground, all he saw and smelled was gasoline-soaked hay. Next, off came the duct tape. He didn't give himself time to think about it—just braced and pulled. Bits of skin came off with the tape. Never in his life had he wanted lip balm more than in that moment.

"Ouch, ouch, ouch, shit, ouch," he groaned, this time clearly audible.

Sight and speech restored, he examined his surroundings. An old silo. That's where they had locked him up. A support pole ran from the base to the domed roof at least thirty feet over his head. As his mysterious friend had suggested, the walls were made of brick. He couldn't see much other than the skeletal outlines of some wooden rafters and supports above, and that was only through a few cracks in between the bricks. Any normal person would have been blinded by complete darkness in there, but Lex had experience struggling to see in dim places.

He took stock of his condition and immediately regretted doing so. Aching legs. Sore arms. Pounding, debilitating headache from whatever they had used to drug him. Side on fire again, and he remembered they had kicked him when they tackled him for their own amusement. He was in rough shape just about everywhere.

He pulled at his sleeve, exposing the EVP recorder. It was still running.

"Finally something goes my way," he said. Seeing the EVP recorder gave him focus and purpose. He knew what he had to do.

He cleared his throat. "This is Alexander 'Lex' Sterling. The date is Friday. Right? Yeah, Friday, March eighteenth. Time is—I don't even know. Late. Really late. Location is middle of Redneck Central, Missouri. This is not an investigation. I've been kidnapped. Yeah, maybe I encouraged it. Maybe I was trying to help and messed up again. Whatever. The point is, this is *evidence*. If I don't make it through this..."

He paused. Saying the words made it all the more real. He had seen what they could do. He knew their cruelty. They were capable of killing, and they blamed him for so many of their problems. He could die tonight. It was that simple. But he realized he didn't even fear for his own safety. All he saw was her.

"Yeah, I might not make it through this. If I don't—Penelope, I love you."

Using his hands as support, he crawled backward toward the pole until his spine pressed against it once again. He curled into a C and began hacking away at the ropes around his ankles.

Cutting through industrial strength ropes with a pocket knife so small it probably wouldn't be confiscated by school security was a lengthy, exhausting process. Just getting through the ropes at his wrists had taken at least fifteen minutes. And they had taken extra precaution with his legs.

Somehow, he knew he couldn't take fifteen minutes this time. With the full strength of his arms and hands, he resolved to finish the task in five minutes. As he set to work, he said, "If I *do* make it through this, Penelope, I swear to the Norse gods, *I'm* picking what we do next, and it's going to be Mexican food and that roadside cemetery. Maybe a movie, too. I hate the theater, so let's be honest. I want to go so we can make out."

The last strand of one of the ropes snapped. *One down, seven to go*, he thought. As he worked on the second one, he continued talking to the recorder as well as to her. "And, if we get through this, I won't make the same mistakes. You can't keep me away, and I won't run off again, either. I don't care what problems, what trouble, what warped cults we end up encountering. You're stuck with me. We just have to survive this first. No big deal, right?"

Penelope held her breath and tried to picture it burning away. But she couldn't. This place was etched in her memory. Dropping one match wouldn't change that.

She lifted the little flame to her face, watched it for one more second to imagine what could have been, and blew it out.

Alpha's face contorted in frustration. "Why?"

"Because it's a part of me. I can't just destroy my past. It shaped who I am. And no, maybe I'm not normal. But it's still me. You're right. I do need to heal. This just isn't the way to do it."

She considered him, the family resemblance obvious. He was Elijah, but older, more lost. "I hope you can figure that out too, some day."

Alpha let out a sharp bark of laughter. He stepped backward and away from her. "Childish. Naïve. You'll see. When everyone else around you breaks away because you couldn't hold onto them, you'll understand. But it's already too late for you, Lois."

"I listened to you, Warren. I considered everything you said, and I did everything you asked," Penelope said. "Where is Ghost?"

He shaped his lips into a malicious grin—the first emotion she'd seen from him. "He is locked in the silo." He pulled out his book of matches, struck a second match, and dropped it to the ground. At his feet, a trail of fire raced through the grass and began eating at the house.

"I kept my promise. What I didn't tell you is I have the only key to the silo around my neck." He lifted a leather thong from under his shirt. "If you had done that yourself, I would have given this to you." He snapped his fingers.

Haze, Griffin, and Titan stalked out of the barn toward her.

"Now, you'll have to get through them to get to the silo. Maybe you'll have just enough time to listen to his last screams of agony."

He's going to die, she thought. *He's going to die because of me.* Everything had been her fault. Joining the Broken. Going to the mall. Shit, meeting Lex in the first place. And now, he would burn to death, the most excruciating death anyone could experience.

"Alpha, please, please, no! I'll do anything." She fell to her knees as the three of them formed a triangle around her. "Please!"

Deaf to her cries, Warren turned away from her and strolled down the gravel driveway. Penelope jumped to her feet and tried to dash after him, but Haze, as swift as a shadow, closed the distance and swung his foot under her legs.

She fell to the gravel, landing on her arms. The thin skin of her elbows and forearms split, and bright-red blood dripped on the road.

Trying to roll back to her side, she felt another standing close. Griffin, lithe and lean, loomed above her as she kissed her brass knuckles. Black bangs hung over one eye, and her other eye, caked in mascara, leered at her.

When Penelope pushed herself into a crawling position, Griffin slammed her brass knuckles square in the center of her back. Haze laughed, high pitched and gleeful, as Penelope crumpled back down into the gravel, falling face first into her own blood.

Splayed on the rocks, she commanded her legs to move. At first, they refused to listen. Her foot flexed. Digging her toes into the sandy dirt, she forced her body up into a plank. Before she could bend her knees under herself to push upright, Griffin punched her again.

When Penelope fell this time, she lost her vision for a moment. Had she blacked out? She didn't know, but she had loss sense of her location just in that brief instant. When her eyes fluttered open again, she turned to face the buildings.

The flames on the house climbed the walls and licked the eaves.

Next would be the barn and the silo.

If she felt pain, it was separate from her awareness. What she was feeling now was adrenaline and little else. Later, she wouldn't move. Later, she would probably be bedridden for days. Now, she had to get up again.

This time, she planted her knees and buried her fingers in the rocks, trying to push up from the ground.

Haze hooked his foot under her and kicked her in the stomach.

Her breath blasted from her lungs. She couldn't breathe. Couldn't. Breathe. For a few agonizing seconds, she wondered if she had somehow punctured a lung. But no, gradually, the air came back to her. Rocks clung to her cheek and lips, and she tasted blood. Her entire face felt wet.

From somewhere far away, she heard them talking about her.

"She's stubborn, I'll give her that," Griffin said.

"Makes things way more interesting," Haze said.

Griffin again. "Well, we need to catch up to Alpha. If she gets up this time, I'll make sure she stays down. Maybe *permanently*."

There was no other choice. She had to get up. As injured and exhausted as she was, she couldn't defeat them. Even if she were fully healthy, she never would have stood a chance. Yet, if she gave up, if she just lay there, Lex would die. It was that simple. She had to do whatever she could, even if it were just to get up and fall down again.

Her arms shaking, she pushed up her midsection. She forced her eyes to stay open as she glanced to her right—just in time to see Griffin's leather combat boot rear back to kick her.

But before it swung forward, it flew to the side, followed by a massive form. Penelope tried to make sense of the scene, and finally her brain clicked. Titan had barreled into Griffin.

Grunts, exclamations, shuffling, swearing. Penelope could barely see any of it as she struggled to maintain consciousness. She knew it was a brief and brutal fight with Titan on one side and Griffin and Haze on the other. Titan's name, apparently, was well deserved, because both of his counterparts were laid out within a couple of minutes.

With a rough jerk, he pulled her to her feet. "Get it together, Lois. Your work isn't done."

Penelope tried to clear her head enough to recognize what was happening around her. She swayed unsteadily on her feet. Her eyes focused on the buildings in front of her. With the gasoline feeding it, the house fire had transformed into a towering blaze. Too hungry to be satisfied with just one building, it had already torn through the barn and was spreading to the silo. A few overzealous flames danced along its roof.

Titan spoke to her in a low, commanding voice. "I have to rejoin Alpha, or he will suspect me. I'll drug these two with so much stuff, they won't remember their entire week, much less what I just did to them. Save him, and I'll call 9-1-1 as soon as we are a safe distance away. Help is coming."

Before Penelope could even begin to piece together what had just transpired, Titan threw the other two team leaders over his shoulders and followed Alpha into the darkness.

She couldn't attempt to figure it out now. Half stumbling and half running, she approached the silo. The closer she got, the louder the silo's growling grew. The intense heat irritated her eyes and her skin. She ran around its exterior until she found the ground level door.

"Lex, Lex!" she cried, pounding on the door with all her might. Where her fists hit, she left smears of blood.

When the last rope snapped, Lex flexed his freed legs. Not a moment too soon. Above, lines of flickering flames clawed along the roof. Once they crossed the barrier, they would eat through the wooden rafters as if they were twigs. All it would take was one spark to fall from above to ignite the hay all around him.

He heard banging on the metal door to his right. And her voice. He rushed to the door. It was locked, just as he had been told. Penelope rattled it from the other side, as well.

"Get out of here!" he screamed at her. "Now!"

"Shut up! No!"

He crouched down to the ground and cleared the years of dirt and rocks that had built up around the door's base. Once he had cleared a spot large enough to push three fingers through, he banged low on the door to get her attention. He felt her fingers wrap around his in a desperate embrace, and he clung to them for a few moments before he unlatched the EVP recorder and shoved it through. Leaning down to the ground, he shouted, "Keep it safe, and go!"

"Screw you, Lex! Forget it!" she yelled through the crack. "I'm not leaving."

He could feel the temperature rising. The fire on the roof was converting the brick silo into a giant oven. Sweat poured from his brow. Smoke, too, trickled in, irritating his skin and airway. At this rate, he would suffocate before he burned to death. And she, being so close to the crumbling, burning structure, was in more immediate danger than he was. If she wasn't going to leave, he had to tell her what to do.

"Help me find some loose bricks around the base," he said. Standing up, he began kicking all the rocks at the ground level with his sneakers, hoping one of them would budge or shift. He patrolled the silo's interior wall twice, but he didn't find anything. After the third time, he struggled to draw in air. Smoke, steam, and gasoline fumes assaulted his lungs.

He coughed until his chest ached. He couldn't keep searching like this. Instead, he fell to the ground by the door again, sucking in outside air and waiting for Penelope. After a few moments, she rejoined him, her voice coming from the other side.

"I found something! A brick is wiggling, but barely. There's a trowel in the barn. I'm going to grab it so I can pry it out."

A barn? Was it on fire as well? "Don't go in there! Do you hear me?" he tried to yell, but his words devolved into desperate coughing.

He feared for her more than himself. While trying to retrieve the trowel, the flames would trap her. She would die, and it would be all his fault.

As he despaired, he glanced up and saw the flames were already on the rafters above him. They crackled and popped in childlike glee as they gobbled up the wooden supports. Any second now, those beams would splinter and fall, and he would be buried under their burning fragments. He would be killed without ever knowing if she were safe.

But a scraping noise caught his attention. To his left, one brick was wiggling. She was there. She had done it. He crawled over on his belly and began pulling at the brick with his own fingers.

No longer by the hole under the door, he was deprived of his one source of cleaner air. He held his breath, knowing that inhaling more smoke could spell his doom. He saw spots as his body begged for oxygen, but he kept digging. With both of them scraping from opposite sides, they were able to knock the brick loose, and Penelope pulled it free.

He breathed in the air wafting in through the opening just long enough to gain some strength before the two of them continued with the second brick. They repeated this process a third, fourth, and fifth time, working silently and with the determination of someone trying to rescue the one thing that mattered in the world.

After the sixth came out, he and Penelope had created a rectangle just large enough for him to squeeze through. Lying on his back, he reached his hands out. Penelope pulled him as he dug his heels into packed earth and pushed forward.

His hands touched cooler air, then his arms. When his head came out, he saw her, bloody and ash-covered, streaks of tears running down her face.

They kept pulling and pushing, exposing his midsection.

He was almost free. They had done it.

From inside, a cacophony of splintering, bursting, and crashing.

The burning wood fell on his legs.

Some part of him screamed. He didn't know he could make such a sound, so primal and instinctive. It wasn't a sound based in thought.

Somewhere far away, Penelope cried out his name over and over again.

She continued to drag him away from the inferno, and with the instinct of a wounded animal, he assisted her by pushing off the ground.

Once they were away from the heat and the roar of the fire was behind them, Penelope buried her face on his chest and cried. In the distance, he heard a siren.

When he glanced down at his legs, he saw a mangled mess of shredded blue jeans, blood, and burned, smoking flesh. He found the strength to wrap his arms around her just before passing out.

20

HE'S DYING, ISN'T HE?

The ambulance bounced and jostled across the windy, country roads with siren blaring. Penelope felt swabs, ointments, and wraps touching various parts of her body. *Bandaging me up—that's the phrase.* One of the emergency technicians placed an oxygen mask over her face and began an IV with a saline solution. She didn't feel the needle's poke.

They had allowed her to sit up, legs strapped to her gurney for safety. She leaned over Lex and held his hand.

Even though they were providing her with some basic emergency care, Lex required most of their focus and attention.

"Kid, let him go. I need to start a heart monitor on his finger. You can have his hand back after."

Much of the ride continued like that, with them telling her to shift this way or that way so they could continue their work. Not once did they tell her to completely move. Something about the fierce determination in her eyes must have let them know it was probably better just to let her have her way.

Their first task was to provide him with an artificial airway by sticking the thick tube down his throat. It appeared uncomfortable and unnatural, but it was doing the work his singed esophagus could not. Two IVs were next, and at least one contained a pain killer with a name Penelope couldn't pronounce.

Other than moving aside incinerated bits of fabric, they provided no treatment to his legs. There was little else they could do for him in the ambulance other than monitor his vital signs.

His burns must be more than EMTs are trained to handle, Penelope realized. Somehow, that made the injuries seem even more horrendous. She focused on the uninjured half of Lex's face. It was deceptively peaceful, and, other than a few black smudges, clean and untouched by the tragedies of the last few days.

It made her wonder what could have been if she had listened to Lex. If she had ignored their invitation to the abandoned mall and believed him when he said the group wasn't worth their time. They could have gone on his slightly weird, slightly cute date idea, and none of this would have happened.

She had thought they were going to take them to the hospital where she was born. Even though that hospital was the closest, they were rerouted back to St. Louis. Barnes Jewish Hospital was close to their homes and had a burn unit. Hearing them mention that made Penelope's stomach churn. She knew that burn unit all too well.

As they neared the end of the three-hour ride, a warm, pinkish glow lit up the interior of the ambulance. It was the sunrise of Saturday morning. Outside, she saw the St. Louis skyline with the Arch, awash in reds, yellows, and pinks in the morning sun. Only then did she realize she was supposed to be home by eleven. Her parents—their worry would turn to panic when they got the call from the hospital.

The paramedics threw open the back doors as soon as they arrived at the hospital and rolled Lex out on his stretcher. Penelope didn't wait to be unstrapped. Throwing the mask off her face and taking her bag of fluids from its hook, she jumped out after them.

"Knock it off, kid. Get in there," a paramedic said.

"I'm going with him. You can't stop me."

"You can say that all you want, but you're in bad shape, little lady. You either sit your own behind back down, or I'll get a security guard to make you sit back down." His tone softened for a second. "It's for his safety as well as yours."

She would have fought all the security guards, honestly, if she wasn't already about to fall over. Just standing there, she had to grip the ambulance for support. Helplessly, she watched them wheel him away before a few more workers came to collect her.

Smoke inhalation, facial cuts requiring a few stitches, a sore back that would need icing, and a broken rib that should have been wrapped days ago. Those were her injuries. Nothing, really. Minor.

They would keep her on fluids and oxygen, as well. They wanted her to stay overnight and would dismiss her Sunday morning. Just to keep watch. Just to be sure.

"Sweetie," a nurse said, "we need to call your parents. We need consent to treat a minor as soon as possible."

Numbly, Penelope gave her the house number. She glanced at the clock. Her dads would reach the hospital in about thirty minutes.

She couldn't decide whether she wanted to see them. It wasn't as if she could tell them the truth, and they would probably panic when they saw her. She didn't fault them for that. It was a natural reaction. But they would misinterpret her stricken expression as fear or pain for herself, and that wasn't the case.

Once they had finished her stitches, they began preparations to admit her so they could free up critical space in the emergency room. Hospitals as big as this one funneled thousands of personal crises through an efficient system of diagnosis, treatment, and transfer either to another department or out the door.

Already, she felt like a cog in the machine. No, not a cog. She was the machine's product, really, being pushed through the gears and levers. Somewhere in that same complex, Lex was being pushed through a different machine. He had no one there to hold his hand, touch his face, or tell him it was all going to be all right. He was just another patient among thousands.

Lying in her hospital bed, she thought about him as well as what version of the evening's events she would tell her dads. She began spinning a story that would free Lex of any responsibility. It was the same story she would probably have to provide for a police statement as well.

They wheeled her up to a room high above the emergency room with a rather dull view of the interstate. It was cheerless and decorated in muted pastels. Everything smelled like a hospital—that sharp stink of antiseptic, cleaner, and chemicals.

An orderly came in and asked her for a breakfast order. To prevent further upset, she picked a bunch of food, but she doubted she was anywhere close to being able to keep down anything.

Just as she made the final edits to her story in her mind, both of her dads rushed into the room. They cried fat tears that spotted her blanket and rubbed the top of her head. They wanted to hug her, but she parted her hospital gown to reveal the bandages around her broken ribs. And Penelope was too tired to cry along with them.

"They told us everything, Penny!" Mike exclaimed.

"They did?" she asked, trying to hide her surprise.

"Of course," Mike replied. "They said you saved him. Your boyfriend? He wrote it all out with a pen and paper. He was doing a paranormal investigation in the middle of nowhere, and he brought a lantern. He fell asleep and tipped the lantern, which started a fire in a silo. You pulled him out. Honey, you're a hero!"

Penelope couldn't help it. She chuckled. Lex had beaten her to it. He had managed to spit out a story that protected her before she could get out her own version. He couldn't even talk. He was one step ahead of her once again. Asshole.

"My baby is in shock," Henry muttered.

"No, I'm fine," she reassured them. "I promise. Did they say how he was doing?"

Her dads exchanged concerned glances, and Penelope felt her stomach fall.

They are going to lie to me, she thought. *Whatever is going on, it's bad enough that they feel the need to lie.*

"He's fine, dear. He said he just wants you to rest and get better," Henry managed to say, hiding the truth behind a kind smile.

For a flash, Penelope resented them for their dishonesty, but she let it go. Instead, she made her mind up in that moment. She was going to sneak out of her room and get to Lex, machines and cogs and processes be damned.

"Oh, that's so good to hear," she lied back to them. "I'm feeling better, too. I'm just tired, that's all. I haven't slept all night."

"Well," Mike said, "we brought you a change of clothes and some books. They said they were going to let you out tomorrow morning. We can stay in here with you, honey, if you want. All day, all night."

A change of clothes was exactly what she needed. She would unhook herself from all this stuff, get dressed, and hurry to the burn ward. After spending three months there, she still knew the hospital better than her high school. By the time they realized she was gone, she would be in his room.

Her first task was getting them out. "I'm so thankful to both of you, but I just need some sleep right now. It would be easier to rest if I was alone. Why don't you two get some breakfast? Give me a little time to sleep, and I'll see you in a few hours?"

"She's so grown up," Henry said with a smile of pride.

"If you're sure, Penny. We know you need your peace and quiet," Mike said. "I'll leave your stuff right here." He set a gym bag on the counter next to her hospital bed.

"I'm sure. Thank you both." She gave them one more disarming smile as they walked out.

As soon as they stepped from her room, Penelope set to work. She knew as soon as she removed her monitors, the nurses would receive about a million alerts at their station. She would have to be quick.

She tore off the oxygen mask, heart monitor, and blood pressure cuff in a few quick motions. Fatigue caused her limbs to quake, but she wouldn't be stopped.

The IV was another matter. She knew how to turn the little knob to stop the fluids, so that wasn't the issue. When she pulled it out, she might start squirting blood everywhere, and she didn't see any bandages within her reach. As she stared at the IV, the machines that had been attached to her began making high-pitched noises.

She had to make a decision before someone came to check on her. She could take the risk or sit here and be discovered.

Tear it out. Do it, she decided. Just as she began to lift the tape from her skin, a nurse barreled into the room. Penelope cursed her bad luck. She hadn't expected her to be that fast.

"Wha—what are you doing?"

Something inside her snapped. "He's dying, isn't he?" she screamed. "You're just letting me sit here like an idiot. He'll die alone, and nobody will tell me anything!"

The nurse responded like she hadn't heard a word Penelope said. "Get in your bed!"

Before she could think about it, she ripped. Out came the IV, and her blood began streaming out of the hole in her skin. She ran for the door.

"I need assistance in Room 5403," the nurse said into the device at her collar. She rushed Penelope and tried to restrain her in a bear hug, but Penelope began squirming, kicking, and thrashing. Within seconds, three more nurses came in the room.

Three? Nothing. Nothing to her. She found a wedge between two of them, squeezed her way through, and ran through the doorway. Another nurse tried to block her, but Penelope managed to duck his grasp, too.

She felt a sharp prick on her arm. Her body went too heavy to hold up. Her knees buckled under her, and she passed out.

When she awoke, a face eerily resembling Lex's leaned over her.

"Morning, sunshine," the female voice drawled. "Or, should I say good evening?"

Penelope pulled herself into a sitting position and immediately regretted it. The evening sunset cast long, bright rays into her eyes. The woman reached forward, adjusted the hospital bed to bring up the back, and positioned her pillows so she could sit upright. She walked over to the window and closed the shade.

"Thanks," Penelope managed to say and reached for the plastic cup of water on the table next to her bed. She pulled her mask away from her face long enough to gulp through a straw.

"No problem," the guest replied.

Once her thirst was quenched, she placed the cup back on the table and studied the woman. In her face, she saw Lex's eyebrows and nose, but slightly thinner lips and a narrower jaw and chin. Her long hair snaked along both sides of her head in tight, intricate braids. Her eyes also resembled Lex's—inquisitive, intelligent, and judgmental.

"Your dads went to get something from downstairs for dinner and asked me to watch over you until they came back," she said in a monotone. "Apparently, they think you need constant adult supervision. What would make them think that, I wonder?"

"Umm."

"I'm being sarcastic. I heard what happened, but it doesn't matter. We have some alone time together, right? We should have just enough time for you to tell me what went down last night."

"Excuse you?" Penelope asked.

"No, dear, excuse *you*. Do you know who I am?"

"The big sister," Penelope said.

"Damn straight I'm the big sister, and I'm one pissed off big sister." She leaned over the hospital bed's rail and toward Penelope. "You better start telling me what happened to my baby brother."

Penelope opened her mouth, then closed it. With Nadine's eyes boring into her, she realized there was no point trying to spin a lie. She would see right through it. "It was all my fault."

"Oh, I gathered that much. Lex has been going out on investigations by himself since he was twelve. He texts me at least twice a day. Until about two weeks ago, his texts were 'School sucks. Found something cool on such and such investigation. Mom is on my case. When are you coming home?' That was it. Then, all of a sudden, I start getting this stuff like, 'Nadine, what is love?'"

She shook her head in disbelief. "He tried to act like he suddenly had this objective interest in the subject. I told him to quit playing. Then he told me about you. 'How do you know when you're in love?' he asked me."

Penelope swallowed. "What did you tell him?"

"I asked him how it felt when he wasn't around you. He said it hurt like hell, and he said it hurt even when he was around you sometimes. I said it was love, or at least as close to it as he's going to understand right now. Anyway, suddenly there's this little girl in my baby brother's life, and now he's in the burn unit. So I'm going to ask it again—*what happened*?"

Penelope inhaled and exhaled. "I can't tell you." Before Nadine could cut her off, Penelope held up her hand. "Please, I don't mean any disrespect. You are the last person on the planet

I want to disrespect right now. It's just that it's his choice what he wants to reveal. It's not my place."

Nadine twisted her lip a little. "I want to be mad at that, but I can't. It makes too much sense, and it shows you actually revere my brother. Fine. I'm going to let this go, but only because he swears you saved him. On that part, I do believe him. We're even now, you got it? After this, if anything happens to him, I won't let you off the hook that easily."

Penelope nodded. "Nadine?"

"Hmm?"

"How is he?"

"He'll be fine, you dramatic lunatic. It will take a while, but he's going to be fine. He's been asking for you about every five seconds. It's driving everybody nuts. They told him you would see him after you were discharged, and if either of you pull any more crap, nobody is seeing anybody." She frowned and examined Penelope until Penelope looked down. "You love him too, don't you?"

"Duh."

"Cool. If you hurt him, I'll kill you. Deal?"

Penelope shrank back from her. "How is that a deal?"

"It's not. Just warning you." She stood up and stretched, revealing her long and lean frame, just like her brother's. Penelope wondered for a moment if their mom was shaped the same way.

Nadine twiddled her fingers at her. "Your dads are coming back. Toodles!" As she exited, she waved to Mike and Henry. "Have a good night, gentlemen. Good luck with that one."

"Yeah, no kidding," Henry grumbled as they both entered the room.

Both of them stared at her with arms folded.

"Just wanted some peace and quiet for sleep, huh?" Mike repeated accusingly.

"Uh." Penelope smiled and looked through her eyelashes. "Yes?"

21

WE'RE ALL WE HAVE LEFT

The next morning, Mike brought her a blank canvas and her paints. Having an outlet for everything she had experienced proved more of a relief than she had initially thought. The painting itself, a depiction of the burning silo, was figurative enough that her parents couldn't identify it as the same silo at her childhood home. It could have been any silo anywhere.

After she had been presented with yet another ultimatum ("Eat your damn breakfast or you can't see your boyfriend later!"), she heard some scurrying and high-pitched protesting in the hallway.

"Penny, two kids are here to see you," Henry said, arms folded. "They say they're your friends. I told them to get lost because you were getting discharged in a couple of hours, but the loud one with the Afro has a listening problem."

"Let them in please?"

Henry huffed, gestured for Mason and Helena to enter, and craned his head around. "Five minutes. That's it," he warned before walking away.

Mason skipped to her bedside, leaped on the bed, and squeezed her. "Yay! You're okay! You're okay!"

"Ow, ow, Drips! Come on, ow!" she complained.

"Sorry, *Penny*. I guess I was a little excited, *Penny*." He started bouncing up and down on the bed. "Can I call you that, too? *Penny*?"

"No, you can't," she grumbled, rubbing her sore sides and back.

Helena, standing behind Mason, snorted out a laugh. Penelope leaned over Mason and gestured for her to sit in a chair. Helena flopped into it and threw her legs over the armrest.

"How are you feeling?" Penelope asked.

"This girl cracks me up," Helena said as she rolled her eyes. "We come to see her in the hospital, and she asks about *me*."

"She's fine. Just grumpy, as usual," Mason said. "At least she's got a good reason today, though. Concussion headaches are the worst. Oh yeah, and she got kicked out of her house."

"Someday I'll find me a man who doesn't put all my business out there," Helena muttered, smirking.

"You can't even be mad at me because we're roomies now. She's staying with us. So, how are they treating you in here? Hopefully better than your dad. Jeez, he was ready to slaughter me!"

"Ghost told us why, though," Helena said. "Ripping out IVs and fighting nurses?" She tsk-tsked her with her index finger. "That's no way for a patient to behave. Are we a bad influence on you, *Penny*?"

"Not you, just Drips," she said with a grin. It dawned on her. "Wait, you talked to Lex?"

"Who do you think told us your room number? His hot sister Nadine led us to his room. We just came from there."

Helena whipped her head around. "You call any woman but me 'hot' again, and I'll serve some of your parts to you for breakfast."

Penelope tried to swallow the ball of emotion in her throat. "How is he?"

Mason grabbed her hand and squeezed it. "Penelope, he looks like shit, and he can't talk with that tube in his throat. He's been using his sister's phone to type out messages to people, so I know he's the same smartass Lex. But brace yourself."

Penelope patted the hand gripping hers and gave him a warm smile. "If he's breathing, I'm happy."

"Gross," Helena said. "And besides, it's not like she looks much better."

"I don't?"

"You haven't seen yourself?" Mason asked. He snatched a handheld mirror from a wash basin on the counter that contained hospital-issued hygienic supplies.

When Mason held it up to Penelope's face, her eyes widened. Her red, swollen forehead and jaw were just starting to turn a blackish, purplish color. Stitches dug into her left brow, right cheekbone, and under her lip. Both her lips were covered in red scabs. She pulled up her hospital gown and examined her back. It was covered in a multicolored swirl of bruises.

Her two visitors watched her in silence. She let out a sigh. Seeing her injuries made the realities waiting for her outside of the hospital immediate and real.

"Guys," she said, "I need a favor."

"Anything," Mason said.

"Yeah, anything," Helena said. "I feel like a total tool for not being there. I'm sorry. I really am." She was staring at the wall as she sniffed, trying to put her tough mask back over her face.

"It's a big one," Penelope warned. "Actually, it's two in one."

"Apparently, this girl didn't hear us the first time," Helena said with raised eyebrows.

Penelope bit her swollen lip before spilling it out. "It's my car. It's still there. If my parents have to go get it, they'll know the house is where I used to live. That will wreck Lex's whole cover story. But it's three hours away and—"

"Done," Mason said. "Easy."

"I should just sit today, anyway," Helena said. "A road trip will force me to stay still."

A few tears formed in the corners of her eyes, and Penelope reached for one of the tissues on her bed stand. "You guys, I—"

"Shut up, Lois," Mason said. "We're Pack. We don't say please or thank you. We don't feel guilty for needing one another. We're all we have left. The three of us and one messed up Ghostboy. We are all that's left of our Pack, and I'll do everything I can to fight for us. I don't know about you, but..." Mason trailed off, making eye contact with Helena.

Helena, however, shook her head back and forth in warning. "Not now, Mason. Later."

"What?" Penelope asked. "What is it?"

"Revenge, that's what," Mason said. Just like that, the joy and jokes were gone from his expression. She saw the rage boiling in his eyes.

"Mason, shut up," Helena sniped as loud as she dared. She sat up in her chair and leaned into their conversation. "Not here. You think she needs that right now?"

"No, no. It's fine." Penelope looked back at Mason, letting her own anger come to the surface. "I want it too. And the first step is this." From under her pillow, she pulled out the EVP recorder. "I told my parents it was Lex's personal fitness tracker. Right before he ended up like this, Lex told me to keep it safe. There must be some information on it we can use."

"We'll check out the files during the car ride," Helena said.

"We'll come by your house later, too," Mason said. "I doubt your parents are going to let you back out."

"There's no way they'll agree to company," Penelope said. "I'm basically on house arrest."

"We're Pack, Lois." Mason patted her on the knee. "Trust me." Snatching the EVP recorder from her, he bounded out of her room.

Her parents walked up to intercept him. Through the glass wall, Penelope could see him chatting with them.

"Watch this," Helena said. "Give him thirty seconds."

"To do what?" Penelope asked, perplexed.

"To win your parents over."

Mike and Henry both had their arms crossed over their chests, and they were staring down at the shorter Drips as if they were Penelope's personal body guards. Mason, acting as if he didn't notice their postures, seemed jovial as he made wide gestures and even reassuringly patted them on the arms a few times. They could only catch a couple of Mason's words and phrases, like "love her so much, like family" and "cookies!" and "dinner? I'll bring a salad."

"Twenty-eight, twenty-nine, thirty," Helena counted.

When Penelope caught sight of her parents again, they couldn't keep the smiles from their faces. Mike had even dropped his arms to his hips.

All three of them reentered the hospital room, and Mason gestured for Helena to join him by the door. "You guys are just great! Thank you so so so so *so* much! We're just super worried about her, and nothing cures better than my cookies. Seriously, the whole family swears by their power."

"That's true," Helena said. "Knocked out my flu once."

"Whatever," Henry said, still trying to act tough. "We'll see you two at six, and you're out not one minute after eight. This girl needs sleep."

"Not a problem, Dad! Bye!"

Once they were both gone, Henry said, "I guess we will have some dinner guests, even if the original guest can't join us." Penelope saw exhaustion lines under his eyes. "Let's just get you showered, dressed, and out of this room, huh?"

Once she was back in her clothes, she felt more like her old self. The prescription bottles and pages of discharge instructions went home with her dads, who agreed to pick her up from the hospital around three that afternoon. She did, however, swallow a few of the bottled pain pills before packing them up. With her favorite black beanie pulled low over her green hair, she walked her dads to the exit leading to the parking lot and made her way back inside toward the burn unit. The closer she approached, the more anxious she became. She couldn't put her finger on the source of the feeling. Whatever the cause, it quickened her steps and her heart rate.

When she approached his room, she saw Nadine standing outside, leaning against the wall. A medical textbook was close to her face. When Nadine looked up, she placed a bookmark on her page and wedged the giant tome under her arm.

"Hey," she greeted. "Sleep well?"

"I mean, I guess. For a hospital." Penelope shrugged.

Nadine grunted in agreement. She scrutinized her from the bottom of her feet to the top of her head. "Under all those stitches, you are a little cutie, aren't you? You resemble my girlfriend when she was younger."

"Well—"

"Never mind. I just did you a big favor, dear. Mom won't be back until later tonight. She had to go to the airport to pick up her baggage, and I'm leaving, too. You'll have all afternoon to talk to him about whatever it is two teenagers talk about."

"Wow, thank you. Really."

Nadine flicked her wrist at her, shooing away her gratitude. "It's nothing. Just remember what I said."

"I will."

As Nadine walked away, Penelope glanced into the room. It was quiet and empty, except for the skinny, long figure on the hospital bed. The tubes, monitors, and bandages obscured most of him. When she approached, though, she saw his face with both eyes closed. The bruising from the fight with Nate had gone down, at least.

Penelope realized she was shaking a little. Seeing him finally helped her understand why she couldn't stay calm. It was two dueling emotions. Assuring herself he was alive and breathing filled her with immeasurable relief, and yet knowing he had come to any harm at all made her so infuriated she couldn't think straight.

She pulled a chair up to his bedside and, with a shuddering breath, leaned over and buried her face in his chest. Warm and solid. She could feel it rising and falling as well as his heartbeat pounding along steadily under her cheek.

After a few moments, Lex stirred, wrapped his tube-ridden arms around her, and shifted over in the hospital bed. He couldn't talk, but he didn't need to say anything. After he tapped next to him with his hand, Penelope climbed into bed, crossing his stomach with her arm and pulling some of his blanket over her legs. He put his own arms over hers and fell back to sleep.

In that moment, all the confusion and chaotic emotion seemed to release their grip on her. The feelings weren't gone, but they were subdued. In their place, they left complete emotional and physical exhaustion. She, too, fell asleep.

Near lunchtime, a nurse's routine check roused them both. Reddening with embarrassment, Penelope shifted out of the bed and claimed the chair next to Lex. After the nurse left, Lex reached for his sister's phone. Penelope laid on his chest again, head nestled under his chin. His arms were resting on her back as he held the phone and opened a text document.

Lex: *Hey.*

Smirking, he passed the phone to her. She held the phone close to her face as she leaned against him.

Penelope: *Hey.*

Lex: *So, how's your weekend going?*

Penelope: *Oh, you know. I've done a lot of lying around. I haven't seen my boyfriend much, which has sucked.*

She glanced up to catch his smirk as he read her message.

Lex: *You have a boyfriend?*

Penelope: *I guess so. He never told me either way.*

He stiffened underneath her.

Lex: *Well, I don't approve of this guy. He must be a real asshole to let you get hurt like that.*

Penelope: *Actually, he's not. He made a point to tell me the first night I met him that he most certainly wasn't a real asshole.*

Lex: *I'm not sure I believe him.*

Penelope felt her stomach flutter as she typed her next words.

Penelope: *I do. Pretty sure I'm in love with him, too.*

Lex: *Sounds serious.*

Penelope: *It's super serious.*

Lex: *Young love is so dumb and childish. Who even believes in that crap anymore? I sure don't.*

Penelope: *I feel sorry for your girlfriend.*

Lex: *I'm not sure I have a girlfriend. She never told me either way.*

Penelope typed back with flying fingers, pounding on the screen. As he watched her, Lex laughed as much as he could with the tube in his mouth.

Penelope: *Lex, I'm in love with you. You're my boyfriend, and I'm your girlfriend.*

Lex: *Dammit, Penelope! You weren't supposed to do that here.*

Penelope: *Why not?*

Lex: *Because I'm like this. Because this place sucks. Because I wanted to tell you somewhere, I dunno, more appropriate. Maybe from a balcony or something?*

Penelope: *That's stupid. What, you have to find a balcony every time you want to tell me how you feel about me?*

She passed the phone back, and he groaned in acquiescence.

Lex: *Fine. You win. I'm in love with you. You're my reporter girl, and I'm your Ghostboy, done extra crispy.*

Penelope: *Was that so hard?*

Lex: *Yes, actually. It was torture. Just awful. Ugh. I'm never doing that crap again.*

Penelope: *Shut up.*

Lex: *Pretty sure I can't right now with this thing in my throat, but they're supposed to take it out tomorrow as long as the swelling stays down. Then, I promise I'll shut up.*

Penelope: *Are you trying to make me feel guilty?*

Lex: *Never. I never, ever want you to feel guilty.*

"Well, I do feel guilty." She responded verbally so he could hear her irritation. "If we're being serious now."

Lex: *Don't do that, Penelope. I'm begging you. Don't.*

"Do what, be serious?"

Lex: *You know what I mean. Do not feel guilty about this. I feel guilty enough for the both of us, but we both have to let go of all that. We're going to do what we can, and that's all we can do.*

She read the words slowly, holding the phone as she let their meaning sink in. Realizing she would never say her words verbally, she took the phone from him.

Penelope: *Lex, we were never supposed to be. It was all part of Alpha's plan because he designed his test that way. He knew you were going to be at the cemetery. It wasn't just some random chance.*

She told him the entire story—the message from the Broken app framing Lex, the chase and fight in the sewers, the word spelled in fire, Alpha's final test.

Lex read it all, then pounded the bed with a fist. Penelope grabbed his hand and bent his arm so it was close to her. She squeezed it until his fingers uncurled. Once she felt his heart rate subside to its normal pace, she released his hand so he could type back to her.

Lex: *I'm going to kill him, Penelope. For everything he did to you. For everything he did to all of us.*

Penelope: *Stop it. You can't be thinking about that now. I just need you to rest and get better.*

Lex: *That's bullshit, and you know it. You're as ready to rip him apart as I am. The only difference is you're a little less messed up than me.*

He told her everything that had transpired between him and the other Broken team leaders.

Lex: *I did get some audio of them on the EVP recorder, but it's not going to be enough to prove anything. It's a start, though. And we will need everything we can find if we are going to clear Elijah and Seth's names.*

Penelope read the message and groaned. "No, Lex! This isn't your fight anymore. You've done enough. Please, just forget about it."

Lex: *You're not being fair. If our places were switched, could you forget about it?*

"No, no, I couldn't."

Lex: *Stop asking me to do the same. I won't be in here forever. One of the legs is burned worse than the other, and the other one is broken in three places. It's going to be a couple of weeks, and that's if there aren't any complications. But I want to help any way I can, and I want in on all of it as soon as I'm out of here. We are stronger together. It's just that simple. We've wasted too much time trying to protect each other and failing miserably at it. From now on, it's you, me, and the rest of the Pack against all of them.*

She realized tears were dampening his hospital gown as they slipped down her nose and onto his chest.

Penelope: *Lex, none of this should have ever happened. But that doesn't change the way I feel about you. I tried to break up with you, and I completely failed at that. I guess you're stuck with me, but that won't make me feel like I deserve you. You wouldn't be like this if it wasn't for me. And we both know I'm way more 'broken' than you. At any time, you can walk away from all this, including me. I wouldn't judge you for it.*

He read the text and shook his head furiously from side to side.

Lex: *See that? That's the crap that must stop right now. You think I don't feel the same way? You think I feel like I deserve you? I don't. I love you. Accept it. And, if that's hard, it's hard for me, too. But, like you said, you're stuck with me now. We're going to make them regret everything they've done to us. Then we're going to do all that stupid stuff teenage couples are supposed to do.*

She wiped her face with some tissues and stood to stare out the hospital room window. His view looked over Forest Park, so it was much more scenic than her view had been. She couldn't see the fire's damage from the vantage point. Out there, it was just a peaceful Sunday afternoon. She wondered where Alpha was right now.

Does he feel guilt, like we do? she wondered. *Or do all his actions seem reasonable and justified?*

She felt Lex watching her as she stared out and pondered. After a few minutes, she sat in a comfy chair next to him and picked up the phone.

Penelope: *Well, we better figure out some stupid stuff we can do now, too. It's spring break starting tomorrow, so we'll have to do something with all our time. I mean, as much time as my parents will allow. I'm in trouble, to say the least.*

Lex waggled his index finger at her, just as Helena had done earlier that morning.

Lex: *Bad Penelope, very bad Penelope, trying to fight your way to my room like an Amazonian warrior. That's not sexy at all. I swear it's not. Ahem.*

Penelope: *Glad to hear my emotional outbursts are arousing to you.*

Lex: *I'm a guy of simple tastes. What can I say? Back to the topic at hand. How to spend our time together. We've been through so much stuff already, but I don't feel like I know basic facts about you.*

Penelope: *Such as?*

Lex: *Your favorite color.*

"Obvious," she drawled, pointing to her hair.

Lex: *Ah, of course. Stupid question. Well, mine is black and blue. I like the contrast.*

Penelope: *What a tortured, emo teen answer. My turn. What do you do for fun, other than chase ghosts and hack apps?*

Lex: *Game. I'm a big gamer.*

She snickered. "You're typecasting yourself here, Lex. Loner teen boy who's addicted to video games and likes the color black? Come on, be original."

He snatched the phone from her.

Lex: *All right, Miss Original, what do you do for fun other than chase nonexistent story leads?*

Penelope: *Paint.*

Lex: *How is that less stereotypical?! That's every emo teen princess's favorite hobby.*

Penelope: *Well, it's still true. And I painted you.*

Lex: *Did you really?*

Penelope: *Really. But you can't see it.*

Lex: *Excuse you? I'm stuck like this, and you're telling me I can't see it?*

"Not like that," she insisted as she tried to wipe the blush from her cheeks. "It's a piece of crap. And embarrassing."

Lex: *Well, I want it. I want this embarrassing piece of crap. Stop putting yourself down, please.*

Penelope: *Fine. I'll bring it tomorrow. But you can't laugh at it.*

Lex: *I'm blushing under all this crap on my face. Seriously. I don't think I've ever been painted before. My turn. Favorite food?*

Penelope: *Tacos. Duh.*

Lex: *Same.*

"Oh my God. It's destiny. We'll be together forever!" she exclaimed.

Lex: *To have and to hot sauce, till guacamole do us part?*

"I do. Anyway, moving on! My turn now."

EPILOGUE

"Pass the aux," Lex demanded, reaching forward.

Mason, in the driver's seat, shook his head. "No way, dude. My turn. It's never my turn."

Lex made a grab-grab motion. "It's my first day out of a wheelchair. You have to be nice to me. Pass it."

With a sulk, Penelope said, "Yup, he's right. *First* day out of the wheelchair."

Mason ignored her tone. "Don't stick up for your man, Lois! This is between us right now."

"I think you should give it to him, too," Helena muttered, her sneakers planted in the middle of the dashboard. "Not because I feel like we owe this moron anything for being here. He shouldn't be here at *all*. I just hate your music."

"Why does everybody hate my music?"

"Shut up, Drips," Lex said. "You're outvoted. Pass it."

"Ugh!" Mason groaned and handed the white cord into Lex's waiting hand.

With a few taps, the car filled with a moody, brooding male voice moaning over life's woes to a bass beat. It was dark music, the type that created a hovering cloud of gray emotion. The sounds made them feel the gravity of the evening to come. They grew quiet and aloof, but also anxious.

At last, they had a lead. After all their months of searching and running into dead ends, they had something. Alpha and the others kept taunting them with clues, then disappearing. Lex, who could do little else other than listen, heard the others tell him story after story of coming so close but losing him.

Alpha wanted them to keep searching for him. It probably gave him some sort of sadistic pleasure to keep them baited this way.

Every near miss made Lex feel more frustrated, impatient, and helpless. As he waited for his legs to heal, they became his worst enemy.

Last week, they had been contacted. Someone wanted to meet. A sealed note with contact information had been slipped under Penelope's front door. Penelope hadn't intended to tell Lex about it, but he had spent so much time with her as he laid in his hospital bed he could read her every emotion, reaction, and discomfort.

He knew she was hiding something the second he saw her. As she doodled swirls and zigzags on his blue leg cast with black sharpie, he pulled the truth out of her.

The truth. Something they had promised to always share. It was a promise they both struggled to keep at times. They never intended to be dishonest. In an effort to protect each other, they tried to shelter each other from the ugliest realities.

"You can't go like this," she had insisted.

"I'm getting rid of this chair at the end of the week, and I'm switching to crutches. I'm going."

In desperation, Penelope enlisted Mason for help, but he refused to talk to Lex. "I get it, Lois. Sorry. If I was him, I'd hobble along, too."

Lex knew about the interaction because Mason had called him, just to try to be the peacemaker.

Seated in the back of the car, he knew she was still angry at him. She was in the other passenger seat, her attention focused out the window. Seeing her so close and not touching her in some way made her feel a thousand miles away, not right across the backseat.

Fine. Be mad, he thought. *You'd do the same thing in my place. Women. Ugh.*

And she sure wasn't angry when, two weeks ago right after getting out the hospital, he left his wheelchair at the bottom of her house stairs and scooted, one stair at a time, up to her bedroom. He had to literally hop from the hallway to her bedside. Her parents had assumed it was safe to leave them home alone together since he was still so messed up.

They had assumed incorrectly.

He so enjoyed screwing with people's assumptions and expectations.

The car lurched to a stop. The crumbling ruins of a church, white brick and stone, loomed outside. Four walls and an open doorway, nothing more.

In the summer heat, vines had taken over the back wall, then spilled over the opening that had been the roof. As a hot wind blew down the city street, the vines rustled, and a little cloud of dust floated upward. The neighboring streetlights lighted the interior of the church well.

"Why here?" Lex asked as he opened the car door.

Mason grabbed Lex's crutches from the trunk and handed them to him. "Well, it's a little nostalgic because Penelope and I met up here in March right before things got crazy. But mostly, I chose it because it's public. I don't trust this guy."

"Smart," Lex muttered as he approached a small set of concrete steps leading to the church's gravel ground floor. He should have anticipated steps.

Penelope, in front of him, pivoted and raised an eyebrow.

"What?" he snapped.

Slowly, she strolled to the top of the steps and crossed her arms. With a dramatic flourish, she gestured to the steps and waited.

He wouldn't admit she was right. Nope, never.

Lex, staring right back at her, tossed the crutches to the top of the few steps, then hopped up each step. When he reached the top, she didn't hand him the crutches, just watched him as he bent over to pick them up.

Helena observed the hostile interaction with growing frustration. "If you two don't cut the crap…" Helena thundered.

"Yeah, seriously," Mason said. "Not now."

Penelope, flicking her longer, black-tipped hair, gave him one last glare before slinking into the church. She joined Helena, who had dyed Penelope's hair last week during a late-night gathering. Lex loved it. He wanted to run his fingers through it.

Fights are stupid, he thought.

Grumbling to himself, Lex plodded along behind the other three.

They reached the back wall and waited. Penelope, leaning against the bricks and vines, stood next to Mason, while Lex propped himself on the other end by Helena. As he lingered, he twirled his own lengthening twists with one hand while using the other to prop himself up.

"We look pretty awesome lined up here," Mason said.

"Shut up, Drips," Penelope said.

"No seriously, we should form a band. The Broken! Their first album, *Crumbling Faith*."

"Except for Crutches over there," Helena said with a smirk. "He's ruining the image."

"Garnet, go to hell."

"Lois, deal with your man before I kick his ass and put him back in the hospital."

When Penelope replied, she didn't share the others' mirth. It was all malice. "Well, he won't listen to me. That's for sure."

"That's it! Kiss and make up. Right now!" Mason said. "I can't take all this tension. Seriously. Lois, you knew he was stubborn the second you met him. Are you surprised?"

"Yup."

"Why?"

"Because I didn't know he was *this* stupid."

With lips twisted to the side, Lex muttered, "You weren't saying that last night."

Helena broke out into a raucous, loud laugh. Mason, too, shrieked like a hyena. Penelope, realizing the joke was at her expense, folded her arms over her stomach and huffed.

They all spotted him at the same time. He strolled up the stairs, one step at a time, and crossed the threshold into the church. Even though there was no roof, doors, or windows, Lex felt the man was somehow invading their space. Yes, they were arguing, but they were Pack, and this man didn't smell like one of them. Lex bristled in apprehension in this stranger's presence.

He was taller than Lex and much wider. Not wide from weight, but sheer size and bulk. Lex recognized him long before he dropped his red hood. When he did reveal his face, the others saw a long ponytail of black curls, thick eyebrows, and pale gray eyes.

"Titan," Lex said, astonished.

"You know him?" Mason asked.

"He saved both of us at the farm," Penelope said, equally shocked. "He gave Lex a pocket knife so he could cut himself free, and he fought off the other team leaders so I could pull Lex out. He called the ambulance, too."

Titan's rumbling voice projected against the wall behind them. "When is the last time any of you talked to Nail?" Despite his volume, his voice had a gentle cadence with a soft accent, which caused him to roll some of his sounds together.

Just hearing Nate's Broken name caused Lex to stare at the ground in regret. Nate had cut himself off from the rest of the Pack after his brother and Elijah had been arrested. Nate blamed Lex for everything, and Lex couldn't do anything about it. The fact that Lex actually agreed with him didn't help much.

"Uhh, gee, a hi would be nice!" Drips retorted. "Here, I'll start. Hey, Titan. Thanks for helping our Pack."

"Yeah. Thank you," Penelope said. Lex realized she was trying to hold back a tidal wave of emotions. Seeing him standing before them was making that night of the fire too real again.

Lex was not ready to thank this man, though. "What do you want?"

"I'm confused," Titan said. "Which do you prefer? Pleasantries or brevity?"

"Brevity," Helena said, "so we can decide what to do with you."

His answer wasn't kind, but it wasn't cruel either. Only honest. "Garnet, you are feared for your ferocity, but I doubt even you are much of a match for me. And who else could pose even the slightest physical threat in your Pack? You even brought a lame wolf with you!" He extended an arm in friendship. "I'm not here for trouble. Let's not waste time with insults and doubts."

Nobody moved toward him, but Drips nodded in agreement. "Fine. We're listening. Make it quick."

"Nail has joined Ozone, and he has vowed to take the rest of you out."

Penelope let out a gasp. Helena groaned loudly. Mason slapped his face with his palm. Lex stared ahead of him.

Ozone, led by the redhead Haze, specialized in quick movement and subtlety. As one of the top three teams, they served as a critical branch of Alpha's army. Lex, unfortunately, had learned of their expertise firsthand when he was captured in his neighborhood. Members of Ozone had chased him down, the women of The Riot herded him with their weapons, and someone in The Void had drugged him.

Lex still couldn't believe how much he had underestimated them. If he hadn't, maybe he never would have ended up in the hospital or stuck with the cast.

"Just let me talk to him. I know I can explain everything," Mason begged. "We're brothers. It's all just been such a mess. If

I just had ten minutes to tell him how sorry we all are and what we're doing to fix it, I know I could make this right."

Titan shook his head, revealing the angles of his square jaw. "I don't think that would work. And, even if I wanted you two to talk, there is no way for me to establish contact without making it obvious that we've had this meeting."

"Why are you telling us this, huh?" Helena shouted. She stomped forward and pointed her index finger at Titan. "Are you just trying to make us feel like shit? We've been chasing you assholes for almost two months now, and we can't find anything. And now, Nail is with the rest of you sick bastards! What are we supposed to do about that, huh? What?"

Mason walked forward and gripped Helena's arm.

She shoved him off and paced the length of the church. Fists clenched, her rage simmered in the surrounding air.

Penelope said, "I think what she's asking is, what do you want us to do, Titan?"

"I want one of you to join The Void."

They all made some sort of noise, mostly variations of "What?" or "Huh?"

"One of you should confess your crimes to Alpha, say you now understand everything he's trying to establish, and offer to serve him and the new order of the Broken with unwavering loyalty. I could probably persuade him to allow you in. You would have a contact inside."

"Why can't you just be this contact for us?" Penelope asked with raised eyebrows.

"I've tried," he said, "but I'm too high ranking. I'm watched too closely."

"Like a former Pack member wouldn't be watched? Please," Helena scoffed.

"At first," he said. "But after repeated tests, Alpha would forget. You would become one of us. You could spread discord from within."

"Stupid idea," Mason asserted. "We're stronger together. There are so few of us left. I'm sure eventually we can figure this out on our own."

"What luck have you had with that so far?" Titan said without rancor.

"Nobody's asking your opinion here, meathead," Helena barked.

"No, he's right," Lex said. "I'll do it."

Everyone turned their heads to him. "Yeah, there we go!" Helena laughed. "Let Crutches go. Great idea."

"Honestly, he is sought more than the rest of you and is more likely to be believed," Titan said.

"Why?" Penelope cut in. Lex was probably the only one who heard the panic in her voice.

"Drips and Garnet had been by Wolf Cub's side since the start of the Broken. No one will believe they are ready to follow Alpha. And Lois, Alpha already tested you, and you failed. He'll never accept that you changed that quickly. Ghost, however, is still a mystery to him, to all of us. Alpha knows he survived, by the way, and he's said repeatedly that his role in this isn't finished."

Lex covered his nervousness with feigned apathy. "Perfect. Cool. I'm in."

Penelope, abandoning any sense of image or unity, rushed over to Lex and grabbed him by his T-shirt. "No! No. Are you crazy? Stop it."

Any resistance against her Lex had been trying to maintain fell apart. He reached up, arms still resting on the crutches, and held her face in his hands. "Let me do this."

"Why?"

"You know why."

"We promised to stop trying to protect each other. We said it never works."

"It doesn't. I'm not trying to protect you. I'm trying to protect all of us. If you could, you would do the same thing."

"Your leg isn't even fully healed," she said, grasping at the one argument she had left.

"My cast comes off in twelve days. You know that."

She pulled out of his hold and stalked over to Titan, his size making her look extra petite. "Tell me he'll be safe."

"I can't do that," Titan said.

"Tell me they won't discover this is all a trick."

"I can't do that, either."

"What *can* you tell me?"

"I can tell you that if this works, we could stop one of the biggest disasters in this city's history." He paused for a moment, letting that thought settle, before he continued. "This is bigger than a few disgruntled teens checking out abandoned buildings. This is bigger than a brother's feud. This is bigger than a fire in an empty sewer. This is bigger than any of us. I'm not promising anything other than the opportunity to do what is right and just. If that isn't enough, go home, Pack puppies. Go home and forget all of this."

"I can't," Lex seethed. "I can't let them go."

"Promise us revenge," Mason said, his voice as low as a growl. "Promise us that."

Titan nodded. "I promise payback. I promise getting even. I promise vengeance."

Even Penelope, the kindest person he had even known, had fire in her eyes. She turned and in two steps returned to Lex's side and threw her arms around him. He lost his grip on his crutches, and they clanged to the ground. Leaning against the back wall for support, he pulled Penelope close to him and kissed her, deeply. She sighed as she clasped the small of his back and pressed her lips against his. He felt all those new aches and hungers for her stir deep within him. But he pulled his lips away, resting his forehead on hers.

"I love you, Ghostboy," she said with a voice was filled with resignation.

"Love you too, reporter girl."

She sighed, then bent over to pick up his crutches. One shuffling step at a time, he moved over to Titan.

"Don't contact him for a while," Titan said. "Wait for us to reach out to you. We don't want to cause you or him any unnecessary risk."

"I got this. Trust me!" he said, trying to sound cheerful.

"You're an idiot, Crutches, but I love you for it," Helena grunted.

"Be careful, man," Drips said. "Please. I can't lose somebody else."

Penelope didn't say anything. They both knew there was nothing else to say or do, other than to let him go.

So he went, following Titan out of the church and into the night.

Keep reading for a sneak peek at

CHILDREN IN THE CAGE,

Book 2 in The Broken Series

1

OPPORTUNITIES FOR SIN

Helena reached up to spin one of her new cartilage piercings to keep the pus from crusting as well as to give her fingers something to do.

"Ephesians 1:7. In Him, we have redemption through His blood, the forgiveness of our trespasses, according to the riches of His grace." Much like the aging air conditioner, the voice droned in the background.

"Jesus preaches we can all be forgiven. Everyone. Regardless of sin, regardless of transgression."

Her father, at the pulpit, wore the brown suit, the one with the two buttons instead of three. In about a month or so, he would rotate in the three-button suits. When she was a kid, she could measure the passing of the seasons by the number of buttons on her dad's jackets. It was the middle of September, but it would be a while before all the two-button suits went away for the year. The summer heat still pressed against the stained glass and leaked through the drafty doors.

The lingering heat was almost as stifling as the atmosphere inside. Hiding in the back pew, she realized, had been pointless. Every person in the sanctuary knew the subject of Pastor Brandon's sermon. She kept watching and waiting for one of them to turn around, but they didn't. None of them turned around, gave her a side glance, or even shifted in her direction. Instead, she could feel the judgment radiating from their bodies like steam.

"Do we, as his flock, attempt to emulate Him in this way? Can we forgive all, regardless of transgression? Our time on Earth presents so many opportunities for sin. Wife can sin against husband. Brother can sin against brother. Child can sin against parent."

Helena clenched her jaw.

"And yet, we must find the strength to forgive. Let us pray."

Heads bowed in obedience.

They're forgiving me, she realized. *They're probably praying for my soul right now.*

She hated them. All of them.

It was strange to look around that place, which had been the backdrop of so much of her childhood, and to see it through a new filter. Nothing was changed. It was the same wood stain on the pews. The same crack right there in the colored window. The same zigzag rip on the dark blue carpeting. And she possessed the same itching desire to misbehave. As the service moved into song, Helena reached into her back pocket and pulled out her phone. The volume was off, and the screen light was low.

Helena: *I can't take this, Drips*

The reply came within seconds.

Mason: *Don't text in church, my hellcat queen.*

Helena knew Mason was giving her grief. They had been a couple for about three years, since they were fourteen. He was an atheist and couldn't stand her parents. With his typical sarcasm and humor, he was trying to cheer her up. Just reading the text made her wish it was still summer.

Helena knew Mason wouldn't like her next text, but she couldn't stop herself from sending it.

Helena: *you sure you don't wanna move out now?*

Mason: *We'll do it after we graduate high school. Come on. Don't do this to me. This was the plan. You said you could make it through this school year.*

Reminding her of their goals didn't make daily stress easier.

Helena: *well that was before the sermon on "redemption"*

Mason: *You shitting me?*

Helena: *NO*

Mason: *I have a concert this afternoon, but you can come if you want. Just because you're living at home doesn't mean you have to STAY home. And Sasha will be there. She misses you. A lot.*

Helena didn't hesitate.

Helena: *text me the address*

Mason: *I thought you hated my music.*

Helena: *it's different when you're playing it*

Mason: *I think you're falling for me, Garnet!* Mason finished the text with five smooching emojis.

Helena: *shut up, Drips, not in the mood, just send it*

Mason: *Yes dear*

When Helena checked the address on her phone, she sucked her teeth with as much volume as she dared. Traveling by foot, the destination was about two hours away. Her parents had sold her car in March when she was kicked out of the house. Over the summer, it hadn't been a big deal because Mason had a car. And it wasn't like they went anywhere without each other, anyway.

Living at home, her parents had no intention of restoring her freedom. Not then and not ever. As a result, she had been forced to think up more creative solutions to solve her transportation issues.

She thought about texting Poe, but she stopped herself. Since Helena didn't need her, she wasn't going to bother her. Poe had enough problems without Helena's crap. After Ghost left the Pack, Poe started to drift away from the group, too. As far as Helena could tell, he stress of not knowing what Ghost was being forced to do with Warren was wearing on Poe. As for the rest of the Pack, who Helena had relied on to always be there for her, they were now growing apart. Some by choice, some not. Wolf Cub and Skin remained locked up in juvie for arson, set up by Warren. And Nail, Skin's twin brother, had run off to join Warren because he blamed Pack for everything that went down. Never mind the fact that Ghost and Poe almost burned alive in that mess.

And all of this surprises me why? The Pack had never been very logical. Instead, they reacted without thinking, usually in some wild attempt to protect someone they loved or to protect their own pride. *Kind of like how I left the church*, she thought, rolling her eyes at her own hypocrisy.

Helena had two feet. And she had headphones and a full cell phone battery. She could walk and listen to music. She preferred the idea of walking for two hours in the late summer heat to staying there for one more second. If she left the service now, she could make it a few minutes after the start of his performance.

Slipping the phone in her pocket, she slid out of the pew and, keeping her head low, ducked out of the sanctuary. Eyes bored into her and heads turned in her direction.

Good. Look. I dare you.

That was what she wanted all along. Helena picked her head up long enough to stare back, giving them glares of cold indifference and defiance. Her green eyes with the golden flecks spiraling from the center could frighten kids, teens, and *adults*. Adults with surface-level sentiments that were supposed to fix all her problems. She could see the truth behind their concern. They thought she and her brothers were complete trash, and her parents were saints for trying to fix them for all these years.

Screw them. All of them. When Helena stared back, she wanted them to see the mistrust and rebellion behind her eyes. They saw, and they reacted. As they always did, they looked away. They couldn't take it.

No one could except for the Pack. Which now was down to where it all started. With Mason.

The sanctuary door shut behind her, banging on its hinges. Helena knew it would do that. She just didn't care enough to catch it. Outside in the commons area, one of the nursery room volunteers bounced a squawking toddler in her arms. The woman, older than her mother and hair tied back in a bun, turned to her with a smile that only reached her lips. "Oh, restroom break? Did you forget to go before the service?"

"Nope." Helena spat the word without breaking stride.

She almost ran down the stairs leading outside and pushed the front door open wide. The mid-morning sun blasted her sensitive eyes. Her satchel, a shoulder bag with a bohemian sun in the center, hung by her side. Pulling out her reflective, round shades, she jogged through the parking lot and began strolling down the side of the highway as close to the edge as she could without walking in the dry grass.

Someone honked, either to scare her or to flirt. Didn't matter. Helena lifted one arm and gave the passing truck the finger.

It took a few moments to untangle her spaghetti cluster headphones. Once they were unknotted, she plugged them into her phone's headphone jack and tapped up her typical metal and screamo playlist. Now she couldn't hear the assholes when they honked. Perfect.

Walking along the asphalt, she felt the heat of the road soaking through her shoes. Last month before the start of her senior year, Helena shaved the underlayers of her hair and sliced arrow designs into the sides with an electric trimmer. She reached into her bag again and tied her top layer of hair with a ponytail holder, revealing the patterns.

With her hair up, her features and accessories became visible. Her eyes were part of a sweeping, delicate facial structure of high cheekbones, narrow chin, and full lips. Yet, few people took the time to notice the natural beauty under the hardware. Five piercings dotted the cartilage of each ear, and she kept a small gage in the earlobes. A ring hung from her nose's columella. She wore eyebrow rings now, too. One on each side, just like Nail's. She had been the one to convince him to get piercings in the first place.

With the music blasting and her thoughts traveling downward into dark memories, she didn't notice the car pull up behind her. She finally turned around when someone tapped on her shoulder.

Her mother.

"Helena, get in the car."

Her mom had the same eye color and facial structure, but the resemblance between mother and daughter stopped there. She wore a button-up white blouse, pleated skirt, and stockings with low heels. Her face was pierced once—earlobes, tiny silver hoops. Helena wore a neon green sports bra under a bright pink tank top with acid-washed overalls and rubber bracelets of various metal bands.

Helena took her time pulling out one of her earbuds. "Why?"

Her mother's voice was quiet and controlled. Everything about her was quiet and controlled. "That was part of the agreement. Pass all classes. Attend church every Sunday. Complete all your chores. Avoid all conflicts at home and school."

"Did you have to look it up before you got in the car to hunt me down? Or did you memorize that waiting for me to screw up?"

"You broke three of the agreements by leaving."

"I don't remember saying it's okay for Dad to talk about me in his sermons. Nobody said *that* was part of the agreement."

"Helena, why do you have to take everything personally?"

"Because it *was* personal!" she shouted. "And all those fakes in there knew it."

"Maybe if you would just stop being *this* you wouldn't have so much guilt."

"Hah! See? It was about me. And I'm not guilty."

"Just get in the car, Helena. Or it's off."

"You're just looking for an excuse, aren't you? You want to kick me out. Then you'd be three for three. Three kids gone the way of the Devil. That way, you don't have to feed them or actually care about them. You can just pray for their souls. That's a lot easier."

When her mother spoke again, her words were slower and quieter. Helena was getting under her skin. "If you keep talking to me like that, you're kicked out. And this time, you won't come back."

"Do it!" she screamed.

There was no immediate reply. Instead, the older woman walked back to the car and opened the door. "I'll leave your things on the front lawn this afternoon. Come over after dinner to collect them, or they will go out with the morning garbage."

The door shut. The engine started. The car rolled away.

Helena watched it until it turned a corner and out of sight.

The earbud continued to blast a guitar riff in her ears. Helena reached in her bag to turn it off and hold the phone in her hands again.

She was numb. She couldn't feel anything, not anymore.

With her thumbs, she texted four words.

Helena: *I screwed up again*

Mason had attended church with Helena one time. Helena's parents hated most of her life choices. The one exception was Mason. (Helena, of course, had neglected to mention Mason believed religion was a social reaction to a terrifying world and a comfort object for all humanity.) So when he walked into service one day, her parents were delighted. Mason, on the other hand, hated every second of it.

Except for the organ. Something about that reverberating, authoritative drone stuck in his memory. That service happened to be a "diversity" service. Mason had burst out laughing when he heard, being the sole non-white face in a five-mile radius.

Yet it did mean some changes to the typical worship song fare. When the organ began to play "Wade in the Water," Mason leaned back in the pew and closed his eyes. Helena got the feeling the sounds were washing over him like the waters in the song. After the service was over, he couldn't stop talking about it. That song, he said, performed in that stale, emotionless place sounded like a funeral dirge or a marching song for undead walking into Hell.

"Judgment! Judgment is a'comin'!" he shouted, pounding his fist in his hand.

Helena, not a musician, let him prattle.

And then he started incorporating the song into his performances.

Mason was a jazz pianist. If you gave him an instrument and about ten minutes of exploration, he could make the beginnings of music. The piano, however, would always be his first and deepest love, even above Helena. She was okay sharing him, but it wasn't like she had a choice. He had been playing instruments since he was five. His mother gave him the passion, and his father gave him the practical skills. Mason's parents had divorced when he was little. Connie was too much of a free spirit for the logical Howard.

Helena could see them now, sitting in different rows in front of her. Mason had neglected to mention that the benefit concert was taking place in a fellowship hall of another church. Two churches in one day were two too many for Helena. Mason also forgot to mention she would be the only white face in there. That second part was intentional payback probably.

At least this church was more tolerable than her father's. The fellowship hall was painted a bright yellow and filled with the home-cooked aromas of baked ham, macaroni, and greens being prepared in the industrial kitchen. After the concert was over, the families and elderly ladies bobbing their heads to Mason's music would fawn over him, then heap their plates. Many of the younger kids sat in the front row, mesmerized by his speed and dexterity.

Helena was more than happy sitting in the back, watching Mason's fingers fiddle over the keys in his typical jovial way. Jazz was play to him. And just like kids passing notes, Mason used "Wade in the Water" as a secret code. That melody meant he knew she was in the audience and that she was going through something tough.

He never actually played the song from beginning to end. Instead, he would loop into it and then loop back out, pulling out key sequences and then running with them. Helena hated jazz unless Mason was playing it. She loved trying to keep track of his twists and turns. She had learned a long time ago, though, to never try to anticipate his next decision. It was his element of surprise that made some adults call him a child genius.

As Mason went into "Wade in the Water," he managed to look up just long enough to sneak her a slight smirk. Helena shook her head at him, smirking back. How little the crowd knew about the youthful pianist. On stage was the Mason they knew with a button-up dress shirt, slacks, and that bouncy Afro bent over the keys.

Helena knew more. It wasn't that the stage Mason wasn't the real Mason. It was. There was just a lot of shit he kept buried under that smile.

Sweat still clung to her brow from the two-hour walk, but she was shivering. She tried to tell herself the church's newer air conditioner was turned up too high, but she also knew her body should have adjusted. Her rattled nerves had to be part of the problem. Regardless, her shivers were just one more reason to get out of there. The goal was to slink outside before Howard waved to her, Sasha squealed and glomped her, or, the worst possibility, Connie cornered her into an explanation.

When Mason's fingers fell into that last chord, letting it linger like a child watching a bubble float away, Helena stood and hurried out of the church. She could find him after.

Back in the heat, she felt more comfortable. A sign reading "Benefit Jazz Concert! Talented young man raising money to support our community" had been pounded into the ground by the road. Before she could sneak around the corner of the building and find a shady spot to sit, the church door opened behind her.

"Garnet," she heard.

And then she was on her.

Pinned.

Good thing Helena had gone through plenty of practice being tackled. Otherwise, she would have lost her footing. It was Sasha, Mason's little sister, arms wrapped around her waist and head pressed against her chest.

"Oh my God. Sasha, get *off*," Helena begged, peeling her fingers one at a time.

Sasha, an eighth grader, was short even compared to her brother. She made up for it in volume. “Were you trying to hide? Throw us aside? Did you move out at all, or did you try?”

“Cut the rhyming crap, Sasha. And *don’t* call me Garnet in public.”

Sasha pursed her lips into a pout, trying to look as harmless and cute as one of those anime characters she adored. “Nobody else is out here yet, Garnet. Why are you leaving?”

“Because I’m trying to avoid your—”

The door opened again. Connie walked out.

“—mother.”

Sasha giggled. “Guess you messed that up.”

TEACHING GUIDE

DURING READING:

Genre

The Ghost and the Wolf has elements of the mystery genre. A typical mystery includes characters with questionable motives, unusual or unsettling settings, problems to solve, and logical solutions to those problems. How does *The Ghost and the Wolf* integrate these elements into the plot as the story progresses? Keep a journal during your reading.

Vocabulary

Below are seven to ten suggested vocabulary words from each chapter. Please note some of the words, such as "crown," have homographs and should be examined in their context. You may want to create a vocabulary journal. You can record the vocabulary word, definition, and use in the text. Then, create your own sentences using the word in a similar manner.

Chapter 1
Submission
Photojournalist
Gauzy
Allegro
Introvert
Ghosting
Reverberated

Traipsed

Chapter 2

Symbolism
Cultures
Lingered
Affirm
Obelisks
Absently
Apathy

Chapter 3

Electromagnetic
Proverbial
Mesmerizing
Skulking
Mausolcums
Arsenic
Ebbed
Delinquent
Fixated

Chapter 4

Illogical
Sketchy
Skidded
Crypts
Deadpanned
Sutured
Knolls
Discreetly
Exhaust

Chapter 5

Lugged
Shockwave
Waddled
Expansive
Reprimanded
Justified
Hubbub
Churning
Conscipuous

Chapter 6
Essence
Torso
Muffled
Askew
Griffiti
Calligraphy
Foreclosure
Panorama

Chapter 7
Hoisted
Irrefutable
Outlet
Impeccably
Periodic
Manipulation
Tresses
Brigade
Pseudoscience

Chapter 8
Philosophy
Violators
Nonchalance
Shimmied
Vacuum
Thrashed
Escort

Chapter 9
Cartilage
Septum
Irises
Consented
Eerie
Rotunda
Maneuvered
Carberateur
Amplifiers

Chapter 10
Resignation
Reserves
Crown
Tension
Dysfunctional
Instincts
Anonymity
Flippant
Decrepit

Chapter 11
Obtained
Undeterred
Accommodated
Acquiesced
Dyslexic
Contort
Bard

Chapter 12
Dank
Reluctantly
Technicolor
Quirked
Ascended
Keening
Audible
Dumbstruck

Chapter 13
Sullenness
Meditative
Foliage
Excursions
Gawkers
Cinders
Hysteria
Pungent

Chapter 14

Revulsion
Heritage
Incriminating
Mangled
Melodrama
Hasty
Formulated
Depiction

Chapter 15
Contradiction
Mortifying
Mirth
Allegedly
Underbelly
Cacophony
Labyrinth
Photographic

Chapter 16
Tagalong
Scrawny
Transgressions
Adrenaline
Quaking
Impassive
Void
Incredulous

Chapter 17
Meticulous
Recumbent
Idling
Desolate
Penetrated
Bolting
Gingerly

Chapter 18
Charred
Compass
Silhouetted

Vulgar
Welfare
Resentment
Brambles

Chapter 19
Emerged
Debilitating
Eaves
Overzealous
Transpired
Fumes
Deprived

Chapter 20
Saline
Esophagus
Inhalation
Stricken
Cog
Antiseptic
Inquisitive

Chapter 21
Figurative
Ultimatum
Hygienic
Intercept
Scrutinized
Dueling
Subside

Epilogue
Sulk
Sadistic
Hobble
Nostalgic
Flourish
Brevity
Subtlety
Expertise
Simmered

AFTER READING:

Discussion/Essay Questions

1. Character Traits: Most of the members of the Pack are dynamic characters. This means their character traits change as the story progresses. How do the Pack members change? Which Pack member changes the most in this story? Who changes the least? What parts of the story drive those changes?

2. Character Roles: Since *The Ghost and the Wolf* is a mystery/thriller, the actual antagonist isn't revealed until the latter half of the story. Also, characters who at first seem to be antagonists turn out to be helpful and well-intentioned by the conclusion. Did you predict any of these character role shifts? If so, at what moment did you realize a character's "true colors"? Since this book is part of a trilogy, do you think any of the characters are still concealing their true motives? Please explain.

3. Conflict Types: Perhaps the most prominent and influential conflict type in this story is character v. self. Choose any character. Examine this character's inner conflict. How does this character express doubt in his/her abilities or potential? How do these doubts influence the character's actions?

4. Setting: Because this story centers on rivaling groups of urban explorers, the various settings in this story are often abandoned, decrepit, and dangerous. Examine how these settings influence the tone of certain scenes in the story. Also, examine the imagery used to describe each setting. What responses did these settings evoke in you as a reader?

5. Point of View: This novel is told in third person limited point of view, with Lex and Penelope as the protagonists. How does the storytelling change when the point of view shifts? By examining their inner dialogue, what major differences do you notice between Lex and Penelope's personalities?

6. **Theme:** The core theme in this novel is related to the alienation of young people, especially those who are disenfranchised in some regard. How does this theme shift and evolve as the story progresses?

7. **Symbolism:** Certain symbols occur at multiple points in this novel. Abandoned buildings, fire, paint brushes, and scars are a few of those symbols. Choose any symbol in the novel and evaluate its meaning in the story. Use the moments when the symbol appears in the story as evidence.

8. **Allusion:** Multiple references to *Romeo and Juliet* can be found in this story. In what ways do the characters mock this classic tragedy while also, sometimes unwillingly, fall in step with some of its tropes?

Research and Project-Based Learning Ideas

1. **Research a Teen Crisis**: The characters in this novel face a variety of hardships common among today's American teenagers. These include racism, homophobia, domestic abuse, learning disabilities, substance abuse, and homelessness. Choose any hardship experienced by a character in this novel. Create an informational research poster about this issue. Include current data, warning signs, and interventions.

2. **Portrait With Symbolism**: Penelope paints a symbolic portrait of Lex in this story. She uses the setting, background, and person's posture to make statements about his personality as well as their recent struggles. Make your own portrait that incorporates symbolism. (Even though Penelope used a canvas and paints, digital media is also encouraged.)

3. **Urban Exploration**: Most major urban centers are affected by the problem of urban decay, which refers to the presence of many abandoned and crumbling buildings. Create a photo collage of different abandoned buildings in your area. Do not

trespass. Instead, take the photos from a sidewalk or side street. Also, do not go alone. Try to capture the "beauty in the broken."

4. Paranormal Investigation: As a serious paranormal investigator, Lex uses a variety of instruments as part of his quest to record paranormal phenomena. While some of his instruments are expensive or rare, others are carried in most people's pockets. A flashlight, audio recorder, and journal can serve as a great "starter kit" for any beginner ghost hunter. Create your own ghost hunting kit. Choose a setting. (Please obtain permission.) Make entries in your journal as the evening progresses, and don't forget to record any measurement shifts. Create an investigation report that includes information about your investigation site.

5. The Broken: What makes you one of the Broken? Record some of your friends giving their own reasons why they are part of The Broken. Use the audio or video as material for a compilation recording. The goal is to encourage unity and acceptance, so please create a piece with an uplifting, inspiring tone.

ACKNOWLEDGEMENTS

To my agent, Stephanie Hansen, who has kept me somewhat sane throughout every step of this epic journey known as navigating the traditional publishing industry.

To the entire Metamorphosis Literary Agency team for reading my cringy rough drafts and recognizing my potential.

To Hannah, Emma, and the rest of the Owl Hollow team for accepting me into their nest. I really feel like I've come home to roost with this publishing company. Hoot hoot!

To my editor, Olivia Swenson, for "getting" it.

To the team at Wattpad HQ for coming to the crazy conclusion that my odd little tale could be enjoyed by more than just my immediate family.

To my immediate family for being my biggest fans.

To my trauma for all the creative inspiration.

And to my co-host and writing wife, L.L. Montez, for being the best support ostrich anyone could ask for.

SHELLY X. LEONN is the author of The Broken Series. After graduating with a Bachelor of Arts in journalism, Shelly worked at her hometown newspaper as the web and youth editor. During her time advising the youth staff, Shelly realized her true calling was teaching. Her years in education have been spent in middle school and high school language arts classrooms. She is also an adjunct professor.

She and her two boys reside in Affton, and she enjoys reading, writing, outdoor activities, anime, video games, and other dorky pastimes.

FIND SHELLY ONLINE AT DRSXL.COM

#TheGhostandtheWolf

Made in the USA
Monee, IL
20 April 2022

95063577R10173